Faust in Plain and Simple English
First Part of the Tragedy

Johann Wolfgang von Goethe

BookCaps™ Study Guides
www.SwipeBook.com

Table of Contents

Dedication

Again ye come, ye hovering Forms! I find ye,
As early to my clouded sight ye shone!
Shall I attempt, this once, to seize and bind ye?
Still o'er my heart is that illusion thrown?
Ye crowd more near! Then, be the reign assigned ye,
And sway me from your misty, shadowy zone!
My bosom thrills, with youthful passion shaken,
From magic airs that round your march awaken.
Of joyous days ye bring the blissful vision;
The dear, familiar phantoms rise again,
And, like an old and half-extinct tradition,
First Love returns, with Friendship in his train.
Renewed is Pain: with mournful repetition
Life tracks his devious, labyrinthine chain,
And names the Good, whose cheating fortune tore them
From happy hours, and left me to deplore them.

They hear no longer these succeeding measures,
The souls, to whom my earliest songs I sang:
Dispersed the friendly troop, with all its pleasures,
And still, alas! the echoes first that rang!
I bring the unknown multitude my treasures;
Their very plaudits give my heart a pang,
And those beside, whose joy my Song so flattered,
If still they live, wide through the world are scattered.

And grasps me now a long-unwonted yearning
For that serene and solemn Spirit-Land:
My song, to faint Aeolian murmurs turning,
Sways like a harp-string by the breezes fanned.
I thrill and tremble; tear on tear is burning,
And the stern heart is tenderly unmanned.
What I possess, I see far distant lying,
And what I lost, grows real and undying.

You've come again, you flickering shapes! I see you
Just as I saw you with blurry eyes years ago!
Shall I try to nail you down again?
Does my heart still think it can be done?
You're getting closer! Well then, I give in to you
And from behind your surrounding mist you move me!
My heart feels young again,
Thanks to the magic breezes your movements stir up.
You show me beautiful visions of happy days;
Sweet things I thought were dead rise up before me
And like something almost completely forgotten
Love comes back, bringing Friendship with him.
I feel Pain again: over and over
Life follows its long and winding path,
And tells me again of the good people whose bad luck
Ripped them away from our good times and left me to
mourn them.
They can't hear the song that follows,
These souls I sang my very first songs to:
They've disappeared, that friendly crowd
And so have the echoes of those songs.
Now I give my song to crowds of unknown people,
And even their applause hurts me,
Reminding me of those I wrote my songs for,
Who are scattered around the world if they're alive at
all.
Now I'm grabbed by an unfulfilled desire
To visit the peaceful solemn Ghost country:
My song trembles on the wind
Like a harp string when a breeze blows on it.
I shiver and shudder and my tears fall one after another,
And my heart's strength grows gently weaker.
The things I own I can see are far away,
And the things I lost are now close at hand.

Prologue On Stage

MANAGER, DRAMATIC POET, MERRY-ANDREW

MANAGER

You two, who oft a helping hand
Have lent, in need and tribulation.
Come, let me know your expectation
Of this, our enterprise, in German land!
I wish the crowd to feel itself well treated,

Especially since it lives and lets me live;
The posts are set, the booth of boards completed.
And each awaits the banquet I shall give.
Already there, with curious eyebrows raised,
They sit sedate, and hope to be amazed.
I know how one the People's taste may flatter,
Yet here a huge embarrassment I feel:
What they're accustomed to, is no great matter,
But then, alas! they've read an awful deal.
How shall we plan, that all be fresh and new,--
Important matter, yet attractive too?
For 'tis my pleasure-to behold them surging,
When to our booth the current sets apace,
And with tremendous, oft-repeated urging,
Squeeze onward through the narrow gate of grace:
By daylight even, they push and cram in
To reach the seller's box, a fighting host,
And as for bread, around a baker's door, in famine,
To get a ticket break their necks almost.
This miracle alone can work the Poet

On men so various: now, my friend, pray show it.

Both of you have often helped me out
When I've needed it or been in trouble.
Now, let me know how you think we'll do
With our new enterprise here in Germany!
I want the crowd to feel they've had their money's
worth,
After all, by being here they give me my living;
The theatre's all set up,
And everyone's waiting to see what I have to offer them.
They're out there already, looking on curiously,
Sitting quietly and hoping for something stunning.
I know how to give them what they want,
But I haven't got it just at the moment:
They're not used to getting anything good,
But unfortunately they have read a lot.
What shall we give them that's fresh and new,
That deals with issues but amuses them as well?
I love to see them rushing up
To our theatre when they're driven here,
And they're pushed on, shouting to each other to hurry,
Squeezing through our turnstiles:
Even in the daytime they crowd and shove
To get to the box office, fighting like a crowd
Outside a baker's when they're starving,
They'd nearly die to get a ticket.
Only a Poet can have this effect on so many different
men:
Come on my friend, work your magic!

POET

Speak not to me of yonder motley masses,
Whom but to see, puts out the fire of Song!
Hide from my view the surging crowd that passes,
And in its whirlpool forces us along!
No, lead me where some heavenly silence glasses
The purer joys that round the Poet throng,--
Where Love and Friendship still divinely fashion
The bonds that bless, the wreaths that crown his
passion!
Ah, every utterance from the depths of feeling
The timid lips have stammeringly expressed,--
Now failing, now, perchance, success revealing,--
Gulps the wild Moment in its greedy breast;
Or oft, reluctant years its warrant sealing,
Its perfect stature stands at last confessed!
What dazzles, for the Moment spends its spirit:
What's genuine, shall Posterity inherit.

Don't tell me about the rough crowd out there,
Just seeing them takes away all inspiration!
Don't let me see the crowd rushing by
That drags us along with it!
No, take me where it's beautifully quiet
And I can enjoy the purer things a Poet needs.
Take me where Love and Friendship still give
Blessings and rewards for the Poet's passion!

I've tried expressing my feelings in every way
My lips have tried to say them all:
Sometimes I've failed, sometimes succeeded
Sometimes inspiration comes right away;
Other times it hides away for years
And comes out perfectly in the end!
Something might look good and amaze for a moment
But if it has genuine worth it will last down the years.

MERRY-ANDREW

Posterity! Don't name the word to me!
If I should choose to preach Posterity,
Where would you get contemporary fun?
That men *will* have it, there's no blinking:
A fine young fellow's presence, to my thinking,
Is something worth, to every one.
Who genially his nature can outpour,
Takes from the People's moods no irritation;
The wider circle he acquires, the more
Securely works his inspiration.
Then pluck up heart, and give us sterling coin!
Let Fancy be with her attendants fitted,--
Sense, Reason, Sentiment, and Passion join,--
But have a care, lest Folly be omitted!

Don't talk to me about things lasting!
If I spent my energy thinking about that
How would anyone have fun in the here and now?
You can't deny that men want to have fun:
I think a fine young man, on the spot,
Has something to offer to one and all.
He can spill out his joyful personality
Without getting annoyed by other people's moods;
The more people listen to him, the more
He gets inspired by his audience.
Take courage and give us the best you've got!
Let your works have all the right elements:
Sense, Reason, Sentiment and Passion all together,
But make sure you don't leave out a bit of fun!

MANAGER

Chiefly, enough of incident prepare!
They come to look, and they prefer to stare.
Reel off a host of threads before their faces,
So that they gape in stupid wonder: then

By sheer diffuseness you have won their graces,

And are, at once, most popular of men.
Only by mass you touch the mass; for any
Will finally, himself, his bit select:
Who offers much, brings something unto many,
And each goes home content with the effect,
If you've a piece, why, just in pieces give it:
A hash, a stew, will bring success, believe it!
'Tis easily displayed, and easy to invent.
What use, a Whole compactly to present?
Your hearers pick and pluck, as soon as they receive it!

The main thing we need is plenty of action!
They come to see things happening.
Give them lots of different plots
So they're amazed even when they don't understand:
then
You've got their approval through sheer volume of
entertainment,
And you'll be popular with them at once.
By giving plenty you'll appeal to plenty, for each one
Will choose the bit he likes:
If you offer a lot everyone will get something from it,
And everyone goes home happy with what they've seen.
Whatever you've got give it some variety,
A mixture is the key to success, believe you me!
It's easy to stage and easy to make up.
What's the point in giving them a neat performance?
They'll tear it into bits as soon as you give it to them
anyway!

POET

You do not feel, how such a trade debases;

How ill it suits the Artist, proud and true!
The botching work each fine pretender traces

Is, I perceive, a principle with you.

Don't you have any feeling for how cheap your attitude
is?
This isn't right for the noble Artist!
This stiched together method which every new sensation
copies
Is, I can see, your way of working.

MANAGER

Such a reproach not in the least offends;
A man who some result intends
Must use the tools that best are fitting.
Reflect, soft wood is given to you for splitting,
And then, observe for whom you write!
If one comes bored, exhausted quite,
Another, satiate, leaves the banquet's tapers,
And, worst of all, full many a wight

Your telling off doesn't bother me at all;
When you want to achieve a particular thing
You must do it in the way most suitable for your aims.
Think about the material you have to work with
And think about the sort of people you're writing for!
Some will turn up bored and shattered,
Some will come stuffed from a big dinner,
And worst of all, many of them

Is fresh from reading of the daily papers.
Idly to us they come, as to a masquerade,
Mere curiosity their spirits warming:
The ladies with themselves, and with their finery, aid,

Without a salary their parts performing.
What dreams are yours in high poetic places?
You're pleased, forsooth, full houses to behold?
Draw near, and view your patrons' faces!

The half are coarse, the half are cold.
One, when the play is out, goes home to cards;
A wild night on a wench's breast another chooses:

Why should you rack, poor, foolish bards,
For ends like these, the gracious Muses?
I tell you, give but more--more, ever more, they ask:

Thus shall you hit the mark of gain and glory.
Seek to confound your auditory!
To satisfy them is a task.--
What ails you now? Is't suffering, or pleasure?

POET
Go, find yourself a more obedient slave!
What! shall the Poet that which Nature gave,
The highest right, supreme Humanity,
Forfeit so wantonly, to swell your treasure?
Whence o'er the heart his empire free?
The elements of Life how conquers he?
Is't not his heart's accord, urged outward far and dim,
To wind the world in unison with him?
When on the spindle, spun to endless distance,
By Nature's listless hand the thread is twirled,
And the discordant tones of all existence
In sullen jangle are together hurled,
Who, then, the changeless orders of creation
Divides, and kindles into rhythmic dance?
Who brings the One to join the general ordination,
Where it may throb in grandest consonance?
Who bids the storm to passion stir the bosom?
In brooding souls the sunset burn above?
Who scatters every fairest April blossom
Along the shining path of Love?
Who braids the noteless leaves to crowns, requiting
Desert with fame, in Action's every field?
Who makes Olympus sure, the Gods uniting?
The might of Man, as in the Bard revealed.

MERRY-ANDREW
So, these fine forces, in conjunction,
Propel the high poetic function,
As in a love-adventure they might play!

Will come in having just read the newspapers.
They drift in here as if they were going to a dance,
They've got no passion, just idle curiosity;
The ladies are only interested in themselves and their clothes,
They're like unpaid actresses playing a part.
You like to have your lofty poetic dream eh?
But you like having a packed theatre as well, don't you?
Have a good look at the people who've come to see your work!
Half are rough and uncultured, half are passionless.
One goes straight from the play home to a game of cards
While another chooses to have a night of passion with some tart:
To amuse people like these, why do you foolish poets
Torture the goddesses of inspiration?
I'm telling you, just give them plenty and they'll want plenty more:
That's the way to get yourself fame and wealth.
Get your listeners confused!
Keeping them satisfied's your job -
Now what's wrong? Pleasure or pain?

Go and find yourself someone else!
Should a Poet take his natural gifts,
The highest things a man can have,
And throw them away to increase your bank balance?
How would he be able to move hearts again?
How could he rule over the elements?
Isn't it his mission to throw his heart out
And then draw the world back to him?
On the spinning wheel flung out endlessly
Are the threads which Nature twists together,
And all the tuneless parts of existence
Are hurled together discordantly.
Who draws all these parts together
And makes sweet music from them?
Who brings the Eternal into the everyday
To let it show its greatest harmony?
Who makes the storm thrill us with passion?
Who makes the sunset light up men's souls?
Who makes the flowers' petals
Part of the way which takes us to love?
Who makes crowns out of the leaves
To reward every good action of man?
What gives even heaven strength and unites the gods?
The spirit of Man, as shown through the Poet.

So, all these wonderful energies
Fuel your poetry
As if it was a love affair!

You meet by accident; you feel, you stay,

And by degrees your heart is tangled;
Bliss grows apace, and then its course is jangled;
You're ravished quite, then comes a touch of woe,
And there's a neat romance, completed ere you know!
Let us, then, such a drama give!
Grasp the exhaustless life that all men live!
Each shares therein, though few may comprehend:
Where'er you touch, there's interest without end.
In motley pictures little light,
Much error, and of truth a glimmering mite,
Thus the best beverage is supplied,
Whence all the world is cheered and edified.
Then, at your play, behold the fairest flower
Of youth collect, to hear the revelation!
Each tender soul, with sentimental power,
Sucks melancholy food from your creation;
And now in this, now that, the leaven works.
For each beholds what in his bosom lurks.
They still are moved at once to weeping or to laughter,

Still wonder at your flights, enjoy the show they see:
A mind, once formed, is never suited after;
One yet in growth will ever grateful be.

POET
Then give me back that time of pleasures,
While yet in joyous growth I sang,--
When, like a fount, the crowding measures
Uninterrupted gushed and sprang!
Then bright mist veiled the world before me,
In opening buds a marvel woke,
As I the thousand blossoms broke,
Which every valley richly bore me!
I nothing had, and yet enough for youth--
Joy in Illusion, ardent thirst for Truth.

Give, unrestrained, the old emotion,
The bliss that touched the verge of pain,
The strength of Hate, Love's deep devotion,--
O, give me back my youth again!

MERRY ANDREW
Youth, good my friend, you certainly require
When foes in combat sorely press you;
When lovely maids, in fond desire,
Hang on your bosom and caress you;
When from the hard-won goal the wreath
Beckons afar, the race awaiting;
When, after dancing out your breath,
You pass the night in dissipating:--

You meet by accident and stay because you feel something
And bit by bit your heart gets caught up.
Happiness swells up but then is let down again;
You're enchanted, then there's a little sadness,
And there you have a good story, easy as anything!
Let's put on a play like that!
Grab hold of the life that men live!
Everyone's part of it, even if not many understand it:
There's endless interest in every part of life.
A varied picture can be made with a little light,
Loads of error and a tiny spark of truth;
That way we can brew the best potion,
Which will cheer and interest the whole world.
Your play will draw in the cream
Of youth, to hear what you have to say!
Each sensitive soul will use their emotional power,
And take sad inspiration from what you've made;
Here and there you'll touch them
So that each will know how he feels inside.
They're of an age when they will weep or laugh at the drop of a hat,
And be amazed by language, and enjoy the play.
Once the mind is set in its ways it is never satisfied,
But one that's still growing will always be grateful for what's offered.

Then take me back to that time of pleasure,
When I sang with joy as I grew,
When I was like a fountain
Spraying out poetry without interruption!
The world was veiled in a bright mist back then,
I could see miracles in a budding bloom
And I picked the flowers of inspiration from them
Which I found in every valley I walked through!
I had nothing, and that was enough for a young man:
I took pleasure in mirages and my panting thirst for Truth.
Give me those old feelings back without limits,
Give me the happiness so strong it was almost painful,
The great force of Hate, the deep power of Love,
Oh, make me young again!

You certainly need to be young, my friend,
When you come under attack in battle,
Or when beautiful girls lovingly want
To hug and kiss you;
When you can see the prize far off
Waiting for you at the end of the race;
When, after you've exhausted yourself dancing,
You spend the night in wine, women and song.

But that familiar harp with soul
To play,--with grace and bold expression,
And towards a self-erected goal
To walk with many a sweet digression,--
This, aged Sirs, belongs to you,
And we no less revere you for that reason:
Age childish makes, they say, but 'tis not true;
We're only genuine children still, in Age's season!

MANAGER
The words you've bandied are sufficient;
'Tis deeds that I prefer to see:
In compliments you're both proficient,
But might, the while, more useful be.
What need to talk of Inspiration?
'Tis no companion of Delay.
If Poetry be your vocation,
Let Poetry your will obey!
Full well you know what here is wanting;
The crowd for strongest drink is panting,
And such, forthwith, I'd have you brew.
What's left undone to-day, To-morrow will not do.
Waste not a day in vain digression:
With resolute, courageous trust
Seize every possible impression,
And make it firmly your possession;
You'll then work on, because you must.
Upon our German stage, you know it,
Each tries his hand at what he will;
So, take of traps and scenes your fill,
And all you find, be sure to show it!
Use both the great and lesser heavenly light,--
Squander the stars in any number,
Beasts, birds, trees, rocks, and all such lumber,
Fire, water, darkness, Day and Night!
Thus, in our booth's contracted sphere,
The circle of Creation will appear,
And move, as we deliberately impel,
From Heaven, across the World, to Hell!

But to play the old instrument with soul
Gracefully, expressively,
To journey towards the goal you've set yourself,
Walking with many sweet turnings on the way,
This, you older men, is what you can do,
And we admire you for it.
They say getting old makes you childish but it's a lie;
We're still children, just mellowed with age!

That's enough throwing words about,
I want to see some action:
You're both experts at flattery
But some hard work is what we need at the moment.
Why do we need to talk about Inspiration?
It doesn't mean you have to hang around waiting.
If you're going to call yourself a Poet
Then make poetry do some work for you!
You know very well what we want here;
The crowd are eagerly waiting for your best stuff
And I need you to start producing it, right now.
If we don't get it done today, tomorrow will be too late.
Don't waste time skirting round the job;
Take all your strength and courage
And grasp every inspiration you see
And claim ownership of it for yourself;
Then you'll work on it, because it's your job.
You know that on the stage here in Germany
Everyone has a go at what he fancies;
So, take what scenery and special effects you want,
And make sure you use it in the show!
Use the light of the sun and moon,
Burn up all the stars you want,
Animals, birds, trees, rocks, all that stuff,
Fire, water, darkness, day and night!
Within the little circle of our theatre,
We'll show the whole universe,
And take our audience across the world
From heaven into hell!

Prologue In Heaven

THE LORD THE HEAVENLY HOST *Afterwards*
MEPHISTOPHELES
(*The* THREE ARCHANGELS *come forward.*)

RAPHAEL
The sun-orb sings, in emulation,
'Mid brother-spheres, his ancient round:
His path predestined through Creation

He ends with step of thunder-sound.
The angels from his visage splendid
Draw power, whose measure none can say;
The lofty works, uncomprehended,

Are bright as on the earliest day.

GABRIEL
And swift, and swift beyond conceiving,
The splendor of the world goes round,
Day's Eden-brightness still relieving
The awful Night's intense profound:
The ocean-tides in foam are breaking,
Against the rocks' deep bases hurled,
And both, the spheric race partaking,
Eternal, swift, are onward whirled!

MICHAEL
And rival storms abroad are surging
From sea to land, from land to sea.
A chain of deepest action forging
Round all, in wrathful energy.
There flames a desolation, blazing
Before the Thunder's crashing way:
Yet, Lord, Thy messengers are praising
The gentle movement of Thy Day.

THE THREE
Though still by them uncomprehended,
From these the angels draw their power,
And all Thy works, sublime and splendid,
Are bright as in Creation's hour.

MEPHISTOPHELES
Since Thou, O Lord, deign'st to approach again
And ask us how we do, in manner kindest,
And heretofore to meet myself wert fain,
Among Thy menials, now, my face Thou findest.
Pardon, this troop I cannot follow after
With lofty speech, though by them scorned and
spurned:
My pathos certainly would move Thy laughter,

The sun is singing in competition
With the other stars as he goes round on his orbit;
His route has been laid down for him since the
beginning of time
And he shoots along with a step like thunder.
From the sun's beauty the angels
Draw a power which no-one can measure;
God's works in the sky, which none can hope to
understand,
Are shining as brightly as the first day of creation.

Quickly, with a speed beyond belief,
The magnificent world spins round,
With the bright day like the first morning
Taking over from the terrible darkness of night;
The waves of the oceans are crashing
Against the foot of the cliffs,
And both, being a part of the earth
Rush on with it forever!

And clashing storms rush around
From the sea to the land and back again.
They make a necklace of fierce energy
Which wraps around the whole world.
There's a flash of lightning, shining
Before the thunder explodes:
But, Lord, your angels sing the praises
Of the beauty of the day you've made.

Though they cannot understand it
The angels gain their strength from these things,
And everything you have made, beautiful and wonderful,
Is as bright as when you first made it.

Since you, Lord, lower yourself to visit us
And ask how we are getting on in the kindest way,
As you used to see me amongst your servants,
You see my face here with them again.
Forgive me, I can't follow the others,
With fine speeches, though they've rejected and mocked
me:
My poor situation would certainly amuse you,

If Thou hadst not all merriment unlearned.
Of suns and worlds I've nothing to be quoted;
How men torment themselves, is all I've noted.
The little god o' the world sticks to the same old way,
And is as whimsical as on Creation's day.
Life somewhat better might content him,
But for the gleam of heavenly light which Thou hast lent him:
He calls it Reason--thence his power's increased,
To be far beastlier than any beast.
Saving Thy Gracious Presence, he to me
A long-legged grasshopper appears to be,
That springing flies, and flying springs,
And in the grass the same old ditty sings.
Would he still lay among the grass he grows in!
Each bit of dung he seeks, to stick his nose in.

If you hadn't forgotten how to laugh.
I've got nothing to say about suns and planets;
All I've learned is how men torture themselves.
Man carries on just the same as ever,
And behaves just as oddly as the day he was made.
He might have a better chance of happiness
If it wasn't for the divine spark You put in him:

He calls it reason, and it gives him the power
To be more beastly than any animal.
Without wanting to offend You, he looks to me
Like a long legged grasshopper,
Leaping about here and there,
And singing the same old song in the grass.
I wish he would stop there in the grass,
But no, he has to stick his nose into everything
unpleasant he can find.

THE LORD
Hast thou, then, nothing more to mention?
Com'st ever, thus, with ill intention?
Find'st nothing right on earth, eternally?

Is that all you have to say?
Do you only ever come with evil in your heart?
Can you never see anything good on earth?

MEPHISTOPHELES
No, Lord! I find things, there, still bad as they can be.

Man's misery even to pity moves my nature;
I've scarce the heart to plague the wretched creature.

No I can't! Everything there is as bad as one can imagine.
The misery of man makes even me feel sorry for him;
I can hardly bring myself to torment the poor thing.

THE LORD
Know'st Faust?

Do you know Faust?

MEPHISTOPHELES
The Doctor Faust?

Faust the Doctor?

THE LORD
My servant, he!

Yes, he's my servant!

MEPHISTOPHELES
Forsooth! He serves you after strange devices:
No earthly meat or drink the fool suffices:
His spirit's ferment far aspireth;
Half conscious of his frenzied, crazed unrest,
The fairest stars from Heaven he requireth,
From Earth the highest raptures and the best,
And all the Near and Far that he desireth
Fails to subdue the tumult of his breast.

Well! He has a strange way of serving you:
The idiot's not happy with what's available on earth:
His desires spread out into the universe;
He's half awake and half mad,
And he wants the most beautiful stars from the sky,
He wants all the greatest pleasures from earth as well.
If he gets all he wants, from near and far,
It still wouldn't satisfy his cravings.

THE LORD
Though still confused his service unto Me,
I soon shall lead him to a clearer morning.

His service to me is still mixed up
But I shall make him see the light soon.

10

Sees not the gardener, even while buds his tree,
Both flower and fruit the future years adorning?

Doesn't the gardener, when he plants a tree,
Have a vision of the fruits and flowers he'll get in years to come?

MEPHISTOPHELES
What will you bet? There's still a chance to gain him,
If unto me full leave you give,
Gently upon *my* road to train him!

What will you bet? I can still trap him,
If you give me full permission,
To take him along my path!

THE LORD
As long as he on earth shall live,
So long I make no prohibition.
While Man's desires and aspirations stir,

He cannot choose but err.

As long as he's still living on earth,
I don't make any rules to control you.
Whilst men still have desires and hopes working on them,
They can't help but make mistakes.

MEPHISTOPHELES
My thanks! I find the dead no acquisition,

And never cared to have them in my keeping.
I much prefer the cheeks where ruddy blood is leaping,
And when a corpse approaches, close my house:
It goes with me, as with the cat the mouse.

Thank you! I'm not interested in getting hold of the dead,
And I don't like having them in my charge.
I like to play with the living
And close my doors to corpses:
I like to play with live things, like a cat with a mouse.

THE LORD
Enough! What thou hast asked is granted.
Turn off this spirit from his fountain-head;
To trap him, let thy snares be planted,
And him, with thee, be downward led;
Then stand abashed, when thou art forced to say:
A good man, through obscurest aspiration,
Has still an instinct of the one true way.

Alright then! I'll give you what you want.
Take this soul away from his inspiration;
Lay out your traps
And drag him down with you;
Then you'll be proved wrong and have to admit
That a good man, even if you cloud his vision,
Still knows how to take the right path.

MEPHISTOPHELES
Agreed! But 'tis a short probation.
About my bet I feel no trepidation.
If I fulfill my expectation,
You'll let me triumph with a swelling breast:
Dust shall he eat, and with a zest,
As did a certain snake, my near relation.

Agreed! It won't take long.
I don't have worries about my bet.
If everything goes according to plan
You'll have to let me enjoy my victory:
He'll eat dust and enjoy it,
Like a certain snake who's related to me.

THE LORD
Therein thou'rt free, according to thy merits;
The like of thee have never moved My hate.
Of all the bold, denying Spirits,
The waggish knave least trouble doth create.
Man's active nature, flagging, seeks too soon the level;
Unqualified repose he learns to crave;
Whence, willingly, the comrade him I gave,
Who works, excites, and must create, as Devil.
But ye, God's sons in love and duty,
Enjoy the rich, the ever-living Beauty!
Creative Power, that works eternal schemes,

Alright, you're free to try in your own way.
Your type has never inspired my hatred.
Of all those spirits who fight against me,
The joking rogue causes me the least trouble.
When a man gets tired, he quickly sinks down
And wants to have nothing but rest;
Then I'm happy for him to have a Devil as a companion
Who stirs him up and gets him working.
But you, my faithful and loving sons,
Enjoy the rich eternal beauty!
My power, which rules the universe,

Clasp you in bonds of love, relaxing never,
And what in wavering apparition gleams
Fix in its place with thoughts that stand forever!

Wraps you in ropes of love forever,
And what you see shining for a moment
Make eternal by keeping it in your thoughts eternally!

(Heaven closes: the ARCHANGELS separate)

MEPHISTOPHELES (*solus*)
I like, at times, to hear The Ancient's word,
And have a care to be most civil:
It's really kind of such a noble Lord
So humanly to gossip with the Devil!

I like to hear God speak from time to time
And I make sure I'm very polite to him:
It's most kind of such a high God
To pass the time of day with the Devil!

I

NIGHT
(*A lofty-arched, narrow, Gothic chamber*. FAUST, in a chair at his desk, restless)

FAUST

I've studied now Philosophy	*Now I've studied Philosophy*
And Jurisprudence, Medicine,--	*And Law, Medicine,*
And even, alas! Theology,--	*And even – unfortunately! – Theology,*
From end to end, with labor keen;	*From top to bottom, working hard;*
And here, poor fool! with all my lore	*And here, like a fool, with all my learning,*
I stand, no wiser than before:	*Am I, no wiser than when I started.*
I'm Magister--yea, Doctor--hight,	*I'm called a teacher – a Doctor even! -*
And straight or cross-wise, wrong or right,	*And one way and another, right or wrong,*
These ten years long, with many woes,	*For ten years, with much grief,*
I've led my scholars by the nose,--	*I've dragged my students around -*
And see, that nothing can be known!	*And now I see that one can understand nothing!*
That knowledge cuts me to the bone.	*Knowing that pains me right down in my soul.*
I'm cleverer, true, than those fops of teachers,	*It's true I'm cleverer than those ridiculous teachers,*
Doctors and Magisters, Scribes and Preachers;	*Doctors, Academics, Clerks and Priests;*
Neither scruples nor doubts come now to smite me,	*I can't be stopped by doubts or scruples,*
Nor Hell nor Devil can longer affright me.	*Nor can Hell or Devils frighten me.*
For this, all pleasure am I foregoing;	*I've given up all pleasure to get here;*
I do not pretend to aught worth knowing,	*Still I don't know anything worthwhile,*
I do not pretend I could be a teacher	*Neither could I be a teacher*
To help or convert a fellow-creature.	*Who could give anything worthwhile to my fellow man.*
Then, too, I've neither lands nor gold,	*As well as that I haven't got money or property,*
Nor the world's least pomp or honor hold--	*Neither do I have any wordly position or title -*
No dog would endure such a curst existence!	*A dog wouldn't put up with this rotten life!*
Wherefore, from Magic I seek assistance,	*So, I want the help of Magic:*
That many a secret perchance I reach	*Hopefully I can learn many secrets*
Through spirit-power and spirit-speech,	*Through the power of Spirits and speaking to them,*
And thus the bitter task forego	*So I can give up the painful job*
Of saying the things I do not know,--	*Of having to talk about things I know nothing of.*
That I may detect the inmost force	*I want to find the inner power*
Which binds the world, and guides its course;	*That holds the world together and directs its path;*
Its germs, productive powers explore,	*I want to find how the world's made and explore its power,*
And rummage in empty words no more!	*And stop wasting my time with meaningless words!*
O full and splendid Moon, whom I	*You wonderful full Moon, whom I*
Have, from this desk, seen climb the sky	*Have often seen climbing into the sky when I'm sitting at my desk,*
So many a midnight,--would thy glow	*Sitting here at so many midnights – I'd love it if your light*
For the last time beheld my woe!	*Was shining on my sadness for the last time!*
Ever thine eye, most mournful friend,	*You've always seen me, my sad friend,*
O'er books and papers saw me bend;	*Hunched over my books and papers;*
But would that I, on mountains grand,	*But I want to stand on great mountains,*
Amid thy blessed light could stand,	*Shining in your beautiful light,*
With spirits through mountain-caverns hover,	*I want to drift through mountain caves with ghosts,*
Float in thy twilight the meadows over,	*Drift over the meadows at twilight,*
And, freed from the fumes of lore that swathe me,	*And instead of being wrapped up with this choking learning*

To health in thy dewy fountains bathe me!

Ah, me! this dungeon still I see.
This drear, accursed masonry,
Where even the welcome daylight strains
But duskly through the painted panes.
Hemmed in by many a toppling heap
Of books worm-eaten, gray with dust,
Which to the vaulted ceiling creep,
Against the smoky paper thrust,--
With glasses, boxes, round me stacked,
And instruments together hurled,
Ancestral lumber, stuffed and packed--
Such is my world: and what a world!
And do I ask, wherefore my heart
Falters, oppressed with unknown needs?

Why some inexplicable smart
All movement of my life impedes?
Alas! in living Nature's stead,
Where God His human creature set,
In smoke and mould the fleshless dead
And bones of beasts surround me yet!
Fly! Up, and seek the broad, free land!
And this one Book of Mystery
From Nostradamus' very hand,
Is't not sufficient company?
When I the starry courses know,
And Nature's wise instruction seek,
With light of power my soul shall glow,
As when to spirits spirits speak.
Tis vain, this empty brooding here,
Though guessed the holy symbols be:
Ye, Spirits, come--ye hover near--
Oh, if you hear me, answer me!
*(He opens the Book, and perceives the sign
of the Macrocosm.)*
Ha! what a sudden rapture leaps from this
I view, through all my senses swiftly flowing!
I feel a youthful, holy, vital bliss
In every vein and fibre newly glowing.
Was it a God, who traced this sign,
With calm across my tumult stealing,
My troubled heart to joy unsealing,
With impulse, mystic and divine,
The powers of Nature here, around my path, revealing?
Am I a God?--so clear mine eyes!
In these pure features I behold
Creative Nature to my soul unfold.
What says the sage, now first I recognize:
"The spirit-world no closures fasten;
Thy sense is shut, thy heart is dead:
Disciple, up! untiring, hasten

*I want to regain health by bathing in the dew by your
light!*
Ah no! I'm still in this dungeon of mine,
This prison of dull, cursed bricks,
Where even when it's bright daylight
It's dusk inside, thanks to the tinted glass.
I'm trapped in here by great tottering heaps
Of dusty, wormy books,
Reaching right up to the ceiling,
Leaning against the smoke blackened wallpaper.
I have magnifiers and boxes stacked around me,
And scientific apparatus all jumbled up,
Old heirlooms stuffed in cases;
This is my world, and what a world it is!
I have to ask, why is my heart so sad,
*Crushed by the weight of wanting things unknown to
me?*
Why does this pain, whose source I don't know,
Handicap me in everything I do?
Alas! Instead of being in the natural world,
Where God put down his creation, Man,
I'm surrounded by smoke, mould, skeletons
And animal bones.
Fly! Go up to the wide free country!
Isn't this mystical book
Written by Nostradamus himself,
Enough for you?
When I learn about astrology
And read what's written in Nature
My soul will throb with power,
As when spirits commune with spirits.
It's no good, this worthless study in here,
Hoping to guess the signs from God:
Gather round me, Spirits!
If you can hear me then answer me!
*(He opens the Book, and perceives the sign of the
Macrocosm [a diagram of the cosmos])*
Ha! What a thrill seeing this gives me,
Tingling through my bones!
I can feel a deep, holy, youthful joy,
Lighting up my blood and muscles.
Did God, who drew out this plan,
Come to lay calm upon my troubled mind,
To open my troubled heart to happiness,
With a mystic and divine power
Showing me the powers of Nature which surround me?
Am I a God? I can see everything so clearly!
Everything in these pure characters here
Shows the ways of nature to my soul!
I understand the wise man's words for the first time:
"The spirit world is never locked:
It's you whose heart and mind are closed.
Learner, wake up! Rush out

To bathe thy breast in morning-red!"
(*He contemplates the sign.*)
How each the Whole its substance gives,
Each in the other works and lives!
Like heavenly forces rising and descending,
Their golden urns reciprocally lending,
With wings that winnow blessing
From Heaven through Earth I see them pressing,
Filling the All with harmony unceasing!
How grand a show! but, ah! a show alone.
Thee, boundless Nature, how make thee my own?
Where you, ye beasts? Founts of all Being, shining,
Whereon hang Heaven's and Earth's desire,
Whereto our withered hearts aspire,--
Ye flow, ye feed: and am I vainly pining?

(He turns the leaves impatiently, and perceives the
sign of the Earth-Spirit)
How otherwise upon me works this sign!
Thou, Spirit of the Earth, art nearer:
Even now my powers are loftier, clearer;
I glow, as drunk with new-made wine:
New strength and heart to meet the world incite me,

The woe of earth, the bliss of earth, invite me,

And though the shock of storms may smite me,
No crash of shipwreck shall have power to fright me!
Clouds gather over me--
The moon conceals her light--
The lamp's extinguished!--
Mists rise,--red, angry rays are darting
Around my head!--There falls
A horror from the vaulted roof,
And seizes me!
I feel thy presence, Spirit I invoke!
Reveal thyself!
Ha! in my heart what rending stroke!
With new impulsion
My senses heave in this convulsion!
I feel thee draw my heart, absorb, exhaust me:

Thou must! thou must! and though my life it cost me!

(He seizes the book, and mysteriously pronounces the
sign of the Spirit. A ruddy flame flashes: the Spirit
appears in the flame)

SPIRIT
Who calls me?

And bathe yourself in the sunrise!"
(He contemplates the sign)
See how everything is a part of the whole,
Everything working and living together!
See the planets rising and setting,
Their golden vessels sharing one to another
The blessings of their light;
I can see it flowing from heaven to earth,
Filling everything with eternal harmony!
What a wonderful show! Ah, but it's just a show,
How can I gain the power of nature for myself?
Where are you? The source of all life,
Which all Heaven and Earth desires,
And our shriveled hearts want to gain,
You flow, you make life grow: am I striving for you in vain?
(He turns the leaves impatiently, and perceives the sign of the Earth-Spirit)
Now this sign has a different effect on me!
You, the Earth, are nearer than the stars,
I feel more powerful, I see things more clearly;
I'm lit up, as if I've had too much new wine:
I have a new strength and more heart to take on the world,
The sorrow and the beauty of the Earth are calling to me,
And though storms might crash down upon me,
No shipwreck will be able to frighten me!
The clouds are gathering overhead,
The light of the moon is hidden,
The lamp's gone out!
There's a fog rising, red lightning
Flashes around my head! Something terrible
Falls down from the ceiling
And grabs hold of me!
I can feel your presence, Spirit I summoned!
Show yourself to me!
Ha! Something slashes at my heart!
I am tossed around
And my senses are whipped up into a storm!
I feel you pulling out my heart; do, consume me, take all of me:
You must, you must, even if it costs me my life!

(He seizes the book, and mysteriously pronounces the sign of the Spirit. A ruddy flame flashes: the Spirit appears in the flame)

Who's summoned me?

FAUST (*with averted head*)
Terrible to see!

SPIRIT
Me hast thou long with might attracted,
Long from my sphere thy food exacted,
And now—

FAUST
Woe! I endure not thee!

SPIRIT
To view me is thine aspiration,
My voice to hear, my countenance to see;
Thy powerful yearning moveth me,
Here am I!--what mean perturbation
Thee, superhuman, shakes? Thy soul's high
calling, where?
Where is the breast, which from itself a world did bear,
And shaped and cherished--which with joy expanded,
To be our peer, with us, the Spirits, banded?
Where art thou, Faust, whose voice has pierced to me,
Who towards me pressed with all thine energy?
He art thou, who, my presence breathing, seeing,
Trembles through all the depths of being,
A writhing worm, a terror-stricken form?

FAUST
Thee, form of flame, shall I then fear?
Yes, I am Faust: I am thy peer!

SPIRIT
In the tides of Life, in Action's storm,
A fluctuant wave,
A shuttle free,
Birth and the Grave,
An eternal sea,
A weaving, flowing
Life, all-glowing,
Thus at Time's humming loom 'tis my hand prepares
The garment of Life which the Deity wears!

FAUST
Thou, who around the wide world wendest,
Thou busy Spirit, how near I feel to thee!

SPIRIT
Thou'rt like the Spirit which thou comprehendest,
Not me!
(*Disappears.*)

FAUST (*overwhelmed*)
Not thee!

This is a dreadful thing to see!

I have felt your presence for a long time,
Drawing your powers from my world,
And now -

No! I can't face you!

You want to see me,
To hear my voice and see my face,
It was your desire which brought me here,
And here I am! What petty fears
Worry you, you superman? Where are those high hopes
of the soul?
Where is the heart which made a whole world
For itself, shaped and loved it, and happily
Wanted to become like we Spirits?
Where are you, Faust, who called to me,
With every fibre of your being?
Is this you, who seeing my living presence
Trembles from head to foot,
A wriggling worm, terrified?

Shall I be frightened of you, fiery shape?
Yes I am Faust: I am your equal!

In the currents of life, in the storm of Action,
I flow like a wave,
Fly like the shuttle of a loom,
Over Birth and Death
An eternal sea,
I shape and flow through life,
Glowing,
At the loom of time I weave
The clothes of Life which God wears!

You travel the world from end to end,
Busy Spirit, and how close I feel to you!

You're like the Spirit you understand, and that's not me!

(Disappears)

Not you!

Whom then?
I, image of the Godhead!
Not even like thee!
(*A knock*).
O Death!--I know it--'tis my Famulus!
My fairest luck finds no fruition:
In all the fullness of my vision
The soulless sneak disturbs me thus!

WAGNER

Pardon, I heard your declamation;
'Twas sure an old Greek tragedy you read?
In such an art I crave some preparation,
Since now it stands one in good stead.
I've often heard it said, a preacher
Might learn, with a comedian for a teacher.

FAUST

Yes, when the priest comedian is by nature,
As haply now and then the case may be.

WAGNER

Ah, when one studies thus, a prisoned creature,
That scarce the world on holidays can see,--
Scarce through a glass, by rare occasion,
How shall one lead it by persuasion?

FAUST

You'll ne'er attain it, save you know the feeling,
Save from the soul it rises clear,
Serene in primal strength, compelling
The hearts and minds of all who hear.
You sit forever gluing, patching;
You cook the scraps from others' fare;
And from your heap of ashes hatching
A starveling flame, ye blow it bare!
Take children's, monkeys' gaze admiring,
If such your taste, and be content;
But ne'er from heart to heart you'll speak inspiring,
Save your own heart is eloquent!

WAGNER

Yet through delivery orators succeed;
I feel that I am far behind, indeed.

FAUST

Seek thou the honest recompense!
Beware, a tinkling fool to be!
With little art, clear wit and sense
Suggest their own delivery;

Who then?
I'm the image of God,
But not like you!
(A knock)
It's Death! I know it! He's come to attend to me!
My luck won't serve me now:
Even as I have my great vision
The soulless sneak comes to disturb it!

(Enter WAGNER, in dressing-gown and night-cap, a lamp in his hand. FAUST turns impatiently)

Excuse me, I heard you making speeches;
Surely you were reading out an old Greek tragedy?
I'd like to be taught how to do that,
As it's so admired these days.
I've often heard people say that a preacher
Can learn a lot from an actor.

Yes he can, when the preacher is an actor by nature;
You find ones now and then who are.

Ah, when one's chained to his books like this,
And hardly goes out in the world even on the holidays,
Looks at the world from a distance;
How can one try to get through to him?

You never will, unless you know how it feels,
Unless your speech comes straight from the heart,
Calm with the strength of nature, drawing to you
The hearts and minds of all your listeners.
You can sit forever, making do,
Taking the crumbs from other's tables;
And when from your pathetic heap of ashes
You get a tiny flame, you'll blow it out!
Take your applause from kids and monkeys,
If that's what you want and it makes you happy,
But you'll never touch other's hearts with your speech
Unless you're speaking from the heart yourself!

Yet orators succeed with the tricks of speech;
I think I'm very backward in all this.

Don't try and be too tricky!
Don't make a chattering fool of yourself!
It doesn't take much skill for wit and sense
To find the right form of speech.

And if thou'rt moved to speak in earnest,
What need, that after words thou yearnest?

Yes, your discourses, with their glittering show,
Where ye for men twist shredded thought like paper,
Are unrefreshing as the winds that blow
The rustling leaves through chill autumnal vapor!

WAGNER
Ah, God! but Art is long,
And Life, alas! is fleeting.
And oft, with zeal my critic-duties meeting,
In head and breast there's something wrong.
How hard it is to compass the assistance
Whereby one rises to the source!
And, haply, ere one travels half the course
Must the poor devil quit existence.

FAUST
Is parchment, then, the holy fount before thee,
A draught wherefrom thy thirst forever slakes?
No true refreshment can restore thee,
Save what from thine own soul spontaneous breaks.

WAGNER
Pardon! a great delight is granted
When, in the spirit of the ages planted,
We mark how, ere our times, a sage has thought,
And then, how far his work, and grandly, we have brought.

FAUST
O yes, up to the stars at last!
Listen, my friend: the ages that are past
Are now a book with seven seals protected:
What you the Spirit of the Ages call
Is nothing but the spirit of you all,
Wherein the Ages are reflected.
So, oftentimes, you miserably mar it!
At the first glance who sees it runs away.
An offal-barrel and a lumber-garret,
Or, at the best, a Punch-and-Judy play,
With maxims most pragmatical and hitting,
As in the mouths of puppets are befitting!

WAGNER
But then, the world--the human heart and brain!

Of these one covets some slight apprehension.

FAUST
Yes, of the kind which men attain!
Who dares the child's true name in public mention?

If you're genuinely going to speak the truth,
Why would you need to scrabble around for clever words?
All these fine speeches
In which thoughts are balled up like paper,
Are as sterile as the chilly winds
Which blow through the dead autumn leaves.

Oh God! Art takes a long time,
And life is sadly short.
I've often tried hard to get my work done,
Only to find my head and heart lack inspiration.
How difficult it is to find the way
Up to the fountain of knowledge!
It seems you can only make half the journey
Before you die.

Do you think inspiration comes from books then?
Is that how you're going to get it?
You can't get true inspiration,
From anything except your own soul.

Excuse me! There's great joy to be had
From looking back to what's been done already,
Studying the thoughts of wise men,
And seeing how far, and how well, we have developed their work.

Oh yes, that'll get you to the stars!
Listen to me, my friend, times gone by
Are like a book that can't be read:
What you call the Spirit of the Ages
Is just the spirit of all men
Reflected at different times.
So often you make a miserable mess of it,
So those who see what you have done recoil from it!
You make it into a dustbin or a dusty attic,
Or, the most you can hope for, a puppet show,
With a bunch of clever clichés,
Such as suit the mouths of puppets!

But what about the world; the human heart and the brain!
One wants to get some little knowledge of them.

Knowledge of the kind which men create, yes!
Who dares speak the truth to the public?

The few, who thereof something really learned,
Unwisely frank, with hearts that spurned concealing,
And to the mob laid bare each thought and feeling,
Have evermore been crucified and burned.
I pray you, Friend, 'tis now the dead of night;
Our converse here must be suspended.

WAGNER
I would have shared your watches with delight,
That so our learned talk might be extended.
To-morrow, though, I'll ask, in Easter leisure,

This and the other question, at your pleasure.
Most zealously I seek for erudition:
Much do I know--but to know all is my ambition.

FAUST (solus)
That brain, alone, not loses hope, whose choice is

To stick in shallow trash forevermore,--
Which digs with eager hand for buried ore,
And, when it finds an angle-worm, rejoices!
Dare such a human voice disturb the flow,

Around me here, of spirit-presence fullest?
And yet, this once my thanks I owe
To thee, of all earth's sons the poorest, dullest!
For thou hast torn me from that desperate state
Which threatened soon to overwhelm my senses:
The apparition was so giant-great,
It dwarfed and withered all my soul's pretences!
I, image of the Godhead, who began--
Deeming Eternal Truth secure in nearness—

Ye choirs, have ye begun the sweet, consoling chant,

Which, through the night of Death, the angels ministrant
Sang, God's new Covenant repeating?

CHORUS OF WOMEN
With spices and precious
Balm, we arrayed him;
Faithful and gracious,
We tenderly laid him:
Linen to bind him
Cleanlily wound we:
Ah! when we would find him,
Christ no more found we!

The few who have found some true learning
And carelessly spoke out with honest hearts,
Showing their true thoughts and feelings to the mob,
Have always ended up burned and crucified.
I beg you, Friend, it's now very late;
Let's leave our chat for now.

I would gladly have sat up with you through the night,
To carry on our intellectual discussions.
I'll ask you tomorrow, as we have the Easter holiday before us,
Many questions, if you'll allow me.
I'm determined to seek enlightenment:
I know a lot, but I want to know everything.

[Exit.]

The only mind which still clings to hope is the one which chooses
To root around in shallow trash forever,
Digging to try and find buried gold,
And is delighted when it finds an earthworm!
Does he really dare to disturb with his voice the atmosphere in here,
Which is swimming with Spirits?
But just for once I'm in your debt
You worthless, dull man.
You tore me away from that terrible condition
Which seemed about to drive me insane:
That Spirit was so terrifying and massive,
It dwarfed my soul and showed up its pretensions!
I, who am made in the image of God, started...
Thinking that I was getting near to discovering Eternal Truth...
What, choirs, have you started that sweet chant of consolation,
Which the angels sang the night Death came into the world
As they repeated God's new covenant with man?

With spices and precious
Ointment, we annointed him;
Faithful and gracious,
We tenderly laid him out:
We wrapped him round
With clean linen for his shroud:
Ah! When we found him,
We did not find Christ!

CHORUS OF ANGELS
Christ is ascended!
Bliss hath invested him,--
Woes that molested him,
Trials that tested him,
Gloriously ended!

Christ has risen to heaven!
He has been filled with joy.
The sorrows he suffered
And his testing trials
Have ended in Glory!

FAUST
Why, here in dust, entice me with your spell,

Ye gentle, powerful sounds of Heaven?
Peal rather there, where tender natures dwell.
Your messages I hear, but faith has not been given;
The dearest child of Faith is Miracle.
I venture not to soar to yonder regions
Whence the glad tidings hither float;
And yet, from childhood up familiar with the note,
To Life it now renews the old allegiance.
Once Heavenly Love sent down a burning kiss
Upon my brow, in Sabbath silence holy;
And, filled with mystic presage, chimed the
church-bell slowly, And prayer dissolved me in a
fervent bliss.
A sweet, uncomprehended yearning
Drove forth my feet through woods and meadows free,
And while a thousand tears were burning,
I felt a world arise for me.

These chants, to youth and all its sports appealing,

Proclaimed the Spring's rejoicing holiday;
And Memory holds me now, with childish feeling,
Back from the last, the solemn way.
Sound on, ye hymns of Heaven, so sweet and mild!
My tears gush forth: the Earth takes back her child!

Why, when I'm stuck here in the dust, do you charm me
with your spell,
You beautiful strong songs from heaven?
Keep your song up there, for the creatures of heaven.
I can hear your words, but I have not been given faith;
Faith creates miracles.
I'm not trying to get to the place
From which these glad tidings come;
And yet, I've known the song since I was a child,
And it brings back that old faith to me.
Once Heavenly Love placed a burning kiss
Upon my forehead, in the silence of a holy Sunday,
And the church bell rang slowly, mystically,
And saying my prayers made me collapse with
happiness.
A delicious desire which I didn't understand
Sent me running off through the woods and meadows,
And as my tears fell like rain
I could feel a whole new world which had been made for
me.
These songs, which called out to youth and all its
interests,
Announced that the Spring holiday was here;
And that memory calls me back, feeling like a child,
From that final dark path.
Sing on, heavenly hymns, so sweet and mild!
My tears are flowing: the earth reclaims her child!

CHORUS OF DISCIPLES
Has He, victoriously,
Burst from the vaulted
Grave, and all-gloriously
Now sits exalted?
Is He, in glow of birth,
Rapture creative near?
Ah! to the woe of earth
Still are we native here.
We, his aspiring
Followers, Him we miss;
Weeping, desiring,
Master, Thy bliss!

Has He, in triumph,
Burst from the arched
Burial chamber and now
Sits exalted in glory?
Is He, with this shining birth
Close to the ecstasy of creation?
Ah! We're still tied
To the sadness of the earth.
We, who want to follow His path,
We miss Him;
Weeping, desiring,
Master, the happiness you give!

CHORUS OF ANGELS
Christ is arisen,
Out of Corruption's womb:

Christ has risen
Out of the corrupt things of earth:

Burst ye the prison,
Break from your gloom!
Praising and pleading him,
Lovingly needing him,
Brotherly feeding him,
Preaching and speeding him,
Blessing, succeeding Him,
Thus is the Master near,--
Thus is He here!

Break out of your prison,
Forget your sadness!
Praising and pleading with Him,
Needing His love,
Feeding Him like a brother,
Praying and travelling with Him,
Blessing and following Him,
The Master is near;
The Master is here!

A STUDENT
Deuce! how they step, the buxom wenches!
Come, Brother! we must see them to the benches.
A strong, old beer, a pipe that stings and bites,
A girl in Sunday clothes,--these three are my delights.

My goodness! Look at the way these busty girls strut!
Come on, brother! Let's get them to sit with us.
A well aged beer, a pipe of strong tobacco,
And a girl in her best clothes – these are the things I
enjoy.

CITIZEN'S DAUGHTER
Just see those handsome fellows, there!
It's really shameful, I declare;--
To follow servant-girls, when they
Might have the most genteel society to-day!

Look at those handsome lads there!
I must say I think it's shameful:
Following servant girls
When they could have much more polite company!

SECOND STUDENT (*to the* First)
Not quite so fast! Two others come behind,--
Those, dressed so prettily and neatly.
My neighbor's one of them, I find,
A girl that takes my heart, completely.
They go their way with looks demure,
But they'll accept us, after all, I'm sure.

Hold your horses! Here are another two -
Those two, dressed up so pretty and elegant.
I see one of them's my neighbour,
A girl who steals my heart away.
There they go, looking so modest,
But I'm sure they'll spend some time with us.

THE FIRST
No, Brother! not for me their formal ways.
Quick! lest our game escape us in the press:
The hand that wields the broom on Saturdays
Will best, on Sundays, fondle and caress.

No, brother! I don't want any high class manners.
Hurry, in case those others get away in the crowd:
The servant's hand that sweeps up on Saturdays
With a bit of luck will be fondling and stroking on
Sundays.

CITIZEN
He suits me not at all, our new-made Burgomaster!
Since he's installed, his arrogance grows faster.
How has he helped the town, I say?
Things worsen,--what improvement names he?
Obedience, more than ever, claims he,
And more than ever we must pay!

I'm not happy with our newly elected Mayor!
Since he got in he's become more and more arrogant.
I ask you, what's he done for the town?
Things just get worse – can he say what's got better?
He wants us to do just what he says,
And the taxes get higher and higher!

BEGGAR (*sings*)
Good gentlemen and lovely ladies,
So red of cheek and fine of dress,
Behold, how needful here your aid is,

My kind gentlemen and beautiful ladies,
So rosy cheeked and smartly dressed,
Look how much your help is needed here,

And see and lighten my distress!
Let me not vainly sing my ditty;
He's only glad who gives away:
A holiday, that shows your pity,
Shall be for me a harvest-day!

See my pain and help me out!
Don't let me sing my song in vain;
The charitable man's a happy man:
For you it's a holiday, a day to show pity,
Which means it's a profitable day for me!

ANOTHER CITIZEN
On Sundays, holidays, there's naught I take delight in,
Like gossiping of war, and war's array,
When down in Turkey, far away,
The foreign people are a-fighting.
One at the window sits, with glass and friends,
And sees all sorts of ships go down the river gliding:
And blesses then, as home he wends
At night, our times of peace abiding.

On Sundays and holidays there's nothing I like better
Than chatting about war and weapons.
Down in Turkey, far away from here,
The foreigners are fighting.
You can sit at the window, with a drink and your friends
And see all sorts of ships sailing down the river:
And when you walk home at night you can give thanks
For the peaceful times we're living in.

THIRD CITIZEN
Yes, Neighbor! that's my notion, too:
Why, let them break their heads, let loose their passions,
And mix things madly through and through,
So, here, we keep our good old fashions!

That's right neighbor! That's my way of thinking too:
Let them break their heads, let their emotions run riot,

And shake everything up in their mad fashion,
As long as we can stick to our good old ways here!

OLD WOMAN (*to the Citizen's Daughter*)
Dear me, how fine! So handsome, and so young!
Who wouldn't lose his heart, that met you?
Don't be so proud! I'll hold my tongue,
And what you'd like I'll undertake to get you.

Goodness me, how lovely! So young and beautiful!
Who wouldn't fall for you when he met you?
Don't look so snobbish! I'll keep quiet,
And I'll get you whatever you fancy.

CITIZEN'S DAUGHTER
Come, Agatha! I shun the witch's sight
Before folks, lest there be misgiving:

'Tis true, she showed me, on Saint Andrew's Night,

My future sweetheart, just as he were living.

Let's go, Agatha! I don't want to be seen with this witch
In front of everybody, in case there's a misunderstanding:
It's true that on Saint Andrew's Night, she magicked up a vision
Of my future lover, just as if he were alive in front of me.

THE OTHER
She showed me mine, in crystal clear,
With several wild young blades, a soldier-lover:
I seek him everywhere, I pry and peer,
And yet, somehow, his face I can't discover.

She showed me mine too, clear as you like,
With several dashing young fighters, a soldier-lover:
I've been looking high and low, searching everywhere,
And yet I can't find him anywhere.

SOLDIERS
Castles, with lofty
Ramparts and towers,
Maidens disdainful
In Beauty's array,
Both shall be ours!
Bold is the venture,
Splendid the pay!
Lads, let the trumpets
For us be suing,--

Castles, with high
Battlements and towers,
High and mighty girls
Dressed up in Beauty,
We'll have them both!
It's a daring adventure,
With wonderful pay!
Lads, let the trumpets,
Ring out for us,

Calling to pleasure,
Calling to ruin.
Stormy our life is;
Such is its boon!
Maidens and castles
Capitulate soon.
Bold is the venture,
Splendid the pay!
And the soldiers go marching,
Marching away!

Calling us to our pleasure
And our ruin.
Our life is chaotic,
But here's the reward!
Girls and castles,
Quickly surrender.
It's a daring adventure,
With wonderful pay!
And the soldiers go marching,
Marching away!

FAUST AND WAGNER
FAUST
Released from ice are brook and river
By the quickening glance of the gracious Spring;
The colors of hope to the valley cling,
And weak old Winter himself must shiver,
Withdrawn to the mountains, a crownless king:
Whence, ever retreating, he sends again
Impotent showers of sleet that darkle
In belts across the green o' the plain.
But the sun will permit no white to sparkle;
Everywhere form in development moveth;
He will brighten the world with the tints he loveth,
And, lacking blossoms, blue, yellow, and red,

The streams and rivers have been freed from the ice
By the sweet warmth of the lovely Spring;
The valley is dressed in the colours of hope,
And the weak old winter gets cold himself,
And retreats to the mountains, a king without a crown:
From there he sends down weak showers of sleet

That darken the green plains at intervals.
But the sun won't allow any snow to settle;
Things are growing everywhere;
He's painting the world in the colors he loves,
And when He hasn't got the blue, yellow and red flowers,

He takes these gaudy people instead.
Turn thee about, and from this height
Back on the town direct thy sight.
Out of the hollow, gloomy gate,
The motley throngs come forth elate:
Each will the joy of the sunshine hoard,
To honor the Day of the Risen Lord!
They feel, themselves, their resurrection:
From the low, dark rooms, scarce habitable;
From the bonds of Work, from Trade's restriction;
From the pressing weight of roof and gable;
From the narrow, crushing streets and alleys;
From the churches' solemn and reverend night,
All come forth to the cheerful light.
How lively, see! the multitude sallies,
Scattering through gardens and fields remote,
While over the river, that broadly dallies,
Dances so many a festive boat;
And overladen, nigh to sinking,
The last full wherry takes the stream.
Yonder afar, from the hill-paths blinking,

He uses these colorful people instead.
Turn round, and from up here,
Look back to the town.
Out of the hollow, dark gate,
The mob pours out, happy:
They'll all enjoy the sunshine,
To celebrate the day of the Lord's Rising!
They feel as if they've been resurrected too,
Taken from their hardly habitable low dark rooms,
From the chains of work and of trade,
From the roofs and ceilings pressing down on them,
From the narrow streets and alleys hemming them in,
From the solemn darkness of the churches,
They all come out into the cheery light.
See how the lively crowd comes out,
Spreading through the gardens and far off fields,
While on the wide, meandering river,
There are many cheerful boats,
And packed until it almost sinks,
The last barge puts out from the shore.
Over there, far off, gleaming from the paths on the hillside,

Their clothes are colors that softly gleam.
I hear the noise of the village, even;
Here is the People's proper Heaven;

The colours of their clothes shine softly.
I can even hear the noise of the village;
This is the real Heaven of the people:

Here high and low contented see!
Here I am Man,--dare man to be!

WAGNER
To stroll with you, Sir Doctor, flatters;
'Tis honor, profit, unto me.
But I, alone, would shun these shallow matters,

Since all that's coarse provokes my enmity.
This fiddling, shouting, ten-pin rolling
I hate,--these noises of the throng:
They rave, as Satan were their sports controlling.
And call it mirth, and call it song!

PEASANTS, UNDER THE LINDEN-TREE
(*Dance and Song.*)
All for the dance the shepherd dressed,
In ribbons, wreath, and gayest vest
Himself with care arraying:
Around the linden lass and lad
Already footed it like mad:
    Hurrah! hurrah!   Hurrah--tarara-la!
The fiddle-bow was playing.
He broke the ranks, no whit afraid,
And with his elbow punched a maid,
Who stood, the dance surveying:
The buxom wench, she turned and said:
"Now, you I call a stupid-head!"
    Hurrah! hurrah!   Hurrah--tarara-la!
"Be decent while you're staying!"

Then round the circle went their flight,
They danced to left, they danced to right:
Their kirtles all were playing.
They first grew red, and then grew warm,
And rested, panting, arm in arm,--
    Hurrah! hurrah!   Hurrah--tarara-la!
And hips and elbows straying.
Now, don't be so familiar here!
How many a one has fooled his dear,
Waylaying and betraying!
And yet, he coaxed her soon aside,
And round the linden sounded wide.
    Hurrah! hurrah!   Hurrah--tarara-la!
And the fiddle-bow was playing.

OLD PEASANT
Sir Doctor, it is good of you,
That thus you condescend, to-day,
Among this crowd of merry folk,
A highly-learned man, to stray.
Then also take the finest can,
We fill with fresh wine, for your sake:

You can see how happy both high and low are!
Here I feel like a man – so let me be one!

It's wonderful to stroll with you, good Doctor;
It's an honor and valuable for me.
But for my part, I'm not interested in these shallow pastimes:
Everything vulgar revolts me.
This fiddle music, shouting, bowling,
I hate them, all these crowd noises:
They rush around as if possessed by the Devil,
And call it humor and call it singing!

The shepherd's all dressed up for the dance,
In ribbons, a wreath and his brightest vest,
Dressing himself with care:
Around the linden tree the lass and lad
Had already danced around madly:
Hurrah! Hurrah! Hurrah! Tra-la!
The fiddler was playing.
He broke through the crowd, good and bold,
And bumped a girl with his elbow,
Who was standing watching the dance:
This buxom lass, she turned and said:
"Now, I call you an idiot!"
Hurrah! Hurrah! Hurrah! Tra-la!
"Just behave yourself while you're here!"
Hurrah! Hurrah! Hurrah! Tra-la!
Then they pranced around the circle,
Dancing left and dancing right,
Their coats and dresses flapping.
They got red in the face, and then got hot,
And rested, panting, arm in arm,
Hurrah! Hurrah! Hurrah! Tra-la!
With hips and elbows touching.
Now, don't you get so saucy!
How many a man's betrayed his wife,
Sneaking and betraying!
But still, he soon persuaded her to go off with him,
And all round the tree the song rang out:
Hurrah! Hurrah! Hurrah! Tra-la!
And the fiddler was playing.

Noble Doctor, you're very good,
To lower yourself, today,
To mix with this merry crowd,
You, a well-educated man.
Here, we'll take the best glass we have
And fill it with fresh wine for you:

I offer it, and humbly wish
That not alone your thirst is slake,--
That, as the drops below its brink,
So many days of life you drink!

Here it is, and I humbly hope,
That it doesn't just slake your thirst,
But that there are as many days in your life
As there are drops of wine in your drink!

FAUST
I take the cup you kindly reach,
With thanks and health to all and each.

I'll have the drink you so kindly offer,
Gratefully, and wish you all good health!
(The People gather in a circle about him.)

OLD PEASANT
In truth, 'tis well and fitly timed,
That now our day of joy you share,
Who heretofore, in evil days,
Gave us so much of helping care.
Still many a man stands living here,
Saved by your father's skillful hand,
That snatched him from the fever's rage
And stayed the plague in all the land.
Then also you, though but a youth,
Went into every house of pain:
Many the corpses carried forth,
But you in health came out again.
No test or trial you evaded:
A Helping God the helper aided.

It really is most appropriate,
That you share our happy day,
The man who in the past, in dark days,
Looked after us so well.
There are many men here who are still alive,
Thanks to the skill of your father,
Who pulled them back from their fever
And stopped the plague everywhere.
And you, even though you were just a boy,
Went into every house where the illness had come:
Many came out of them as corpses,
But you came out with your health intact.
You didn't shirk the hardest tests:
You were helped by a helping God.

ALL
Health to the man, so skilled and tried.
That for our help he long may abide!

Good health to the man, so clever and experienced,
Long may he continue to give us his help!

FAUST
To Him above bow down, my friends,
Who teaches help, and succor sends!
(He goes on with WAGNER.)

Give your thanks to Him above, my friends,
Who teaches us to help and sends his comfort!

WAGNER
With what a feeling, thou great man, must thou
Receive the people's honest veneration!
How lucky he, whose gifts his station
With such advantages endow!
Thou'rt shown to all the younger generation:
Each asks, and presses near to gaze;

The fiddle stops, the dance delays.
Thou goest, they stand in rows to see,
And all the caps are lifted high;
A little more, and they would bend the knee
As if the Holy Host came by.

How good you must feel, you great man,
Taking the honest respect of the people!
How lucky a man is, whose gifts
Raise him to such a high position!
They show you off to all their children;
They ask about you and crowd in to get a glimpse of you;
The fiddle stops, they put off their dancing.
When you leave, they line your path to see you,
And every man raises his cap to you;
If they had any more respect,
They'd kneel down as if God and his angels were passing through.

FAUST
A few more steps ascend, as far as yonder stone!--
Here from our wandering will we rest contented.

Climb up a few more steps, up to that stone there!
We'll stop for a good rest from our walk.

Here, lost in thought, I've lingered oft alone,
When foolish fasts and prayers my life tormented.
Here, rich in hope and firm in faith,
With tears, wrung hands and sighs, I've striven,
The end of that far-spreading death
Entreating from the Lord of Heaven!
Now like contempt the crowd's applauses seem:
Couldst thou but read, within mine inmost spirit,
How little now I deem,
That sire or son such praises merit!
My father's was a sombre, brooding brain,
Which through the holy spheres of Nature groped
and wandered, And honestly, in his own fashion,
pondered
With labor whimsical, and pain:
Who, in his dusky work-shop bending,
With proved adepts in company,
Made, from his recipes unending,
Opposing substances agree.
There was a Lion red, a wooer daring,
Within the Lily's tepid bath espoused,
And both, tormented then by flame unsparing,
By turns in either bridal chamber housed.
If then appeared, with colors splendid,
The young Queen in her crystal shell,
This was the medicine--the patients' woes soon ended,

And none demanded: who got well?
Thus we, our hellish boluses compounding,
Among these vales and hills surrounding,
Worse than the pestilence, have passed.
Thousands were done to death from poison of my
giving;
And I must hear, by all the living,
The shameless murderers praised at last!

WAGNER
Why, therefore, yield to such depression?
A good man does his honest share
In exercising, with the strictest care,
The art bequeathed to his possession!
Dost thou thy father honor, as a youth?
Then may his teaching cheerfully impel thee:
Dost thou, as man, increase the stores of truth?
Then may thine own son afterwards excel thee.

FAUST
O happy he, who still renews
The hope, from Error's deeps to rise forever!
That which one does not know, one needs to use;

And what one knows, one uses never.
But let us not, by such despondence, so

I've often stopped up here, meditating alone,
When I've been disturbed by foolish prayers and fasting.
Here, filled with hope and belief,
Crying, wringing my hands and sighing, I've tried
To put an end to the death spreading through the land,
Calling on God for help!
Now the crowd's praise feels like an insult:
If you could see into my mind
You'd see how I think
That neither the father nor the son deserve such praise.
My father had a gloomy sort of mind
Which wandered around the world of Nature groping for
truth,

And got his answers through honest laborious work.
Bent over in his dusty workshop,
With other recognised experts,
Through endless trials he made
Different substances meld together.
So the "Red Lion", like a daring suitor,
Was dipped into a lukewarm bath of "Lily",
And then they were both tormented with flame,
In this "bridal chamber".
Then a splendidly coloured potion appeared,
Like a young Queen in the glass vessel,
This was the medicine we made – and the patients'
suffering was over,
And there was no-one to ask, "who was cured?"
So, with these devilish pills we'd made,
We roamed around these hills and valleys,
And were worse than the plague itself.
Thousands died through taking the poisons I gave them,

And I have to listen to the survivors
Praising these shameless murderers.

Why give in to such gloomy thoughts?
A good man can only do his best
By carefully employing
The skills which he has been granted!
Did you respect your father when you were a child?
Then may what he taught you push you forward:
As a man, do you add to the general store of learning?
Then may your son become even better than you.

How happy the man is, who keeps on hoping
Even though he's drowned in a sea of Error!
One always wants to use the things one doesn't
understand,
And what one does understand one doesn't use.
But let's not let such gloomy thoughts

The fortune of this hour embitter!
Mark how, beneath the evening sunlight's glow,
The green-embosomed houses glitter!
The glow retreats, done is the day of toil;
It yonder hastes, new fields of life exploring;
Ah, that no wing can lift me from the soil,
Upon its track to follow, follow soaring!
Then would I see eternal Evening gild
The silent world beneath me glowing,
On fire each mountain-peak, with peace each valley
filled,
The silver brook to golden rivers flowing.
The mountain-chain, with all its gorges deep,
Would then no more impede my godlike motion;
And now before mine eyes expands the ocean
With all its bays, in shining sleep!
Yet, finally, the weary god is sinking;
The new-born impulse fires my mind,--
I hasten on, his beams eternal drinking,
The Day before me and the Night behind,
Above me heaven unfurled, the floor of waves
beneath me,--
A glorious dream! though now the glories fade.
Alas! the wings that lift the mind no aid
Of wings to lift the body can bequeath me.
Yet in each soul is born the pleasure
Of yearning onward, upward and away,
When o'er our heads, lost in the vaulted azure,
The lark sends down his flickering lay,--
When over crags and piny highlands
The poising eagle slowly soars,
And over plains and lakes and islands
The crane sails by to other shores.

WAGNER
I've had, myself, at times, some odd caprices,
But never yet such impulse felt, as this is.
One soon fatigues, on woods and fields to look,
Nor would I beg the bird his wing to spare us:
How otherwise the mental raptures bear us
From page to page, from book to book!
Then winter nights take loveliness untold,
As warmer life in every limb had crowned you;
And when your hands unroll some parchment rare
and old,
All Heaven descends, and opens bright around you!

FAUST
One impulse art thou conscious of, at best;
O, never seek to know the other!
Two souls, alas! reside within my breast,
And each withdraws from, and repels, its brother.
One with tenacious organs holds in love

Darken this happy hour!
Look how the evening sunlight
Makes the houses glitter amongst the trees.
The light retreats, the working day is done;
It flies over there to explore new lands.
Ah, I wish I had wings that could lift me from the earth
And fly off after it, soaring on its track!
Then I would see the ageless evening coloring
The silent world below me with glowing gold,
Setting flames on every mountain top, filling every valley
with peace,
And the silver streams would flow into golden rivers.
The mountain range, with all its deep gorges,
Would not be able to block my Godlike path;
And now the ocean appears before me,
With its bays all shining in the calm!
Yet, finally, the tired sun is sinking,
But I have a new idea in mind,
I rush on, absorbing all his eternal light,
Day ahead and Night behind,
Above me the wide skies of heaven, the waves a floor
below,
What a glorious dream! But the glories are fading now.
Alas! The mind has wings of imagination,
But that can't give the body wings.
We all have within us when we're born
The pleasure of imagining that we can fly,
When over our heads, lost in the overarching blue,
We hear the lark singing his warbling song,
Or when over the crags and pine covered slopes
The elegant eagle slowly soars,
And when over plains and lakes and islands,
The crane sails by on his way to other shores.

I've had some odd feelings myself from time to time,
But I've never felt anything like that.
One quickly gets bored of looking at woods and fields,
And I wouldn't ask for the wings of a bird:
It's different when we fly inside our minds,
From page to page and book to book!
Then winter nights become unimaginably lovely,
And blissful warmth flows through your limbs,
And when your hands open some rare old book,

Then you're truly in Heaven!

You only feel one desire at the best of times;
Don't try and find yourself another!
Unfortunately there are two souls within me,
And each one hates the other.
One grips tight to, and loves,

And clinging lust the world in its embraces;
The other strongly sweeps, this dust above,
Into the high ancestral spaces.
If there be airy spirits near,
'Twixt Heaven and Earth on potent errands fleeing,
Let them drop down the golden atmosphere,
And bear me forth to new and varied being!
Yea, if a magic mantle once were mine,
To waft me o'er the world at pleasure,
I would not for the costliest stores of treasure--
Not for a monarch's robe--the gift resign.

The things of the earth;
The other shakes the dust off his feet,
And soars up into the heavens.
If there are Spirits which can fly nearby,
Running swift errands between heaven and earth,
Let them drop down through the golden skies,
And carry me up to a new way of being!
If I were given a magic cloak,
Which could carry me over the world at my command,
I wouldn't give it up for the world's greatest treasure,
Not even for a kingship.

WAGNER
Invoke not thus the well-known throng,
Which through the firmament diffused is faring,
And danger thousand-fold, our race to wrong.
In every quarter is preparing.
Swift from the North the spirit-fangs so sharp
Sweep down, and with their barbéd points assail you;
Then from the East they come, to dry and warp
Your lungs, till breath and being fail you:

Don't call up that familiar crowd
Which races through the skies,
That poses so many dangers to humanity,
Dangers they're getting ready right now.
From the North the sharp toothed winds
Sweep down, and stab you with their spears;
Then they blow from the East , drying out
And twisting your lungs, until breath and life both leave
you;

If from the Desert sendeth them the South,
With fire on fire your throbbing forehead crowning,
The West leads on a host, to cure the drouth

If they come up from the desert in the South
They'll set your throbbing forehead on fire,
And the West wind brings a swarm of rainclouds to end
the drought,

Only when meadow, field, and you are drowning.
They gladly hearken, prompt for injury,--
Gladly obey, because they gladly cheat us;
From Heaven they represent themselves to be,
And lisp like angels, when with lies they meet us.
But, let us go! 'Tis gray and dusky all:
The air is cold, the vapors fall.
At night, one learns his house to prize:--
Why stand you thus, with such astonished eyes?
What, in the twilight, can your mind so trouble?

And drowns the meadows and fields, and you.
They'll hear us calling and be ready to hurt us;
They'll be glad to come so they can cheat us;
They pretend to come from Heaven,
And speak with the voices of angels as they lie to us.
But let's go! It's gray dusk all around:
The air's cold, the dew is falling.
At night, one learns to love one's house.
Why are you standing there with your eyes bulging?
What in the twilight has unsettled you so much?

FAUST
Seest thou the black dog coursing there, through corn
and stubble?

Do you see that black dog, tracking through the corn
and stubble?

WAGNER
Long since: yet deemed him not important in the least.

I saw him ages ago, but thought nothing of him.

FAUST
Inspect him close: for what tak'st thou the beast?

Have a close look: what do you make of it?

WAGNER
Why, for a poodle who has lost his master,
And scents about, his track to find.

I'm guessing he's a poodle that's lost his master,
And is sniffing around to get on his track.

FAUST

Seest thou the spiral circles, narrowing faster,
Which he, approaching, round us seems to wind?

A streaming trail of fire, if I see rightly,
Follows his path of mystery.

WAGNER
It may be that your eyes deceive you slightly;
Naught but a plain black poodle do I see.

FAUST
It seems to me that with enchanted cunning
He snares our feet, some future chain to bind.

WAGNER
I see him timidly, in doubt, around us running,

Since, in his master's stead, two strangers doth he find.

FAUST
The circle narrows: he is near!

WAGNER
A dog thou seest, and not a phantom, here!
Behold him stop--upon his belly crawl--His
tail set wagging: canine habits, all!

FAUST
Come, follow us! Come here, at least!

WAGNER
'Tis the absurdest, drollest beast.
Stand still, and you will see him wait;
Address him, and he gambols straight;
If something's lost, he'll quickly bring it,--
Your cane, if in the stream you fling it.

FAUST
No doubt you're right: no trace of mind, I own,

Is in the beast: I see but drill, alone.

WAGNER
The dog, when he's well educated,
Is by the wisest tolerated.
Yes, he deserves your favor thoroughly,--
The clever scholar of the students, he!
(*They pass in the city-gate.*)

Do you see the circles, ever narrowing,
Which he seems to be wrapping around us as he
approaches?
If my eyes don't deceive me a streaming tail of fire
Is following his mysterious path.

I think your eyes are deceiving you:
All I can see is a plain black poodle.

I think that with magic cunning
He's making a loop round our feet, so that in future a
chain can be tied round them.

What I see is him cautiously and timidly running around
us,
Since instead of his master he can see two strangers.

The circle's getting narrower, he's close now!

You're seeing a dog, not a ghost!
Look at him stopping, going down on his belly
With his tail wagging – the habits of a dog!

Come on then, at least come to us!

It's the daftest, funniest beast:
Stand still, and he stops and waits,
Talk to him and he dances about;
If you lose something he'll bring it to you quickly,
Even your cane if you've thrown it in the river.

No doubt you're right. I can't see any sort of
independent mind
In the beast: I can only see what he's been trained to do.

The well trained dog,
Is loved by wise men.
Yes, he deserves your approval,
He's one of the clever students!

III

THE STUDY

FAUST
(*Entering, with the poodle.*)
Behind me, field and meadow sleeping,
I leave in deep, prophetic night,
Within whose dread and holy keeping
The better soul awakes to light.
The wild desires no longer win us,
The deeds of passion cease to chain;
The love of Man revives within us,
The love of God revives again.
Be still, thou poodle; make not such racket and riot!
Why at the threshold wilt snuffing be?
Behind the stove repose thee in quiet!
My softest cushion I give to thee.
As thou, up yonder, with running and leaping
Amused us hast, on the mountain's crest,

So now I take thee into my keeping,
A welcome, but also a silent, guest.
Ah, when, within our narrow chamber
The lamp with friendly lustre glows,
Flames in the breast each faded ember,
And in the heart, itself that knows.
Then Hope again lends sweet assistance,
And Reason then resumes her speech:
One yearns, the rivers of existence,
The very founts of Life, to reach.
Snarl not, poodle! To the sound that rises,
The sacred tones that my soul embrace,
This bestial noise is out of place.
We are used to see, that Man despises
What he never comprehends,
And the Good and the Beautiful vilipends,
Finding them often hard to measure:
Will the dog, like man, snarl *his* displeasure?
But ah! I feel, though will thereto be stronger,
Contentment flows from out my breast no longer.
Why must the stream so soon run dry and fail us,
And burning thirst again assail us?
Therein I've borne so much probation!
And yet, this want may be supplied us;
We call the Supernatural to guide us;
We pine and thirst for Revelation,
Which nowhere worthier is, more nobly sent,
Than here, in our New Testament.
I feel impelled, its meaning to determine,--
With honest purpose, once for all,
The hallowed Original
To change to my beloved German.

I leave the field and meadow sleeping
In the deep prophetic night behind me,
Whose dreadful atmosphere
Awakes a better soul in man.
We no longer let wild desires triumph,
Or get tangled up with passionate deeds;
The love of Man comes back to us,
And so does the love of God.
Keep still, poodle, stop making such a fuss and racket!
Why do you keep sniffing around the door?
Go and sit quietly behind the stove!
I've given you my softest cushion for a bed.
As you amused us so much out there,
With your running and jumping about on the
mountaintop,
I've taken you in as my pet,
A welcome guest, if you'll be quiet.
Ah, when in this narrow room
The lamp glows with a friendly light,
An answering glow starts up in every chest
And also in the self-aware heart.
Hope comes back to help us out,
And Reason speaks to us again:
A man yearns to reach the river of life,
The very fountains of being.
Stop snarling, poodle! With the sounds in here,
The holy music which caresses my soul,
Your animal noises are out of place.
We often see that men hate
What they can't understand,
And scorn the Good and the Beautiful,
Because they can't assess their worth:
Is the dog snarling his displeasure like they do?
But oh! Even though I want it more than ever,
I can feel no contentment in my heart.
Why does the stream run out so quickly,
So that we become thirsty yet again?
It's happened to me enough times!
Yet the gap can be filled;
We call on the Spirits to guide us;
We yearn for Revelation
Which can be found in no better place
Than here, in our New Testament.
I feel the need to reveal its meaning,
With honest intentions I'm going
To translate this sacred original
Into my beloved German.

(*He opens a volume, and commences.*)
'Tis written: "In the Beginning was the *Word*."
Here am I balked: who, now can help afford?
The *Word?*--impossible so high to rate it;
And otherwise must I translate it.
If by the Spirit I am truly taught.
Then thus: "In the Beginning was the *Thought*"
This first line let me weigh completely,
Lest my impatient pen proceed too fleetly.
Is it the *Thought* which works, creates, indeed?
"In the Beginning was the *Power*," I read.
Yet, as I write, a warning is suggested,
That I the sense may not have fairly tested.
The Spirit aids me: now I see the light!
"In the Beginning was the *Act*," I write.
If I must share my chamber with thee,
Poodle, stop that howling, prithee!
Cease to bark and bellow!
Such a noisy, disturbing fellow
I'll no longer suffer near me.
One of us, dost hear me!
Must leave, I fear me.
No longer guest-right I bestow;
The door is open, art free to go.
But what do I see in the creature?
Is that in the course of nature?
Is't actual fact? or Fancy's shows?
How long and broad my poodle grows!
He rises mightily:
A canine form that cannot be!
What a spectre I've harbored thus!
He resembles a hippopotamus,
With fiery eyes, teeth terrible to see:
O, now am I sure of thee!
For all of thy half-hellish brood
The Key of Solomon is good.

SPIRITS (*in the corridor*)

Some one, within, is caught!
Stay without, follow him not!
Like the fox in a snare,
Quakes the old hell-lynx there.
Take heed--look about!
Back and forth hover,
Under and over,
And he'll work himself out.
If your aid avail him,
Let it not fail him;
For he, without measure,
Has wrought for our pleasure.

(He opens a volume, and commences)
It's written here: "In the beginning was the Word."
Now here I'm blocked, who can help me with this one?
The Word? *I can't rate that so highly,*
I'll have to translate it differently,
If I'm really to follow what the Spirit wants.
So I'll put, "In the beginning was the Thought."
Now let me weigh up my first line,
In case I'm rushing on too fast.
Is it Thought *which works and creates?*
"In the beginning was the Power," *I read.*
Yet as I write it I get the feeling
That I haven't got the sense out of it yet.
The Spirit inspires me, now I see the light!
I'll put, "In the beginning was the Act."
If I've got to share my room with you,
Poodle, please stop that howling!
Stop your barking and bellowing!
Someone who makes such a row
I won't put up with.
Now listen to me!
One of us, you hear,
Must leave, I'm afraid.
I withdraw your guest privileges;
There's the open door, you're free to go.
But what do I see in the beast now?
Is this reality? Or is it my imagination?
How tall and wide my poodle's growing!
He swells massively:
That can't be a dog!
What a demon I've let into my home!
He looks like a hippopotamus,
With burning eyes and terrible teeth:
Oh, now I know what you are!
The magick book of Solomon
Is what summons you up.

Somebody's trapped in there!
Stay out here, don't follow him!
Like a fox caught in a trap,
The old hellhound is rumbling in there.
Now keep your eyes open!
Float to and fro,
Up and down,
And he'll find his way out.
If you know how to help him,
Make sure you don't fail him;
For it's sure that what's happening,
Is meant for us to get involved.

FAUST

First, to encounter the beast,
The Words of the Four be addressed:
Salamander, shine glorious!
Wave, Undine, as bidden!
Sylph, be thou hidden!
Gnome, be laborious!
Who knows not their sense
(These elements),--
Their properties
And power not sees,--
No mastery he inherits
Over the Spirits.
Vanish in flaming ether,
Salamander!
Flow foamingly together,
Undine!
Shine in meteor-sheen,
Sylph!
Bring help to hearth and shelf.
Incubus! Incubus!
Step forward, and finish thus!
Of the Four, no feature
Lurks in the creature.
Quiet he lies, and grins disdain:
Not yet, it seems, have I given him pain.
Now, to undisguise thee,
Hear me exorcise thee!
Art thou, my gay one,
Hell's fugitive stray-one?
The sign witness now,
Before which they bow,
The cohorts of Hell!
With hair all bristling, it begins to swell.
Base Being, hearest thou?
Knowest and fearest thou
The One, unoriginate,
Named inexpressibly,
Through all Heaven impermeate,
Pierced irredressibly!
Behind the stove still banned,
See it, an elephant, expand!
It fills the space entire,
Mist-like melting, ever faster.
'Tis enough: ascend no higher,--
Lay thyself at the feet of the Master!
Thou seest, not vain the threats I bring thee:
With holy fire I'll scorch and sting thee!
Wait not to know
The threefold dazzling glow!
Wait not to know
The strongest art within my hands!

First, to take on the beast,
Address him with the Words of the Four:
Salamander, beast of the fire, shine out your light!
Undine, the water nymph, swim close by!
Slyph, spirit of the air, disappear!
Gnome, creature of the earth, dig down deep!
The person who doesn't know the virtues
Of these elements,
Their properties,
And doesn't know their power,
Can't hope to rule
Over the Spirits.
Vanish into the flame,
Salamander!
Flow into the foaming water,
Undine!
Burn like a shooting star,
Sylph!
Bring help to the hearth and home,
Incubus! Incubus!
Come to the front and make it end!
Of these Four, I can't see any element
Of them in this creature.
He lies undisturbed and grins his contempt:
It looks like I haven't given him any trouble yet.
Now, to see your true form,
Listen to my exorcism!
Are you, my saucy lad,
A stray from Hell?
Look now at this sign
Which makes the demons of hell
Bow down before it!
Its hair's all on end, it's swelling up.
You depraved creature, can you hear?
Do you know and fear
The One who was not created
With a name that can't be spoken
Who's woven into the fabric of Heaven
Run right through?
It's still stuck behind the stove,
Look at it, swelling to elephant size!
It fills the whole space,
I can see it will melt like a mist.
That's enough: don't get any taller,
Lie down at your Master's feet!
You can see I'm not making empty threats:
I'll burn and sting you with the Holy Fire!
Don't wait around to suffer
The dazzling light of the Trinity!
Don't wait to feel
The strength which I have at my fingertips!

34

MEPHISTOPHELES
(while the vapor is dissipating, steps forth from behind the stove, in the costume of a Travelling Scholar)
Why such a noise? What are my lord's commands? | *Why all the racket? What does my master desire?*

FAUST
This was the poodle's real core, | *This is the poodle's true nature,*
A travelling scholar, then? The *casus* is diverting. | *A travelling scholar? This amuses me.*

MEPHISTOPHELES
The learned gentleman I bow before: | *I take my hat off to the learned gentleman:*
You've made me roundly sweat, that's certain! | *You've made me sweat, that's for sure!*

FAUST
What is thy name? | *What's your name?*

MEPHISTOPHELES
A question small, it seems, | *That's not much of a question, to my mind,*
For one whose mind the Word so much despises; | *For someone who shuns the power of the Word;*
Who, scorning all external gleams, | *Who rejects all surface things,*
The depths of being only prizes. | *And only wants to touch the deepest parts of existence.*

FAUST
With all you gentlemen, the name's a test, | *With your type, the name's a key,*
Whereby the nature usually is expressed. | *Which gives away the secret of your true nature.*
Clearly the latter it implies | *That can be clearly seen*
In names like Beelzebub, Destroyer, Father of Lies. | *In names like Beelzebub, Destroyer, Father of Lies.*
Who art thou, then? | *Who are you, then?*

MEPHISTOPHELES
Part of that Power, not understood, | *Part of that power which is not understood,*
Which always wills the Bad, and always works the Good. | *That always wants evil, and always causes good.*

FAUST
What hidden sense in this enigma lies? | *What can this riddle mean?*

MEPHISTOPHELES
I am the Spirit that Denies! | *I'm the Spirit that Destroys!*
And justly so: for all things, from the Void | *And am right to do so: everything that was created out of the Void*

Called forth, deserve to be destroyed: | *Deserves to be destroyed:*
'Twere better, then, were naught created. | *It would be better then if nothing had ever been made.*
Thus, all which you as Sin have rated,-- | *So, everything you call Sin –*
Destruction,--aught with Evil blent,-- | *Is Destruction – anything you call evil –*
That is my proper element. | *That's how I do my work.*

FAUST
Thou nam'st thyself a part, yet show'st complete to me? | *You said you were a part of something, but you're showing yourself whole to me?*

MEPHISTOPHELES
The modest truth I speak to thee. | *I'm telling you the truth, in all humility.*
If Man, that microcosmic fool, can see | *If Man is such a fool as to see*

Himself a whole so frequently,
Part of the Part am I, once All, in primal Night,--

Part of the Darkness which brought forth the Light,
The haughty Light, which now disputes the space,
And claims of Mother Night her ancient place.
And yet, the struggle fails; since Light, howe'er it
weaves, Still, fettered, unto bodies cleaves:
It flows from bodies, bodies beautifies;
By bodies is its course impeded;
And so, but little time is needed,
I hope, ere, as the bodies die, it dies!

FAUST
I see the plan thou art pursuing:
Thou canst not compass general ruin,
And hast on smaller scale begun.

MEPHISTOPHELES
And truly 'tis not much, when all is done.
That which to Naught is in resistance set,--
The Something of this clumsy world,--has yet,
With all that I have undertaken,
Not been by me disturbed or shaken:
From earthquake, tempest, wave, volcano's brand,

Back into quiet settle sea and land!
And that damned stuff, the bestial, human brood,--
What use, in having that to play with?
How many have I made away with!
And ever circulates a newer, fresher blood.
It makes me furious, such things beholding:
From Water, Earth, and Air unfolding,
A thousand germs break forth and grow,
In dry, and wet, and warm, and chilly;
And had I not the Flame reserved, why, really,
There's nothing special of my own to show!

FAUST
So, to the actively eternal
Creative force, in cold disdain
You now oppose the fist infernal,
Whose wicked clench is all in vain!
Some other labor seek thou rather,
Queer Son of Chaos, to begin!

MEPHISTOPHELES
Well, we'll consider: thou canst gather
My views, when next I venture in.
Might I, perhaps, depart at present?

FAUST
Why thou shouldst ask, I don't perceive.

His little world as being everything -
Well, I'm a fraction of that which was once really
everything, the first night,
A part of the darkness from which the Light was made,
The arrogant Light, which now fights for space,
With Mother Night, who was here first.
Yet it can't win the fight: whatever it does, Light is still
attached to bodies:
It comes from bodies, makes bodies beautiful;
Bodies can block its path,
And so, after a little while,
I hope that, like all bodies, it'll die!

I see what you're up to:
You can't destroy everything at once,
So you're starting with something small.

And really, it's not much, when all's said and done.
Look what's put up in opposition to Nothingness:
The Somethings of this clumsy world – but
With everything I've tried
It hasn't been upset or shaken.
When there are earthquakes, storms, waves, the burning
of volcanoes,
The sea and land just settle down quietly afterwards!
And as for this damned beastly race of humans,
What fun are they to play with?
How many I've captured!
And yet always more of them come.
It makes me mad to see such things:
From the Water, Earth and the Air
A thousand seeds break open and grow,
Whether it's dry or wet, warm or cold;
Really, if I didn't have the flame of old,
I'd have nothing to show at all!

So, against the eternal living
Creative force, with cold contempt
You set up the Devil's fist,
Whose wickedness works in vain!
Find something else to do,
You strange Son of Disorder, rather than starting on me!

Well, we'll think about it: you can get
My opinions next time I visit you.
May I leave for now?

I don't see why you have to ask.

Though our acquaintance is so recent,
For further visits thou hast leave.
The window's here, the door is yonder;
A chimney, also, you behold.

MEPHISTOPHELES
I must confess that forth I may not wander,
My steps by one slight obstacle controlled,--
The wizard's-foot, that on your threshold made is.

FAUST
The pentagram prohibits thee?
Why, tell me now, thou Son of Hades,
If that prevents, how cam'st thou in to me?
Could such a spirit be so cheated?

MEPHISTOPHELES
Inspect the thing: the drawing's not completed.
The outer angle, you may see,
Is open left--the lines don't fit it.

FAUST
Well,--Chance, this time, has fairly hit it!
And thus, thou'rt prisoner to me?
It seems the business has succeeded.

MEPHISTOPHELES
The poodle naught remarked, as after thee he speeded;
But other aspects now obtain:
The Devil can't get out again.

FAUST
Try, then, the open window-pane!

MEPHISTOPHELES
For Devils and for spectres this is law:
Where they have entered in, there also they withdraw.
The first is free to us; we're governed by the second.

FAUST
In Hell itself, then, laws are reckoned?
That's well! So might a compact be
Made with you gentlemen--and binding,--surely?

MEPHISTOPHELES
All that is promised shall delight thee purely;
No skinflint bargain shalt thou see.
But this is not of swift conclusion;
We'll talk about the matter soon.
And now, I do entreat this boon--
Leave to withdraw from my intrusion.

Although we've just met,
You have my permission to visit again.
There's the window, there's the door;
A chimney too, as you can see.

I must admit that I can't leave;
My steps are blocked by one little thing,
The magic symbol on your doorstep.

The pentagram blocks your way?
Tell me then, Son of Hell,
If it blocks you now, how did you manage to get in?
Can Spirits like you be tricked?

If you look, you'll see the drawing's not complete.
The point at the far end
Is open – the lines don't join up.

Well well, luck's been on my side this time!
So, you're my prisoner?
It seems my magic symbol has worked.

In the shape of a poodle, it had no effect,
But the conditions are changed;
As a Devil I can't get back out.

Try the open window then!

For Devils and ghosts these are the rules:
They have to leave by the same way they entered.
We're free to come in, but we're bound by the laws
on leaving.

So even in Hell there are binding laws?
That's good! So might a deal be struck
With you gentlemen, and it would be binding?

All that we promise will be just for your pleasure;
You won't be getting a poor deal.
But we can't rush all this;
We'll talk about it soon.
And now, I beg you for this favor:
Let me end my visit.

FAUST

One moment more I ask thee to remain,
Some pleasant news, at least, to tell me.

I ask you just to hang on one moment;
Tell me something pleasant, at least.

MEPHISTOPHELES

Release me, now! I soon shall come again;
Then thou, at will, mayst question and compel me.

Set me free, now! I'll come back,
Then you can question and order me as you like.

FAUST

I have not snares around thee cast;
Thyself hast led thyself into the meshes.
Who traps the Devil, hold him fast!
Not soon a second time he'll catch a prey so precious.

I didn't put the net around you;
You walked into it yourself.
If you've caught the Devil, hang on to him!
You won't get a second chance to catch such rare prey.

MEPHISTOPHELES

An't please thee, also I'm content to stay,
And serve thee in a social station;
But stipulating, that I may
With arts of mine afford thee recreation.

If it's your wish, I'm happy to stay,
And to be at your disposal;
On the condition that
You'll let me amuse you with my skills.

FAUST

Thereto I willingly agree,
If the diversion pleasant be.

I certainly agree to that,
As long as the entertainment is pleasant.

MEPHISTOPHELES

My friend, thou'lt win, past all pretences,
More in this hour to soothe thy senses,
Than in the year's monotony.
That which the dainty spirits sing thee,
The lovely pictures they shall bring thee,
Are more than magic's empty show.
Thy scent will be to bliss invited;
Thy palate then with taste delighted,
Thy nerves of touch ecstatic glow!
All unprepared, the charm I spin:
We're here together, so begin!

My friend, in all honesty you'll get
More to please you in an hour
Than you would in a year of everyday life.
The songs the dainty spirits will sing for you,
The lovely pictures they will bring to you,
Are more than just empty magic tricks.
You will smell things that call you to enjoyment,
Then you'll taste things that will give you pleasure,
And you'll feel things that will have you in ecstasy!
So, starting from scratch, I work my magic:
We're both here, so let's get started!

SPIRITS

Vanish, ye darking
Arches above him!
Loveliest weather,
Born of blue ether,
Break from the sky!
O that the darkling
Clouds had departed!
Starlight is sparkling,
Tranquiller-hearted
Suns are on high.
Heaven's own children
In beauty bewildering,
Waveringly bending,
Pass as they hover;

Disappear, you dark
Ceiling above him!
Let the loveliest weather
Made from the blue air,
Cover the sky!
Banish
The dark clouds!
Starlight sparkles,
And soft suns
Fill the sky.
The angels
With unearthly beauty,
Swaying and bowing,
Pass floating by.

Longing unending
Follows them over.
They, with their glowing
Garments, out-flowing,
Cover, in going,
Landscape and bower,
Where, in seclusion,
Lovers are plighted,
Lost in illusion.
Bower on bower!
Tendrils unblighted!
Lo! in a shower
Grapes that o'ercluster
Gush into must, or
Flow into rivers
Of foaming and flashing
Wine, that is dashing
Gems, as it boundeth
Down the high places,
And spreading, surroundeth
With crystalline spaces,
In happy embraces,
Blossoming forelands,
Emerald shore-lands!
And the winged races
Drink, and fly onward--
Fly ever sunward
To the enticing
Islands, that flatter,
Dipping and rising
Light on the water!
Hark, the inspiring
Sound of their quiring!
See, the entrancing
Whirl of their dancing!
All in the air are
Freer and fairer.
Some of them scaling
Boldly the highlands,
Others are sailing,
Circling the islands;
Others are flying;
Life-ward all hieing,--
All for the distant
Star of existent
Rapture and Love!

MEPHISTOPHELES
He sleeps! Enough, ye fays! your airy number

Have sung him truly into slumber:
For this performance I your debtor prove.--
Not yet art thou the man, to catch the Fiend and hold

The heart yearns
To follow them.
They, with their shining
Clothes streaming out,
Cover as they pass,
The gardens and pavilions,
Where, in privacy,
Lovers join together,
Lost in the magic.
Leaves upon leaves!
Their stems unharmed!
Look! Like a shower
The grapes overhead,
Are crushed into sweetness, or
Flow into rivers
Of foaming, shining
Wine, that flashes like jewels
At it rushes down
From the high places,
And, spreading out, surrounds
The clear spaces,
With happy embraces,
The fertile plains,
The emerald shores!
And the angels
Drink, and fly on,
Flying always towards the sun,
To the inviting
Islands that call them,
Bobbing up and down,
Light on the water!
Listen to the inspiring
Sound of their song!
See the enchanting
Whirl of their dance!
All in the air are
More free, more lovely.
Some of them are bravely
Climbing the mountains,
Others are sailing
Around the islands,
Others are flying;
They're all going to Life,
Off to the distant
Star of living,
Pleasure and Love!

He's asleep! That's enough, you fairies! Your sweet songs
Have lulled him to sleep.
I'm indebted to you for your efforts.
You're not the man yet who can catch the Devil and keep

him!-- With fairest images of dreams infold him,

Plunge him in seas of sweet untruth!
Yet, for the threshold's magic which controlled him,
The Devil needs a rat's quick tooth.
I use no lengthened invocation:
Here rustles one that soon will work my liberation.
The lord of rats and eke of mice,
Of flies and bed-bugs, frogs and lice,
Summons thee hither to the door-sill,
To gnaw it where, with just a morsel
Of oil, he paints the spot for thee:--
There com'st thou, hopping on to me!
To work, at once! The point which made me craven
Is forward, on the ledge, engraven.
Another bite makes free the door:
So, dream thy dreams, O Faust, until we meet once
more!

FAUST (awaking)
Am I again so foully cheated?
Remains there naught of lofty spirit-sway,
But that a dream the Devil counterfeited,
And that a poodle ran away?

him!
Give him the sweetest dreams
Drown him in sweet lies!
Now, to pass the spell at the door,
I need to use a rat's teeth.
I won't bother with a lengthy spell:
Here scuttles he who can set me free.
The lord of rats and also of mice,
Of flies and bedbugs, frogs and lice,
Calls you here to the doorstep,
To chew on it where a spot of oil
Shows the place:
Here you come, hopping over me!
Get to work! The place which blocked me
Is on the front edge of the step:
One more bite and the door is unlocked,
So, sweet dreams, Faust, until we meet again!

Have I been cruelly tricked again?
Is there nothing left of all that angelic beauty,
Except for a dream the Devil conjured up,
And a poodle that ran away?

IV

THE STUDY

FAUST MEPHISTOPHELES

FAUST
A knock? Come in! Again my quiet broken?

Someone knocking? Come in! Must I be disturbed again?

MEPHISTOPHELES
'Tis I!

It's me!

FAUST
Come in!

Come in!

MEPHISTOPHELES
Thrice must the words be spoken.

You must say that three times.

FAUST
Come in, then!

Come in, then!

MEPHISTOPHELES
Thus thou pleasest me.
I hope we'll suit each other well;
For now, thy vapors to dispel,
I come, a squire of high degree,
In scarlet coat, with golden trimming,
A cloak in silken lustre swimming,
A tall cock's-feather in my hat,
A long, sharp sword for show or quarrel,--
And I advise thee, brief and flat,
To don the self-same gay apparel,
That, from this den released, and free,
Life be at last revealed to thee!

I'm pleased with you for that,
I think we'll get on very well:
For now, to blow away your cobwebs,
I come dressed as a young nobleman,
In a red coat with gold braid,
A cloak of shimmering silk,
With a tall cock's feather in my hat
And a long sharp sword, for show or for fighting,
And I'm telling you bluntly,
Dress yourself in the same flashy outfit,
So you can get out of this hole, and when you're free,
The truth of life will be shown to you!

FAUST
This life of earth, whatever my attire,
Would pain me in its wonted fashion.
Too old am I to play with passion;
Too young, to be without desire.
What from the world have I to gain?
Thou shalt abstain--renounce--refrain!
Such is the everlasting song
That in the ears of all men rings,--
That unrelieved, our whole life long,
Each hour, in passing, hoarsely sings.
In very terror I at morn awake,
Upon the verge of bitter weeping,
To see the day of disappointment break,
To no one hope of mine--not one--its promise keeping:--
That even each joy's presentiment

However I'm dressed, this earthly life,
Would pain me as it always does.
I'm too old to throw myself into life,
And too young to have lost all my passion.
What can the world give to me?
You must abstain, reject, stop!
This is the song
That's always ringing in men's ears,
Never stopping throughout our lives,
It croaks at us every hour.
I wake up in the mornings terrified,
Close to crying bitter tears,
Seeing another disappointing daybreak,
With nothing I hoped for – not one thing – having come to pass:
Even joys I'm looking forward to,

With wilful cavil would diminish,
With grinning masks of life prevent
My mind its fairest work to finish!
Then, too, when night descends, how anxiously
Upon my couch of sleep I lay me:
There, also, comes no rest to me,
But some wild dream is sent to fray me.
The God that in my breast is owned
Can deeply stir the inner sources;
The God, above my powers enthroned,
He cannot change external forces.
So, by the burden of my days oppressed,
Death is desired, and Life a thing unblest!

MEPHISTOPHELES
And yet is never Death a wholly welcome guest.

FAUST
O fortunate, for whom, when victory glances,
The bloody laurels on the brow he bindeth!
Whom, after rapid, maddening dances,
In clasping maiden-arms he findeth!
O would that I, before that spirit-power,
Ravished and rapt from life, had sunken!

MEPHISTOPHELES
And yet, by some one, in that nightly hour,
A certain liquid was not drunken.

FAUST
Eavesdropping, ha! thy pleasure seems to be.

MEPHISTOPHELES
Omniscient am I not; yet much is known to me.

FAUST
Though some familiar tone, retrieving
My thoughts from torment, led me on,
And sweet, clear echoes came, deceiving
A faith bequeathed from Childhood's dawn,
Yet now I curse whate'er entices
And snares the soul with visions vain;
With dazzling cheats and dear devices
Confines it in this cave of pain!
Cursed be, at once, the high ambition
Wherewith the mind itself deludes!
Cursed be the glare of apparition
That on the finer sense intrudes!
Cursed be the lying dream's impression
Of name, and fame, and laurelled brow!
Cursed, all that flatters as possession,
As wife and child, as knave and plow!
Cursed Mammon be, when he with treasures

Ebb away in the face of life's pettiness,
Life pulls its stupid faces at me, and stops
Me from finishing my best work!
Then, when night falls, I anxiously
Lay down on my bed to sleep:
But even there I can't get rest,
Some wild dream comes along to try my nerves.
The God that lives within me,
Can see deeply into life;
The God who lives beyond my understanding,
Can't change the world for me.
So, bowed down by the weight of years,
I long for Death, and Life is just a curse!

But nobody completely welcomes Death.

It's a lucky man who wins a victory,
And puts the bloody crown upon his head!
Who, after breathless crazy dancing,
Finds himself in the girl's arms!
Oh I wish that I, to that power of Death,
Had succumbed at such a moment!

And yet, in the dark hour of the night, someone
Didn't drink a certain liquid.

Ha! Eavesdropping seems to be your thing!

I'm not all-knowing, but I know a lot.

Although some remembered song called back
My thoughts from their torture, led me on,
And their sweet echoes conjured up a false image
Of the faith I had as a child,
Now I curse these things that suck you in
And trap your soul with untrue visions;
With dazzling tricks and clever seduction
Imprison it in this tortured cage!
This lofty illusion be damned
That lets the mind deceive itself!
And damn those glaring visions
That crush our finer senses!
Damn the lying dreams, that make us think
We'll get fame and fortune and all their rewards!
Damn the false idea that we can own anything,
Be it wife and child, land or servant!
And be damned to wealth, who shows us treasures

To restless action spurs our fate!
Cursed when, for soft, indulgent leisures,
He lays for us the pillows straight!
Cursed be the vine's transcendent nectar,--
The highest favor Love lets fall!
Cursed, also, Hope!--cursed Faith, the spectre!
And cursed be Patience most of all!

CHORUS OF SPIRITS (*invisible*)
Woe! woe!
Thou hast it destroyed,
The beautiful world,
With powerful fist:
In ruin 'tis hurled,
By the blow of a demigod shattered!
The scattered
Fragments into the Void we carry,
Deploring
The beauty perished beyond restoring.
Mightier
For the children of men,
Brightlier
Build it again,
In thine own bosom build it anew!
Bid the new career
Commence,
With clearer sense,
And the new songs of cheer
Be sung thereto!

MEPHISTOPHELES
These are the small dependants
Who give me attendance.
Hear them, to deeds and passion
Counsel in shrewd old-fashion!
Into the world of strife,
Out of this lonely life
That of senses and sap has betrayed thee,
They would persuade thee.
This nursing of the pain forego thee,
That, like a vulture, feeds upon thy breast!
The worst society thou find'st will show thee
Thou art a man among the rest.
But 'tis not meant to thrust
Thee into the mob thou hatest!
I am not one of the greatest,
Yet, wilt thou to me entrust
Thy steps through life, I'll guide thee,--
Will willingly walk beside thee,--
Will serve thee at once and forever
With best endeavor,
And, if thou art satisfied,
Will as servant, slave, with thee abide.

Which drive us on to hasty acts!
Damn him when for our lazy indulgence
He plumps up the pillows for us!
Be damned to the sweet wine from the vine
And be damned to the highest feelings of Love!
Be damned, Hope! Be damned, Faith, you ghost!
And be damned to Patience most of all!

Sorrow! Sorrow!
You've smashed it,
The beautiful world,
With a powerful fist:
It's laid in ruins,
By the blow of a demigod!
We'll carry the scattered fragments
Off into the Void,
Mourning,
For a beauty which can never be repaired.
Stronger
For your children,
Brighter,
Build it again,
Build it again in your heart!
Start the work again,
Begin,
With clearer vision,
And new hymns of happiness,
Sing them to it!

These are the little creatures
Who travel with me.
Listen to them, urging action and feelings,
With their age old wisdom!
To come outside,
Away from this lonely life
Which has dried up your sense and energy
They're calling you.
Stop hoarding the pain
That gnaws on your soul like a vulture!
Even the worst society you find will show you,
That you're a part of humanity.
But I don't mean the throw you
Into the mob you despise!
I'm not one of the greats,
But if you trust me
To direct your steps, I'll guide you –
I'll gladly walk beside you –
I serve you now and always,
Always doing my best,
And if you're happy with me,
I'll stay with you as your servant, your slave.

FAUST

And what shall be my counter-service therefor?

And what do I have to do in return?

MEPHISTOPHELES

The time is long: thou need'st not now insist.

We've got plenty of time, we can work that out later.

FAUST

No--no! The Devil is an egotist,
And is not apt, without a why or wherefore,
"For God's sake," others to assist.
Speak thy conditions plain and clear!
With such a servant danger comes, I fear.

Oh no you don't! The Devil is selfish,
And doesn't, without any reason,
Help out others as if he were a Christian!
Lay out your terms, plain and clear!
I'm afraid having you as a servant will be dangerous.

MEPHISTOPHELES

Here, an unwearied slave, I'll wear thy tether,
And to thine every nod obedient be:
When *There* again we come together,
Then shalt thou do the same for me.

Here, *a tireless slave, I'll be bound to you,*
And obey your every whim:
Then when we meet again There,
You'll do the same for me.

FAUST

The *There* my scruples naught increases.
When thou hast dashed this world to pieces,
The other, then, its place may fill.
Here, on this earth, my pleasures have their sources;
Yon sun beholds my sorrows in his courses;
And when from these my life itself divorces,
Let happen all that can or will!
I'll hear no more: 'tis vain to ponder

If there we cherish love or hate,
Or, in the spheres we dream of yonder,
A High and Low our souls await.

That There *doesn't bother me.*
When you have smashed this world to bits,
That other might then take its place.
My pleasures have their sources on this earth;
The sun sees my sorrows as it goes round;
When my life is separated from them
Let whatever happens, happen.
I don't want to hear any more; there's no point in wondering
If love or hate's our lot in the hereafter,
Or if in that afterlife we dream of,
Our souls will be sent High or Low.

MEPHISTOPHELES

In this sense, even, canst thou venture.
Come, bind thyself by prompt indenture,
And thou mine arts with joy shalt see:
What no man ever saw, I'll give to thee.

With that attitude, you can start the adventure.
Come on, agree quickly,
And you'll enjoy seeing my arts:
I'll show you things no other man has seen.

FAUST

Canst thou, poor Devil, give me whatsoever?
When was a human soul, in its supreme endeavor,
E'er understood by such as thou?
Yet, hast thou food which never satiates, now,--
The restless, ruddy gold hast thou,
That runs, quicksilver-like, one's fingers through,--
A game whose winnings no man ever knew,--
A maid that, even from my breast,
Beckons my neighbor with her wanton glances,
And Honor's godlike zest,
The meteor that a moment dances,--
Show me the fruits that, ere they're gathered, rot,
And trees that daily with new leafage clothe them!

Can you, you poor Devil, give me all this?
When were the highest works of the human soul,
Ever understood by the likes of you?
But you have food which never satisfies,
You have the shifting money,
Which runs through one's fingers like water –
No-one ever profited from this game –
It's like a girl who, even when she is in my arms,
Is making eyes at my neighbor,
And the noble concept of Honour,
Burns out like a shooting star.
Show me those fruits that rot before they're harvested,
And the trees which sprout again each day!

MEPHISTOPHELES
Such a demand alarms me not:
Such treasures have I, and can show them.
But still the time may reach us, good my friend.
When peace we crave and more luxurious diet.

Such demands don't worry me:
I have these things and can give them to you.
But still, my good friend, we may come to a point,
When we desire peace and better food.

FAUST
When on an idler's bed I stretch myself in quiet.
There let, at once, my record end!
Canst thou with lying flattery rule me,
Until, self-pleased, myself I see,--
Canst thou with rich enjoyment fool me,
Let that day be the last for me!
The bet I offer.

When I lie myself down to rest,
Let that be the end of my life!
If you can fool me with flattery,
Until I'm completely self-satisfied,
If you can trick me with rich pleasures,
Then let that day be my last!
This is the deal I offer you.

MEPHISTOPHELES
Done!

Agreed!

FAUST
And heartily!
When thus I hail the Moment flying:
"Ah, still delay--thou art so fair!"
Then bind me in thy bonds undying,
My final ruin then declare!
Then let the death-bell chime the token.
Then art thou from thy service free!
The clock may stop, the hand be broken,
Then Time be finished unto me!

Completely!
So when I call to the fleeting Moment,
"Wait, you're still so lovely!"
Then wrap me in your eternal chains,
And call time on my life!
Then let the death bell ring for me.
Then you'll be free from your service!
Let the clock stop, break its hands,
That will be the end of time for me!

MEPHISTOPHELES
Consider well: my memory good is rated.

Be careful what you say: I won't forget it.

FAUST
Thou hast a perfect right thereto.
My powers I have not rashly estimated:
A slave am I, whate'er I do--
If thine, or whose? 'tis needless to debate it.

You have every right to remember it.
I'm not fooling myself:
I'm a slave whatever happens –
Whether I'm yours or another's, there's no need to
argue over it.

MEPHISTOPHELES
Then at the Doctors'-banquet I, to-day,
Will as a servant wait behind thee.
But one thing more! Beyond all risk to bind thee,

Give me a line or two, I pray.

Then at the Doctors' dinner today,
I'll wait on you like a servant.
But just one more thing! To make the contract
watertight,
Please write me a couple of lines.

FAUST
Demand'st thou, Pedant, too, a document?
Hast never known a man, nor proved his word's intent?
Is't not enough, that what I speak to-day
Shall stand, with all my future days agreeing?
In all its tides sweeps not the world away,
And shall a promise bind my being?

You pedant, you need a written contract?
Can't you take a man's word for it?
Isn't it enough to know that what I've said,
Will stay the same forever?
Just as the world keeps wearing away,
Doesn't my promise last forever?

Yet this delusion in our hearts we bear:
Who would himself therefrom deliver?
Blest he, whose bosom Truth makes pure and fair!
No sacrifice shall he repent of ever.
Nathless a parchment, writ and stamped with care,
A spectre is, which all to shun endeavor.
The word, alas! dies even in the pen,
And wax and leather keep the lordship then.
What wilt from me, Base Spirit, say?--
Brass, marble, parchment, paper, clay?

The terms with graver, quill, or chisel, stated?
I freely leave the choice to thee.

That's what we tell ourselves
And never want to change it.
He's blessed who knows pure truth,
And he'll never give it up for anything.
Still, a document, properly witnessed,
Is a ghost which all men try to escape.
Alas, the promise dies as it goes through the pen,
And the books then have all the power.
Alright, you low Devil, what do you want?
Shall I write on brass, marble, parchment, paper or clay?
Shall I use an engraving tool, a quill, a chisel?
I'm glad to leave the choice to you.

MEPHISTOPHELES
Why heat thyself, thus instantly,
With eloquence exaggerated?
Each leaf for such a pact is good;
And to subscribe thy name thou'lt take a drop of blood.

Why get angry so quickly,
And speak in such an exaggerated way?
Any scrap of paper will do,
And you can sign it with a drop of blood.

FAUST
If thou therewith art fully satisfied,
So let us by the farce abide.

If that's going to make you happy,
We'll go ahead with this farce.

MEPHISTOPHELES
Blood is a juice of rarest quality.

Blood is the finest fluid.

FAUST
Fear not that I this pact shall seek to sever?
The promise that I make to thee
Is just the sum of my endeavor.
I have myself inflated all too high;
My proper place is thy estate:
The Mighty Spirit deigns me no reply,
And Nature shuts on me her gate.
The thread of Thought at last is broken,
And knowledge brings disgust unspoken.
Let us the sensual deeps explore,
To quench the fervors of glowing passion!
Let every marvel take form and fashion
Through the impervious veil it wore!
Plunge we in Time's tumultuous dance,
In the rush and roll of Circumstance!
Then may delight and distress,
And worry and success,
Alternately follow, as best they can:
Restless activity proves the man!

Are you still worried I'll break the deal?
The promise that I'm making you
Is the best I have to offer.
I've become so arrogant,
That my rightful place is now with you.
The great Spirit will not answer me,
And Nature's barred her doors to me.
All my speculations have ended,
And I'm sick of Knowledge.
Let's plumb the depths of the senses,
Until all passion's spent!
Bring on every miraculous thing,
Let's see through the disguise it once wore!
Let's throw ourselves into the river of Time,
Into the rolling waves of events!
Let delight and distress,
Worry and success,
Follow one after the other with their best show,
Restless activity is the thing for Man!

MEPHISTOPHELES
For you no bound, no term is set.
Whether you everywhere be trying,
Or snatch a rapid bliss in flying,
May it agree with you, what you get!

For you there are no limitations.
Whether you want to try everything,
Or snatch a quick bite as you fly by,
Let's hope you enjoy what you get!

Only fall to, and show no timid balking.

FAUST
But thou hast heard, 'tis not of joy we're talking.
I take the wildering whirl, enjoyment's keenest pain,
Enamored hate, exhilarant disdain.
My bosom, of its thirst for knowledge sated,
Shall not, henceforth, from any pang be wrested,
And all of life for all mankind created
Shall be within mine inmost being tested:
The highest, lowest forms my soul shall borrow,
Shall heap upon itself their bliss and sorrow,
And thus, my own sole self to all their selves expanded,
I too, at last, shall with them all be stranded!

MEPHISTOPHELES
Believe me, who for many a thousand year
The same tough meat have chewed and tested,
That from the cradle to the bier
No man the ancient leaven has digested!
Trust one of us, this Whole supernal
Is made but for a God's delight!
He dwells in splendor single and eternal,
But *us* he thrusts in darkness, out of sight,
And *you* he dowers with Day and Night.

FAUST
Nay, but I will!

MEPHISTOPHELES
A good reply!
One only fear still needs repeating:
The art is long, the time is fleeting.
Then let thyself be taught, say I!
Go, league thyself with a poet,
Give the rein to his imagination,
Then wear the crown, and show it,
Of the qualities of his creation,--
The courage of the lion's breed,
The wild stag's speed,
The Italian's fiery blood,
The North's firm fortitude!
Let him find for thee the secret tether
That binds the Noble and Mean together.
And teach thy pulses of youth and pleasure
To love by rule, and hate by measure!
I'd like, myself, such a one to see:
Sir Microcosm his name should be.

FAUST
What am I, then, if 'tis denied my part
The crown of all humanity to win me,
Whereto yearns every sense within me?

Just throw yourself into it, and don't hesitate.

But you've heard, I'm not out for happiness.
I'll have the chaos, the exquisite pain,
I want the hatred of love, the joy of frustration.
My heart, which has had enough of knowledge,
Won't reject any feeling from now on,
And all of the life which has been made for man,
I'll try, with all my soul:
My soul will become the highest and the lowest,
And experience all their joy and sadness.
And so, when I've become like all of them,
I'll be abandoned with them in the end.

Believe me, who for thousands of years
Has chewed on this tough meat:
From the cradle to the grave
No man has ever been able to digest it!
Take it from one who knows, the whole universe,
Is made only for God's pleasure!
He *lives in alone in the light forever,*
But us *he casts into the darkness, out of sight,*
And you *he forces to have Day and Night.*

Believe me, I'm going to try!

A good answer!
There's only one thing which must be said again:
There's much to learn, and time is short.
But let yourself be taught, I say!
Go into business with a poet,
Let his imagination have free rein,
Then copy what he says and be like
The things he has invented;
Have the courage of a lion,
The speed of the stag,
The fiery blood of an Italian,
The stoicism of a northener!
Let him show you the secret chain
Which ties the high and the low together.
Teach your young hot passions
To love to his lines, and hate to his beat!
I'd like to see such a man myself:
I'd call him Mr. All-in-one.

Who am I then, if I'm not allowed,
To experience everything man can,
Which is what I want most of all?

MEPHISTOPHELES

Why, on the whole, thou'rt--what thou art.
Set wigs of million curls upon thy head, to raise thee,
Wear shoes an ell in height,--the truth betrays thee,
And thou remainest--what thou art.

Why, generally, you are – what you are.
Put on a big curly wig to look taller,
Wear shoes with yard high heels, the truth will out,
And you're still – what you are.

FAUST

I feel, indeed, that I have made the treasure
Of human thought and knowledge mine, in vain;
And if I now sit down in restful leisure,
No fount of newer strength is in my brain:
I am no hair's-breadth more in height,
Nor nearer, to the Infinite.

I definitely feel that all my study
Of human thought and knowledge was a waste of time;
If I sit down at my ease now,
I'm not in any way more clever:
I'm not a hair's breadth taller,
And no closer to understanding the Infinite.

MEPHISTOPHELES

Good Sir, you see the facts precisely
As they are seen by each and all.
We must arrange them now, more wisely,
Before the joys of life shall pall.
Why, Zounds! Both hands and feet are, truly--
And head and virile forces--thine:
Yet all that I indulge in newly,
Is't thence less wholly mine?
If I've six stallions in my stall,
Are not their forces also lent me?
I speed along, completest man of all,
As though my legs were four-and-twenty.
Take hold, then! let reflection rest,
And plunge into the world with zest!
I say to thee, a speculative wight
Is like a beast on moorlands lean,
That round and round some fiend misleads to evil plight,
While all about lie pastures fresh and green.

Dear man, this is exactly
How everyone feels.
We must arrange the facts of life differently,
Before their attraction starts to fade.
Good heavens! Your hands and your feet are, truly,
Yours, and so are your head and your potency:
And if I try something new,
Who's to say it's not mine?
If I have six stallions pulling my carriage,
Isn't their power loaned to me?
I speed along, the greatest of them all,
As if I had twenty four legs.
Grab hold! Stop the philosophizing,
And throw yourself gleefully into the world!
I'm telling you, the thinker
Is like a beast on a bare hillside,
That some Devil leads round and round in circles,

While all around there are fresh green pastures for the taking.

FAUST

Then how shall we begin?

How shall we start?

MEPHISTOPHELES

We'll try a wider sphere.
What place of martyrdom is here!
Is't life, I ask, is't even prudence,
To bore thyself and bore the students?
Let Neighbor Paunch to that attend!
Why plague thyself with threshing straw forever?
The best thou learnest, in the end
Thou dar'st not tell the youngsters--never!
I hear one's footsteps, hither steering.

We'll try a wider field of operations.
What torture chamber this is!
I ask you, is it living, is it even wise,
To bore yourself and your students?
Let your fat-headed neighbor attend to that!
Why flog yourself to death with this labour?
The best stuff you learn
You'd never dare tell the youngsters anyway!
I hear someone coming.

FAUST

To see him now I have no heart.

I don't want to see him now.

MEPHISTOPHELES

So long the poor boy waits a hearing,
He must not unconsoled depart.
Thy cap and mantle straightway lend me!
I'll play the comedy with art.
(*He disguises himself.*)
My wits, be certain, will befriend me.
But fifteen minutes' time is all I need;
For our fine trip, meanwhile, prepare thyself with speed!
[*Exit* FAUST]

MEPHISTOPHELES

(*In* FAUST'S *long mantle.*)
Reason and Knowledge only thou despise,
The highest strength in man that lies!
Let but the Lying Spirit bind thee
With magic works and shows that blind thee,
And I shall have thee fast and sure!--
Fate such a bold, untrammelled spirit gave him,
As forwards, onwards, ever must endure;
Whose over-hasty impulse drave him
Past earthly joys he might secure.
Dragged through the wildest life, will I enslave him,
Through flat and stale indifference;
With struggling, chilling, checking, so deprave him
That, to his hot, insatiate sense,
The dream of drink shall mock, but never lave him:

Refreshment shall his lips in vain implore--
Had he not made himself the Devil's, naught could save him,
Still were he lost forevermore!
(*A STUDENT enters.*)

STUDENT

A short time, only, am I here,
And come, devoted and sincere,
To greet and know the man of fame,
Whom men to me with reverence name.

MEPHISTOPHELES

Your courtesy doth flatter me:
You see a man, as others be.
Have you, perchance, elsewhere begun?

STUDENT

Receive me now, I pray, as one
Who comes to you with courage good,
Somewhat of cash, and healthy blood:
My mother was hardly willing to let me;
But knowledge worth having I fain would get me.

The poor boy's been waiting so long to see you,
He mustn't leave empty handed.
Give me your cap and gown!
I'll play the part skilfully.
(He disguises himself)
My cunning will help me out here;
All I need is fifteen minutes –
You go and prepare for our adventure!

So, you hate Reason and Knowledge,
The things which make men strongest!
Let this lying Devil tie you up
With magic tricks and blinding shows,
And you'll be in my power for sure!
Fate gave him such a proud and haughty spirit,
That must be pressing forever onwards;
This hasty nature has made him
Miss the earthly pleasures he might have had.
I'll drag him through the wildest life, and enslave him
By denying him its pleasures;
I fight him, block him, freeze him, and that will ruin him,
So that to his greedy senses,
It'll be like dreaming of drink, but never quenching your thirst:
He'll beg for refreshment in vain:
If he hadn't sold himself to the Devil, he'd still be beyond redemption,
Still be damned forever!

I'm only making a brief visit,
And I've come, devoted and sincere,
To be introduced to the famous man,
Whom so many speak so well of.

Your politeness flatters me:
I'm just a man, like any other.
Tell me, have you begun studying elsewhere?

Please, welcome me as a person
Who comes to you with a good heart,
A little money and good health:
My mother didn't want me to come,
But I want to learn the things worth knowing.

MEPHISTOPHELES
Then you have reached the right place now.

Then you're in the right place.

STUDENT
I'd like to leave it, I must avow;
I find these walls, these vaulted spaces
Are anything but pleasant places.
Tis all so cramped and close and mean;
One sees no tree, no glimpse of green,
And when the lecture-halls receive me,
Seeing, hearing, and thinking leave me.

I must say I'd like to leave it;
I find these places with their walls and ceilings
Are far from pleasant.
It's all so cramped, stuffy and mean,
You can't see the trees or the grass,
And when I go into a classroom,
I seem to lose all my sense.

MEPHISTOPHELES
All that depends on habitude.
So from its mother's breasts a child
At first, reluctant, takes its food,
But soon to seek them is beguiled.
Thus, at the breasts of Wisdom clinging,
Thou'lt find each day a greater rapture bringing.

It's just a matter of getting used to it.
A child's reluctant, at first,
To take its food from its mother's breast,
But it soon learns to seek it out.
So, if you cling to the breast of Wisdom,
You'll find it gets better by the day.

STUDENT
I'll hang thereon with joy, and freely drain them;
But tell me, pray, the proper means to gain them.

I'll happily cling to them and gladly drain them,
But please tell me the best way to find them.

MEPHISTOPHELES
Explain, before you further speak,
The special faculty you seek.

Before you go any further,
Tell me specifically what you want to study.

STUDENT
I crave the highest erudition;
And fain would make my acquisition
All that there is in Earth and Heaven,
In Nature and in Science too.

I want to learn the highest wisdom;
I want to get for myself
All the knowledge of Heaven and Earth,
And Nature and Science, too.

MEPHISTOPHELES
Here is the genuine path for you;
Yet strict attention must be given.

That's the right way to go,
But you'll have to work hard.

STUDENT
Body and soul thereon I'll wreak;
Yet, truly, I've some inclination
On summer holidays to seek
A little freedom and recreation.

I'll throw myself into it, body and soul;
Though I must admit,
In the summer holidays I want
To have a little fun.

MEPHISTOPHELES
Use well your time! It flies so swiftly from us;
But time through order may be won, I promise.

Use your time wisely! It runs out all too fast;
But I promise, you can gain time through being
disciplined.

So, Friend (my views to briefly sum),
First, the *collegium logicum*.
There will your mind be drilled and braced,
As if in Spanish boots 'twere laced,
And thus, to graver paces brought,

So, my lad, to sum up my plans:
First, you must study at the College of Logic.
There your mind will be put through its paces
As if it were laced up in Army boots,
And so it'll be slowed down

'Twill plod along the path of thought,
Instead of shooting here and there,
A will-o'-the-wisp in murky air.
Days will be spent to bid you know,
What once you did at a single blow,
Like eating and drinking, free and strong,--
That one, two, three! thereto belong.
Truly the fabric of mental fleece
Resembles a weaver's masterpiece,
Where a thousand threads one treadle throws,
Where fly the shuttles hither and thither.
Unseen the threads are knit together.
And an infinite combination grows.
Then, the philosopher steps in
And shows, no otherwise it could have been:
The first was so, the second so,
Therefore the third and fourth are so;
Were not the first and second, then
The third and fourth had never been.
The scholars are everywhere believers,
But never succeed in being weavers.
He who would study organic existence,
First drives out the soul with rigid persistence;
Then the parts in his hand he may hold and class,
But the spiritual link is lost, alas!
Encheiresin natures, this Chemistry names,
Nor knows how herself she banters and blames!

So your thoughts plod along,
Instead of shooting about everywhere,
Like a will-o'-the-wisp in the fog.
You'll have to spend days in learning
Things you used to grasp at once,
As easy as eating or drinking, freely,
Like learning your ABC.
The fabric of logic
Is like the work of a master weaver:
One push on the pedal throws out a thousand threads,
And the shuttles fly about all over the place.
The threads are woven together unseen,
Building in infinite complexity.
Then the philosopher takes the stand
And shows that this is how it must be.
The first thread went here, the second there,
So the third must go there and the fourth here;
If it wasn't for the first and second
The third and fourth couldn't exist.
Scholars believe in many things,
But they make lousy weavers.
The man who wants to study the nature of matter
Throws away the idea of the soul;
The bits and pieces he has left he can name and list,
But there's no spirit to hold them together, alas!
"Natural treatment", the chemists call it,
Not knowing how stupid it makes them look!

STUDENT
I cannot understand you quite.

I'm not sure I follow you.

MEPHISTOPHELES
Your mind will shortly be set aright,
When you have learned, all things reducing,
To classify them for your using.

You'll understand alright,
When you've learned to boil everything down
To a set of lists.

STUDENT
I feel as stupid, from all you've said,
As if a mill-wheel whirled in my head!

Listening to you talk I feel stupid,
As if my brains were scrambled!

MEPHISTOPHELES
And after--first and foremost duty--Of
Metaphysics learn the use and beauty!
See that you most profoundly gain
What does not suit the human brain!
A splendid word to serve, you'll find
For what goes in--or won't go in--your mind.
But first, at least this half a year,
To order rigidly adhere;
Five hours a day, you understand,
And when the clock strikes, be on hand!
Prepare beforehand for your part
With paragraphs all got by heart,

The next thing you must do after that,
Is to learn the use and Beauty of Metaphysics!
Make sure you learn inside out
That which doesn't come naturally to the human brain!
You'll find there a splendid word to describe
What goes in – or won't go in – your mind.
But first, for six months at least,
You must show discipline!
Five hours a day, you understand,
And be ready when the clock strikes!
Get yourself prepared in advance
With texts committed to memory,

So you can better watch, and look
That naught is said but what is in the book:
Yet in thy writing as unwearied be,
As did the Holy Ghost dictate to thee!

STUDENT
No need to tell me twice to do it!
I think, how useful 'tis to write;
For what one has, in black and white,
One carries home and then goes through it.

MEPHISTOPHELES
Yet choose thyself a faculty!

STUDENT
I cannot reconcile myself to Jurisprudence.

MEPHISTOPHELES
Nor can I therefore greatly blame you students:
I know what science this has come to be.
All rights and laws are still transmitted
Like an eternal sickness of the race,--
From generation unto generation fitted,
And shifted round from place to place.
Reason becomes a sham, Beneficence a worry:
Thou art a grandchild, therefore woe to thee!
The right born with us, ours in verity,
This to consider, there's, alas! no hurry.

STUDENT
My own disgust is strengthened by your speech:
O lucky he, whom you shall teach!
I've almost for Theology decided.

MEPHISTOPHELES
I should not wish to see you here misguided:
For, as regards this science, let me hint
'Tis very hard to shun the false direction;
There's so much secret poison lurking in 't,
So like the medicine, it baffles your detection.
Hear, therefore, one alone, for that is best, in sooth,
And simply take your master's words for truth.
On *words* let your attention centre!
Then through the safest gate you'll enter
The temple-halls of Certainty.

STUDENT
Yet in the word must some idea be.

MEPHISTOPHELES
Of course! But only shun too over-sharp a tension,
For just where fails the comprehension,
A word steps promptly in as deputy.

So that you can make sure
Nothing is said that isn't in the book:
But also you must write and write,
As if taking dictation from the Holy Ghost!

I don't need telling twice!
I think it's very useful to write things down,
Then you take what you've got, in black and white,
And take it home to go over it again.

But you must choose a speciality!

I can't bring myself to study Law.

I can't really blame you students for that:
I know how this subject has ended up.
All the rights and laws are handed down
Like a hereditary sickness of mankind,
Forced on every generation,
And moved around from place to place.
Reason becomes nonsense, Kindness an illness:
You are a grandchild, unlucky for you!
The rights we're born with, the true rights of man,
Nobody seems in any hurry to study.

What you say increases my distaste for it:
Your student will be a lucky man!
I've virtually settled on Theology.

I don't want to see you given bad advice:
With regard to this branch of learning, let me say
It's very hard not to go off the rails;
There's so much poison hidden in it
That you can't tell the good from bad.
Just listen to one man, that's really the best way,
And just believe what your master tells you.
Focus on the words!
That's the safest way
To get to the truth.

But there must be something backing up the words.

Naturally! But don't get too wrapped up in that,
For just when your understanding fails,
A word can fill the gap.

With words 'tis excellent disputing;
Systems to words 'tis easy suiting;
On words 'tis excellent believing;
No word can ever lose a jot from thieving.

You can make great arguments with words,
And you can bend systems to fit them;
Words are the things to believe in;
No word can be affected by theft.

STUDENT
Pardon! With many questions I detain you.
Yet must I trouble you again.
Of Medicine I still would fain
Hear one strong word that might explain you.
Three years is but a little space.
And, God! who can the field embrace?
If one some index could be shown,
'Twere easier groping forward, truly.

Excuse me! I'm plaguing you with questions,
But I must ask more.
I'd still like to know, regarding Medicine,
Have you a good word to say?
Three years isn't much time,
And God knows who can master the subject?
If only one could get some guidance,
It'd make the study so much easier.

MEPHISTOPHELES (*aside*)
I'm tired enough of this dry tone,--
Must play the Devil again, and fully.
(*Aloud*)
To grasp the spirit of Medicine is easy:
Learn of the great and little world your fill,
To let it go at last, so please ye,
Just as God will!
In vain that through the realms of science you may drift;
Each one learns only--just what learn he can:
Yet he who grasps the Moment's gift,
He is the proper man.
Well-made you are, 'tis not to be denied,
The rest a bold address will win you;
If you but in yourself confide,
At once confide all others in you.
To lead the women, learn the special feeling!
Their everlasting aches and groans,
In thousand tones,
Have all one source, one mode of healing;

And if your acts are half discreet,
You'll always have them at your feet.
A title first must draw and interest them,
And show that yours all other arts exceeds;
Then, as a greeting, you are free to touch and test them,

While, thus to do, for years another pleads.

You press and count the pulse's dances,
And then, with burning sidelong glances,
You clasp the swelling hips, to see
If tightly laced her corsets be.

(Aside) I've had enough of this dry discussion,
I'm going back to being a Devil again.
(Aloud) It's easy enough to grasp the principle of
Medicine:
Learn all you want of things both big and small,
And then just let it attend to itself, as God does!

It's no good drifting along through Science,
Picking up what you can here and there:
The one who can grasp the Moment,
That's the real Man.
You're a well built chap, it must be said,
And for the rest clever speech will serve you well;
Just trust in yourself,
And at once everyone else will trust in you.
You need to learn about women!
Their eternal aches and moans,
Expressed a thousand ways,
Only have one source, and there's only one way to cure
them;
If you're at all discreet about it,
You can wrap them round your little finger.
First of all, get yourself a title that'll interest them,
To show your Art is better than all the rest;
Then when you meet you're allowed to feel and prod
them,
In a way another might have to plead for years before
he's permitted.
You can hold her wrist and count her heartbeat,
And then, with a smouldering look,
You can squeeze her hips,
To see how tightly laced her corsets are.

STUDENT
That's better, now! The How and Where, one sees.

Now, that's more like it! One can see how this can be
done.

MEPHISTOPHELES
My worthy friend, gray are all theories,
And green alone Life's golden tree.

My worthy friend, all theories are dull,
And only the golden tree of Life shines green.

STUDENT
I swear to you, 'tis like a dream to me.
Might I again presume, with trust unbounded,
To hear your wisdom thoroughly expounded?

I promise you, this is a dream come true for me.
Can I ask, with all my faith in you,
To hear you explaining your wisdom again?

MEPHISTOPHELES
Most willingly, to what extent I may.

Certainly, as much as I can.

STUDENT
I cannot really go away:
Allow me that my album first I reach you,--
Grant me this favor, I beseech you!

I really can't leave without asking -
Can I just pass you my book?
I beg that you'll sign it for me.

MEPHISTOPHELES
Assuredly.

Of course.

(*He writes, and returns the book.*)

STUDENT (*reads*)

"Eritis sicut Deus, scientes bonum et malum."
(*Closes the book with reverence, and withdraws*)

"You'll be like God, knowing both good and evil."

MEPHISTOPHELES
Follow the ancient text, and the snake thou wast
ordered to trample! With all thy likeness to God,
thou'lt yet be a sorry example!
(FAUST *enters.*)

Follow the ancient text, and the snake you were told to kill!
For all you look like God, you'll come to a sticky end!

FAUST
Now, whither shall we go?

Now, where shall we go?

MEPHISTOPHELES
As best it pleases thee.
The little world, and then the great, we'll see.
With what delight, what profit winning,
Shalt thou sponge through the term beginning!

Wherever you like.
We'll visit the little world, then the great one.
What joys you'll have, what profit you'll get,
You'll soak it up like a sponge this time!

FAUST
Yet with the flowing beard I wear,
Both ease and grace will fail me there.
The attempt, indeed, were a futile strife;
I never could learn the ways of life.
I feel so small before others, and thence
Should always find embarrassments.

Yet with this long beard of mine,
I don't feel I have looks or style.
It's not worth making any effort,
I could never learn how to fit in.
I feel so small compared to others, so
I always feel embarrassed.

MEPHISTOPHELES
My friend, thou soon shalt lose all such misgiving:
Be thou but self-possessed, thou hast the art of living!

My friend, you'll soon have no worries,
If you've got self-confidence, you've mastered how to

FAUST
How shall we leave the house, and start?
Where hast thou servant, coach and horses?

MEPHISTOPHELES
We'll spread this cloak with proper art,
Then through the air direct our courses.
But only, on so bold a flight,
Be sure to have thy luggage light.
A little burning air, which I shall soon prepare us,
Above the earth will nimbly bear us,
And, if we're light, we'll travel swift and clear:
I gratulate thee on thy new career!

live!

How shall we leave the house and get started?
Have you got a servant, a coach, horses?

We'll lay out this cloak with magic skill,
And then we'll fly through the air.
Just make sure that on this daring flight,
You don't bring too much baggage.
I'll quickly conjure up some hot air,
Which will lift us up above the earth,
And as long as we're light we'll travel safe and fast:
I congratulate you on your new life!

V

AUERBACH'S CELLAR IN LEIPZIG

CAROUSAL OF JOLLY COMPANIONS

FROSCH
Is no one laughing? No one drinking?
I'll teach you how to grin, I'm thinking.
To-day you're like wet straw, so tame;
And usually you're all aflame.

Is no one laughing? No one drinking?
I think I'll have to teach you to laugh.
You're a bunch of wet rags today;
Usually you're tearing up the place!

BRANDER
Now that's your fault; from you we nothing see,
No beastliness and no stupidity.

Well, it's your fault, we're not seeing,
Your usual beastly buffoonery.

FROSCH
(*Pours a glass of wine over BRANDER'S head.*)
There's both together!

There you go, two for the price of one!

BRANDER
Twice a swine!

That makes you a double pig!

FROSCH
You wanted them: I've given you mine.

Well you asked for it, now you've got it.

SIEBEL
Turn out who quarrels--out the door!
With open throat sing chorus, drink and roar!

Up! holla! ho!

Chuck out the bickerers – chuck 'em out the door!
Open up your throats for shouting, drinking and
laughter!
Hip hip hooray!

ALTMAYER
Woe's me, the fearful bellow!
Bring cotton, quick! He's split my ears, that fellow.

For heaven's sake, what a racket!
Bring me some cotton wool, quickly! That fellow's
going to burst my eardrums!

SIEBEL
When the vault echoes to the song,
One first perceives the bass is deep and strong.

When the song echoes round the cellar,
The first thing you hear is the strength of the bass.

FROSCH
Well said! and out with him that takes the least offence!

Ah, tara, lara da!

Too right! And chuck out anyone who wants to argue
about it!
Hip hip hooray!

ALTMAYER
Ah, tara, lara, da!

Ah, hip hip hooray!

FROSCH
The throats are tuned, commence!
(*Sings.*)
The dear old holy Roman realm,

We're all tuned up, let's get started!
(Sings)
The dear old holy Roman realm,

How does it hold together?

BRANDER

A nasty song! Fie! a political song--
A most offensive song! Thank God, each morning,
therefore,
That you have not the Roman realm to care for!

At least, I hold it so much gain for me,
That I nor Chancellor nor Kaiser be.
Yet also we must have a ruling head, I hope,
And so we'll choose ourselves a Pope.
You know the quality that can
Decide the choice, and elevate the man.

FROSCH (*sings*)
Soar up, soar up, Dame Nightingale!
Ten thousand times my sweetheart hail!

SIEBEL
No, greet my sweetheart not! I tell you, I'll resent it.

FROSCH
My sweetheart greet and kiss! I dare you to prevent it!

(*Sings.*)
Draw the latch! the darkness makes:
Draw the latch! the lover wakes.
Shut the latch! the morning breaks.

SIEBEL
Yes, sing away, sing on, and praise, and brag of her!

I'll wait my proper time for laughter:
Me by the nose she led, and now she'll lead you after.

Her paramour should be an ugly gnome,
Where four roads cross, in wanton play to meet her:
An old he-goat, from Blocksberg coming home,
Should his good-night in lustful gallop bleat her!
A fellow made of genuine flesh and blood
Is for the wench a deal too good.
Greet her? Not I: unless, when meeting,
To smash her windows be a greeting!

BRANDER (*pounding on the table*)
Attention! Hearken now to me!
Confess, Sirs, I know how to live.
Enamored persons here have we,
And I, as suits their quality,
Must something fresh for their advantage give.
Take heed! 'Tis of the latest cut, my strain,

How does it hold together?

A nasty song! Ugh! A political song –
A most offensive song! You should give thanks each
morning
That you don't have to look after the Holy Roman
Empire!
I think I'm a lucky fellow,
That I'm not a Chancellor or a Kaiser.
But I suppose we have to have a ruler,
So we'll choose a Pope for ourselves.
We know the qualities that are needed
To win the vote and put him in office.

Soar up, soar up, Dame Nightingale!
Ten thousand times my sweetheart hail!

Don't you go singing to my sweetheart! I warn you, I
won't have it.

My sweetheart greet and kiss! Go on, I dare you try
and stop me!
(Sings)
Shoot the bolt! It's dark inside:
Shoot the bolt! The lover wakes
Shoot the bolt! The morning's here!

Go on then, sing away, sing her praises and boast she's
yours!
I'll have the last laugh:
She led me up the garden path and she'll do the same to
you.
She should have an ugly goblin for a lover,
Wooing her down at the crossroads:
Some old goat on his way home from Blocksberg,
Should spend his night giving her a gallop!
A real man, all flesh and blood,
Is far too good for the likes of her.
Greet her? Not me, unless when you meet someone,
Smashing their window is seen as a greeting!

Listen up! Pay attention to me!
Admit, my friends, that I know how to live.
There are lovers sitting amongst us here,
So, in honor of their staus,
I must give them something fresh to enjoy.
Listen up, I've got a new song,

And all strike in at each refrain!
(*He sings*.)
There was a rat in the cellar-nest,
Whom fat and butter made smoother:
He had a paunch beneath his vest
Like that of Doctor Luther.
The cook laid poison cunningly,
And then as sore oppressed was he
As if he had love in his bosom.

CHORUS (*shouting*)
As if he had love in his bosom!

BRANDER
He ran around, he ran about,
His thirst in puddles laving;
He gnawed and scratched the house throughout.
But nothing cured his raving.
He whirled and jumped, with torment mad,
And soon enough the poor beast had,
As if he had love in his bosom.

CHORUS
As if he had love in his bosom!

BRANDER
And driven at last, in open day,
He ran into the kitchen,
Fell on the hearth, and squirming lay,
In the last convulsion twitching.
Then laughed the murderess in her glee:
"Ha! ha! he's at his last gasp," said she,
"As if he had love in his bosom!"

CHORUS
As if he had love in his bosom!

SIEBEL
How the dull fools enjoy the matter!
To me it is a proper art
Poison for such poor rats to scatter.

BRANDER
Perhaps you'll warmly take their part?

ALTMAYER
The bald-pate pot-belly I have noted:
Misfortune tames him by degrees;
For in the rat by poison bloated
His own most natural form he sees.

And I want you all to join in the chorus!
(He sings)
There was rat with a nest in the cellar,
Who grew round on fat and butter
He had a belly beneath his vest
That was like Martin Luther's.
The cook laid down a poison trap,
And then he suffered from a pain,
As if he had love in his bosom.

As if he had love in his bosom!

So he ran all round and about
Quenching his thirst in puddles
He gnawed and scratched all through the house
But nothing could cure his madness.
He spun around, gone mad with pain
And soon enough the poor brute
Had had enough,
As if he had love in his bosom.

As if he had love in his bosom!

And at last in the light of day,
He ran into the kitchen,
He fell on the hearth and thrashed about,
Twitching with his last convulsion.
Then his killer laughed with happiness:
"Ha ha! He's had it now," she said,
"As if he had love in his bosom."

As if he had love in his bosom!

How pleased all these dullards are!
I think we should lay down some poison
To get rid of these poor rats.

Perhaps you'll take their side?

I see the bald headed fatty:
He's been brought down by fate;
In the rat swollen up with poison,
He sees an image of himself.

FAUST AND MEPHISTOPHELES
MEPHISTOPHELES
Before all else, I bring thee hither
Where boon companions meet together,
To let thee see how smooth life runs away.
Here, for the folk, each day's a holiday:
With little wit, and ease to suit them,
They whirl in narrow, circling trails,
Like kittens playing with their tails?
And if no headache persecute them,
So long the host may credit give,
They merrily and careless live.

Before anything else, I've brought you here
Where good pals gather together,
To show you how easily life slips away.
For these people, every day's a holiday:
They haven't much brains, and plenty of leisure,
They dance around in little circles
Like kittens chasing their tails.
As long as they don't get hangovers
And the landlord still runs a tab,
They live happily, without a care.

BRANDER
The fact is easy to unravel,
Their air's so odd, they've just returned from travel:
A single hour they've not been here.

It's easy to work those two out;
They stand out so, they've just got back from a trip:
They haven't been here an hour.

FROSCH
You've verily hit the truth! Leipzig to me is dear:

Paris in miniature, how it refines its people!

I think you've hit the nail on the head! I'm very attached
to Leipzig:
A miniature Paris, how it makes its citizens civilized!

SIEBEL
Who are the strangers, should you guess?

Who do you reckon these strangers are?

FROSCH
Let me alone! I'll set them first to drinking,
And then, as one a child's tooth draws, with cleverness,
I'll worm their secret out, I'm thinking.
They're of a noble house, that's very clear:
Haughty and discontented they appear.

Leave it to me! I'll get them drinking,
And then as one pulls a child's tooth, cunningly,
I'll get their secret from them.
They're clearly noblemen:
They have that snobbish and unhappy look.

BRANDER
They're mountebanks, upon a revel.

They're snake-oil salesmen, out on a spree.

ALTMAYER
Perhaps.

Could be.

FROSCH
Look out, I'll smoke them now!

Watch me, I'll unmask 'em!

MEPHISTOPHELES (*to* FAUST)
Not if he had them by the neck, I vow,
Would e'er these people scent the Devil!

I swear these people wouldn't recognise the devil,
If he was strangling them.

FAUST
Fair greeting, gentlemen!

A good day, gentlemen!

SIEBEL
Our thanks: we give the same.

Thank you, and the same to you.

(*Murmurs, inspecting MEPHISTOPHELES from the side.*)

In one foot is the fellow lame?

Has this chap got a game leg?

MEPHISTOPHELES
Is it permitted that we share your leisure?
In place of cheering drink, which one seeks vainly here,
Your company shall give us pleasure.

May we share your evening with you?
One can't seem to get a decent drink round here,
So we'd enjoy your company instead.

ALTMAYER
A most fastidious person you appear.

You seem to be a fussy sort of chap.

FROSCH
No doubt 'twas late when you from Rippach started?
And supping there with Hans occasioned your delay?

I suppose it was late when you set out from Rippach?
You must have been eating with Hans, that's what made
you late?

MEPHISTOPHELES
We passed, without a call, to-day.
At our last interview, before we parted
Much of his cousins did he speak, entreating
That we should give to each his kindly greeting.
(*He bows to* FROSCH)

We passed by without stopping today,
But last time we spoke, before we left,
He told us much about his cousins, and asked,
That we should pass on his kind regards to them all.

ALTMAYER (*aside*)
You have it now! He understands.

He did you there! You've been rumbled.

SIEBEL
A knave sharp-set!

A cunning rascal!

FROSCH
Just wait awhile: I'll have him yet.

Just you wait, I'll get him.

MEPHISTOPHELES
If I am right, we heard the sound
Of well-trained voices, singing chorus;
And truly, song must here rebound
Superbly from the arches o'er us.

If I'm not mistaken, we heard the sound
Of expert voices singing in harmony;
Music must echo beautifully
Around these arched vaults.

FROSCH
Are you, perhaps, a virtuoso?

Are you an expert musician, by any chance?

MEPHISTOPHELES
O no! my wish is great, my power is only so-so.

Oh no! I'd like to be, but my skills aren't much.

ALTMAYER
Give us a song!

Give us song!

MEPHISTOPHELES
If you desire, a number.

I'll give you a number if you like.

SIEBEL
So that it be a bran-new strain!

Give us something new!

MEPHISTOPHELES
We've just retraced our way from Spain,
The lovely land of wine, and song, and slumber.
(*Sings*.)
There was a king once reigning,
Who had a big black flea—

FROSCH
Hear, hear! A flea! D'ye rightly take the jest?
I call a flea a tidy guest.

MEPHISTOPHELES (*sings*)
There was a king once reigning,
Who had a big black flea,
And loved him past explaining,
As his own son were he.
He called his man of stitches;
The tailor came straightway:
Here, measure the lad for breeches.
And measure his coat, I say!

BRANDER
But mind, allow the tailor no caprices:
Enjoin upon him, as his head is dear,
To most exactly measure, sew and shear,
So that the breeches have no creases!

MEPHISTOPHELES
In silk and velvet gleaming
He now was wholly drest--
Had a coat with ribbons streaming,
A cross upon his breast.
He had the first of stations,
A minister's star and name;
And also all his relations
Great lords at court became.
And the lords and ladies of honor
Were plagued, awake and in bed;
The queen she got them upon her,
The maids were bitten and bled.
And they did not dare to brush them,
Or scratch them, day or night:
We crack them and we crush them,
At once, whene'er they bite.

CHORUS (*shouting*)
We crack them and we crush them,
At once, whene'er they bite!

FROSCH
Bravo! bravo! that was fine.

We've just come back from Spain,
That beautiful slumbering country of wine and song.
(Sings)
There was once a ruling king
Who had a big black flea –

Ha, do your hear him? A flea! Do you get it?
I have fleas as guests myself.

There was once a ruling king
Who had a big black flea,
And loved him to distraction,
As if he were his own son.
He called for his sewing man:
The tailor came running:
Here, measure the lad for pants,
And for a coat, I say!

But don't let the tailor get away with shoddy work:
Make sure, on pain of death,
That he measures up properly, cuts and sews,
So the pants don't bag!

Resplendent in silk and velvet
He was now completely dressed,
With a fine ribboned coat,
And a cross upon his chest.
He had a high position,
A minster's decorations and title,
And also all his relations,
Were made great lords of the court.
So the lords and ladies of the court
Were tormented both day and night;
The queen she got the fleas,
And the maids were bitten and bled.
They didn't dare to brush them off
Or scratch at them, day or night:
But we can smash them down and squash them,
As soon as we feel their bite.

But we can smash them down and squash them,
As soon as we feel their bite!

Bravo! Bravo! That was a good 'un.

SIEBEL
Every flea may it so befall!

May every flea have the same fate!

BRANDER
Point your fingers and nip them all!

Pinch your fingers and squidge the lot!

ALTMAYER
Hurrah for Freedom! Hurrah for wine!

Hurrah that we're free! Hurrah for wine!

MEPHISTOPHELES
I fain would drink with you, my glass to Freedom clinking,
If 'twere a better wine that here I see you drinking.

I'd gladly drink a toast to Freedom with you,
If there was better wine available than what I see here.

SIEBEL
Don't let us hear that speech again!

Oh, don't start that again!

MEPHISTOPHELES
Did I not fear the landlord might complain,
I'd treat these worthy guests, with pleasure,
To some from out our cellar's treasure.

If I wasn't worried about upsetting the landlord,
I'd be glad to treat you all
To some wine from our private stock.

SIEBEL
Just treat, and let the landlord me arraign!

You bring out the wine, I'll sort out the landlord!

FROSCH
And if the wine be good, our praises shall be ample.
But do not give too very small a sample;
For, if its quality I decide,
With a good mouthful I must be supplied.

And if it's good wine it'll be well praised.
But don't give us little glasses;
If I have to judge its quality,
I'll need a decent mouthful.

ALTMAYER (*aside*)

They're from the Rhine! I guessed as much, before.

They're from the Rhine, just as I suspected.

MEPHISTOPHELES
Bring me a gimlet here!

Bring me a piercing tool!

BRANDER
What shall therewith be done?
You've not the casks already at the door?

What are you going to do with it?
You haven't got your casks ready outside?

ALTMAYER
Yonder, within the landlord's box of tools, there's one!

There, in the landlord's toolkit, there's one!

MEPHISTOPHELES (*takes the gimlet*)
(*To* FROSCH)
Now, give me of your taste some intimation.

Now, give me some idea of what you like.

FROSCH
How do you mean? Have you so many kinds?

What do you mean? Have you lots of different ones?

MEPHISTOPHELES
The choice is free: make up your minds.

You've got a free choice, so make up your minds.

ALTMAYER (*to* FROSCH)
Aha! you lick your chops, from sheer anticipation.

Aha, you're licking your chops in anticipation!

FROSCH
Good! if I have the choice, so let the wine be Rhenish!

Good! If it's my choice, let's have some of the Rhine wine!

Our Fatherland can best the sparkling cup replenish.

Our country produces the best stuff.

MEPHISTOPHELES
(*boring a hole in the edge of the table, at the place where* FROSCH *sits*)
Get me a little wax, to make the stoppers, quick!

Get me a little wax, to make the stoppers, quickly!

ALTMAYER
Ah! I perceive a juggler's trick.

Ah! I smell a bit of sleight of hand!

MEPHISTOPHELES (*to* BRANDER)
And you?

And you?

BRANDER
Champagne shall be my wine,
And let it sparkle fresh and fine!

I'll have some champagne,
Let it be crisp and sparkling!

MEPHISTOPHELES
(bores: in the meantime one has made the wax stoppers, and plugged the holes with them)

BRANDER
What's foreign one can't always keep quite clear of,
For good things, oft, are not so near;
A German can't endure the French to see or hear of,
Yet drinks their wines with hearty cheer.

One can't always avoid what's foreign,
For good things are often not local;
A German can't abide sight nor sound of a Frenchman,
But he gladly sups their wine.

SIEBEL
(*as* MEPHISTOPHELES *approaches his seat*)
For me, I grant, sour wine is out of place;
Fill up my glass with sweetest, will you?

I can't stand any sour wines;
Top me up with the sweetest, will you?

MEPHISTOPHELES (*boring*)
Tokay shall flow at once, to fill you!

You'll be filled up with Tokay!

ALTMAYER
No--look me, Sirs, straight in the face!
I see you have your fun at our expense.

Come on gents, look me in the eye!
I can see you're having a laugh at our expense.

MEPHISTOPHELES
O no! with gentlemen of such pretence,
That were to venture far, indeed.
Speak out, and make your choice with speed!
With what a vintage can I serve you?

Oh no! With such grand gentlemen,
That would be taking a liberty.
Quickly, speak up and make your choice!
What vintage can I offer you?

ALTMAYER
With any--only satisfy our need.
(*After the holes have been bored and plugged*)

I'll take anything, as long as you actually produce it.

MEPHISTOPHELES (*with singular gestures*)
Grapes the vine-stem bears,
Horns the he-goat wears!
The grapes are juicy, the vines are wood,
The wooden table gives wine as good!
Into the depths of Nature peer,--
Only believe there's a miracle here!
Now draw the stoppers, and drink your fill!

The vines grow grapes,
The billy goat has horns!
Grapes are juicy and vines are made of wood,
This wooden table gives wine just as good!
Look into the depths of Nature,
And believe the miracle you see!
Now draw the stoppers, and drink all you want!

ALL
(as they draw out the stoppers, and the wine which has been desired flows into the glass of each)
O beautiful fountain, that flows at will!

What a wonderful fountain, flowing to order!

MEPHISTOPHELES
But have a care that you nothing spill!
(*They drink repeatedly*)

But make sure you don't spill any!

ALL (*sing*)
As 'twere five hundred hogs, we feel
So cannibalic jolly!

We feel like five hundred pigs,
We're as jolly as cannibals!

MEPHISTOPHELES
See, now, the race is happy--it is free!

See how the people are happy, they're set free!

FAUST
To leave them is my inclination.

I should like to leave them.

MEPHISTOPHELES
Take notice, first! their bestiality
Will make a brilliant demonstration.

Before you do, watch them! Their beastliness
Will prove a point well.

SIEBEL
(drinks carelessly: the wine spills upon the earth, and turns to flame)
Help! Fire! Help! Hell-fire is sent!

Help! Fire! Help! A fire's come from Hell!

MEPHISTOPHELES (charming away the flame)
Be quiet, friendly element!
(*To the revellers*)
A bit of purgatory 'twas for this time, merely.

Calm yourself, friendly element!
(To the revellers)
That was just a bit of Purgatory, for now.

SIEBEL
What mean you? Wait!--you'll pay for't dearly!
You'll know us, to your detriment.

What do you mean? Hold on, you'll pay for this!
You'll find out what we're made of, and it won't do you
any good!

FROSCH
Don't try that game a second time upon us!

You'd better not try that trick again!

ALTMAYER
I think we'd better send him packing quietly.

I think we'd better send him packing quietly.

SIEBEL
What, Sir! you dare to make so free,
And play your hocus-pocus on us!

What, Sir! You think you can take the liberty
Of playing your tricks on us?

MEPHISTOPHELES
Be still, old wine-tub.

Calm down, you old wine bucket.

SIEBEL
Broomstick, you!
You face it out, impertinent and heady?

You tool!
You're going to brazen it out are you?

BRANDER
Just wait! a shower of blows is ready.

Just you wait! You've got a beating coming!

ALTMAYER
(*draws a stopper out of the table: fire flies in his face.*)
I burn! I burn!

I'm burning!

SIEBEL
'Tis magic! Strike--
The knave is outlawed! Cut him as you like!

It's magic! Have at him –
He's broken the law! Slash at him as you please!

(*They draw their knives, and rush upon* MEPHISTOPHELES)

MEPHISTOPHELES (*with solemn gestures*)
False word and form of air,
Change place, and sense ensnare!
Be here--and there!
(*They stand amazed and look at each other.*)

Tricky words take the place of air,
Swap round and trap the senses!
Be here – and there!

ALTMAYER
Where am I? What a lovely land!

Where am I? What a beautiful country!

FROSCH
Vines? Can I trust my eyes?

Are those vines? Can I believe what I'm seeing?

SIEBEL
And purple grapes at hand!

And purple grapes on them!

BRANDER
Here, over this green arbor bending,
See what a vine! what grapes depending!
(*He takes* SIEBEL *by the nose: the others do the
same reciprocally, and raise their knives*)

Look at this, bending over this green arbor!
What a vine! What grapes hanging from it!

MEPHISTOPHELES (*as above*)
Loose, Error, from their eyes the band,
And how the Devil jests, be now enlightened!
(*He disappears with* FAUST: *the revellers start and separate.*)

Trickery, take the blinds from their eyes,
And let them see how the devil jokes!

SIEBEL
What happened?

ALTMAYER
How?

FROSCH
Was that your nose I tightened?

BRANDER (*to* SIEBEL)
And yours that still I have in hand?

ALTMAYER
It was a blow that went through every limb!
Give me a chair! I sink! my senses swim.

FROSCH
But what has happened, tell me now?

SIEBEL
Where is he? If I catch the scoundrel hiding,
He shall not leave alive, I vow.

ALTMAYER
I saw him with these eyes upon a wine-cask riding
Out of the cellar-door, just now.
Still in my feet the fright like lead is weighing.
(*He turns towards the table.*)
Why! If the fount of wine should still be playing?

SIEBEL
'Twas all deceit, and lying, false design!

FROSCH
And yet it seemed as I were drinking wine.

BRANDER
But with the grapes how was it, pray?

ALTMAYER
Shall one believe no miracles, just say!

What happened?

What's going on?

Was that your nose I twisted?

Is this yours I'm holding?

That was a blow that went right through me!
Give me a chair! I'm falling! My head's spinning!

But can somebody tell me what happened?

Where is he? If I catch the villain hiding,
I swear he won't get out of here alive.

I saw him with my own eyes riding on a wine barrel,
Out of the cellar door, just a moment ago.
The fright has turned my feet to lead.
(He turns to the table)
What! The wine's still running!

It was all a con, a lying trick!

But I felt as though I was drinking wine.

But what was that business with the grapes?

Who's going to say they don't believe in miracles now?

VI

WITCHES' KITCHEN
(Upon a low hearth stands a great caldron, under which a fire is burning. Various figures appear in the vapors which rise from the caldron. An ape sits beside it, skims it, and watches lest it boil over. The he-ape, with the young ones, sits near and warms himself. Ceiling and walls are covered with the most fantastic witch-implements)

FAUST MEPHISTOPHELES

FAUST
These crazy signs of witches' craft repel me!
I shall recover, dost thou tell me,
Through this insane, chaotic play?
From an old hag shall I demand assistance?
And will her foul mess take away
Full thirty years from my existence?
Woe's me, canst thou naught better find!
Another baffled hope must be lamented:
Has Nature, then, and has a noble mind
Not any potent balsam yet invented?

These horrid signs of witchcraft disgust me!
Are you telling me I'll get anything good
From these mad, confused practices?
Shall I ask some old hag for help?
Will her disgusting potions
Make me thirty years younger?
This is hopeless, haven't you anything better to offer?
I must mourn for another dream denied:
Hasn't Nature, or a clever mind,
Invented any better cure than this?

MEPHISTOPHELES
Once more, my friend, thou talkest sensibly.
There is, to make thee young, a simpler mode and apter;

But in another book 'tis writ for thee,
And is a most eccentric chapter.

You're talking sense again my friend.
There is a simpler and better way to make you young again;
But that's going to be in another part of our story,
And it's a pretty weird chapter.

FAUST
Yet will I know it.

But I want to know about it.

MEPHISTOPHELES
Good! the method is revealed
Without or gold or magic or physician.
Betake thyself to yonder field,
There hoe and dig, as thy condition;
Restrain thyself, thy sense and will
Within a narrow sphere to flourish;
With unmixed food thy body nourish;
Live with the ox as ox, and think it not a theft
That thou manur'st the acre which thou reapest;--
That, trust me, is the best mode left,
Whereby for eighty years thy youth thou keepest!

Good! You can find the secret,
Without money, magic or a doctor.
Get yourself off to that field over there,
Make it your job to dig and hoe;
Pull yourself in, let your brains and ambition
Be kept in a narrow orbit;
Feed yourself on pure food, and don't think it a crime
To crap on the fields which you harvest:
Trust me, that's the best way,
To keep young for eighty years!

FAUST
I am not used to that; I cannot stoop to try it--
To take the spade in hand, and ply it.
The narrow being suits me not at all.

I'm not used to that; I can't lower myself to trying it,
To take up a spade, and use it;
That little life is of no interest to me.

MEPHISTOPHELES
Then to thine aid the witch must call.

Then you need to ask the witch for help.

FAUST
Wherefore the hag, and her alone?
Canst thou thyself not brew the potion?

Why the witch and only the witch?
Can't you make the potion yourself?

MEPHISTOPHELES
That were a charming sport, I own:
I'd build a thousand bridges meanwhile, I've a notion.

That'd be a nice pastime for me, eh?
Perhaps I could run up a thousand bridges at the same time?

Not Art and Science serve, alone;
Patience must in the work be shown.
Long is the calm brain active in creation;
Time, only, strengthens the fine fermentation.
And all, belonging thereunto,
Is rare and strange, howe'er you take it:
The Devil taught the thing, 'tis true,
And yet the Devil cannot make it.
(*Perceiving the Animals*)
See, what a delicate race they be!
That is the maid! the man is he!
(*To the Animals*)
It seems the mistress has gone away?

Art and Science aren't enough;
This work needs patience as well.
The brain has to devote itself for a long time to creation;
And only time can bring the best results out.
And everything that comes from it
Is rare and wonderful, wherever it comes from.
It's true the Devil wrote the recipe,
But he can't do the cooking.
(Perceiving the animals)
What delicate creatures these are!
This is the female, that's the male.
(To the animals)
It looks like you're mistress isn't home?

THE ANIMALS
Carousing, to-day!
Off and about,
By the chimney out!

She's off on a spree, today!
Out and about,
She left by the chimney!

MEPHISTOPHELES
What time takes she for dissipating?

How long does her pleasure last?

THE ANIMALS
While we to warm our paws are waiting.

As long as the time we take to warm our paws.

MEPHISTOPHELES (*to* FAUST)
How findest thou the tender creatures?

What do you make of these sweet beasts?

FAUST
Absurder than I ever yet did see.

They're the weirdest things I've ever seen.

MEPHISTOPHELES
Why, just such talk as this, for me,
Is that which has the most attractive features!
(*To the Animals*)
But tell me now, ye cursed puppets,
Why do ye stir the porridge so?

Why, for me this sort of chat
Is the best one can get!
(To the animals)
Now tell me, you devilish puppets,
Why are you stirring the porridge like that?

THE ANIMALS
We're cooking watery soup for beggars.

We're cooking watery soup for beggars.

MEPHISTOPHELES
Then a great public you can show.

Then you won't want for customers.

68

THE HE-APE
(*comes up and fawns on* MEPHISTOPHELES)

O cast thou the dice!	*Oh, roll the dice!*
Make me rich in a trice,	*Make me rich in the blink of an eye,*
Let me win in good season!	*Let me win this time!*
Things are badly controlled,	*Everything's in a mess,*
And had I but gold,	*And if I only had money,*
So had I my reason.	*I'd have brains as well.*

MEPHISTOPHELES

How would the ape be sure his luck enhances.	*Why does the ape think all his problems could be solved*
Could he but try the lottery's chances!	*If he could just play the lottery!*

(In the meantime the young apes have been playing with a
large ball, which they now roll forward)

THE HE-APE

The world's the ball:	*The world's the ball:*
Doth rise and fall,	*Up and down it goes,*
And roll incessant:	*Rolling forever:*
Like glass doth ring,	*It echoes*
A hollow thing,--	*Like a hollow glass.*
How soon will't spring,	*How soon will it slip*
And drop, quiescent?	*And fall down still?*
Here bright it gleams,	*Here it shines bright,*
Here brighter seems:	*Here brighter still:*
I live at present!	*I'm alive, for now!*
Dear son, I say,	*My dear son, I tell you,*
Keep thou away!	*Keep away!*
Thy doom is spoken!	*This is your fate:*
'Tis made of clay,	*It's made of clay,*
And will be broken.	*And will be broken.*

MEPHISTOPHELES

What means the sieve?	*What's that sieve for?*

THE HE-APE (*taking it down*)

Wert thou the thief,	*If you were a thief,*
I'd know him and shame him.	*I'd be able to spot you at once.*

(*He runs to the SHE-APE, and lets her look through it.*) (*He runs to the SHE-APE, and lets her look through it*)

Look through the sieve!	*Look through the sieve!*
Know'st thou the thief,	*Do you know the thief,*
And darest not name him?	*But dare not name him?*

MEPHISTOPHELES (approaching the fire)

And what's this pot?	*And what about this pot?*

HE-APE AND SHE-APE

The fool knows it not!	*The idiot doesn't know what it is!*
He knows not the pot,	*He doesn't know what a pot is,*
He knows not the kettle!	*Can't name a kettle!*

MEPHISTOPHELES

Impertinent beast!	*You cheeky brute!*

THE HE-APE
Take the brush here, at least,
And sit down on the settle!
(*He invites MEPHISTOPHELES to sit down.*)

Here, move that brush
And sit down on the bench!

FAUST
(who during all this time has been standing before a mirror, now approaching and now retreating from it)
What do I see? What heavenly form revealed
Shows through the glass from Magic's fair dominions!
O lend me, Love, the swiftest of thy pinions,
And bear me to her beauteous field!
Ah, if I leave this spot with fond designing,
If I attempt to venture near,
Dim, as through gathering mist, her charms appear!--

What this? What angel can I see
Through this glass from the beautiful magic lands?
Love, give me your swiftest wings,
And carry me to her beautiful home!
Ah, if I leave this spot,
Meaning to get a closer look,
Suddenly her beauty is dimmed as if I'm looking through
a mist!

A woman's form, in beauty shining!
Can woman, then, so lovely be?
And must I find her body, there reclining,
Of all the heavens the bright epitome?
Can Earth with such a thing be mated?

Can any woman be so lovely?

Does her reclining form
Embody all that's heavenly?
Can an earthly creature mate with such a vision?

MEPHISTOPHELES
Why, surely, if a God first plagues Himself six days,
Then, self-contented, *Bravo*! says,
Must something clever be created.
This time, thine eyes be satiate!
I'll yet detect thy sweetheart and ensnare her,
And blest is he, who has the lucky fate,
Some day, as bridegroom, home to bear her.
(FAUST *gazes continually in the mirror.*
MEPHISTOPHELES, stretching himself out on the
settle, and playing with the brush, continues to speak)
So sit I, like the King upon his throne:
I hold the sceptre, here,--and lack the crown alone.

Why, surely if God slaves away for six days,
Then gives himself a self satisfied pat on the back,
Something good must have been made.
You drink your fill of looking at her!
I'll find your sweetheart and trap her for you,
And good luck to him who has the fortune
To carry her home as his bride.
(FAUST gazes continually in the mirror.
MEPHISTOPHELES, stretching himself out on the
settle, and playing with the brush, continues to speak)
So I sit here like a King on his throne.
Here's my sceptre, all I need's a crown.

THE ANIMALS
(who up to this time have been making all kinds of fantastic movements together, bring a crown to
MEPHISTOPHELES *with great noise.*)
O be thou so good
With sweat and with blood
The crown to belime!
(They handle the crown awkwardly and break it into
two pieces, with which they spring around)
'Tis done, let it be!
We speak and we see,
We hear and we rhyme!

Would you do us the honor,
Of gluing this crown to your head,
With sweat and blood!
(They handle the crown awkwardly and break it into two
pieces, with which they spring around)
It's done, that's over!
We can speak, we can see,
We can hear and we can sing!

FAUST (*before the mirror*)
Woe's me! I fear to lose my wits.

Oh God! I think I'm going out of my mind.

MEPHISTOPHELES (*pointing to the Animals*)
My own head, now, is really nigh to sinking.

My head's starting to spin, too.

THE ANIMALS
If lucky our hits,
And everything fits,
'Tis thoughts, and we're thinking!

If our lucky guesses hit the mark,
And fit in with everything else,
That counts as thought, it means we can think!

FAUST (*as above*)
My bosom burns with that sweet vision;
Let us, with speed, away from here!

My heart burns with that sweet vision;
Let's hurry away from this place!

MEPHISTOPHELES (*in the same attitude*)
One must, at least, make this admission--
They're poets, genuine and sincere.

One's got to give them this much, at least:
They're proper poets, no doubt about it!

(*The caldron, which the SHE-APE has up to this time neglected to watch, begins to boil over: there ensues a great flame, which blazes out the chimney. The* WITCH *comes careering down through the flame, with terrible cries*)

THE WITCH
Ow! ow! ow! ow!
The damnéd beast--the curséd sow!
To leave the kettle, and singe the Frau!
Accurséd fere!
(*Perceiving* FAUST *and* MEPHISTOPHELES)
What is that here?
Who are you here?
What want you thus?
Who sneaks to us?
The fire-pain
Burn bone and brain!
(She plunges the skimming-ladle into the caldron, and scatters flames towards FAUST, MEPHISTOPHELES, and the Animals. The Animals whimper)

Ow! Ow! Ow! Ow!
You damned brute, you stupid pig!
Neglecting the kettle, burning your mistress!
Oh, you cursed scum!
(*Perceiving* FAUST *and* MEPHISTOPHELES)
What's all this?
Who are you?
What are you after?
Who comes sneaking in here?
Come on fire,
Burn their brains and bones!
(*She plunges the skimming-ladle into the caldron, and scatters flames towards FAUST, MEPHISTOPHELES, and the Animals. The Animals whimper*)

MEPHISTOPHELES
(reversing the brush, which he has been holding in his hand, and striding among the jars and glasses)
In two! in two!
There lies the brew!
There lies the glass!
The joke will pass,
As time, foul ass!
To the singing of thy crew.
(*As the* WITCH *starts back, full of wrath and horror*)
Ha! know'st thou me? Abomination, thou!
Know'st thou, at last, thy Lord and Master?
What hinders me from smiting now
Thee and thy monkey-sprites with fell disaster?
Hast for the scarlet coat no reverence?
Dost recognize no more the tall cock's-feather?
Have I concealed this countenance?--
Must tell my name, old face of leather?

Crash! Bang! Wallop!
There's your potion spilled!
There's your glass broken!
Here's a joke for you
You foul ass,
And all done in time to the singing of your mob!
(*As the* WITCH *starts back, full of wrath and horror*)
Ha! You know me now then? You filth!
Do you recognize your Lord and Master?
Why shouldn't I now call down
Foul punishment on you and your monkey-imps?
Haven't you any respect for the scarlet coat?
Don't you know the meaning of the tall cock's-feather?
Is my face hidden?
Do I have to say who I am, old leatherface?

THE WITCH
O pardon, Sir, the rough salute!

Oh, forgive me sir, for the rough greeting!

Yet I perceive no cloven foot;
And both your ravens, where are *they* now?

MEPHISTOPHELES
This time, I'll let thee 'scape the debt;
For since we two together met,
'Tis verily full many a day now.
Culture, which smooth the whole world licks,
Also unto the Devil sticks.
The days of that old Northern phantom now are over:
Where canst thou horns and tail and claws discover?
And, as regards the foot, which I can't spare, in truth,
'Twould only make the people shun me;
Therefore I've worn, like many a spindly youth,
False calves these many years upon me.

THE WITCH (*dancing*)
Reason and sense forsake my brain,
Since I behold Squire Satan here again!

MEPHISTOPHELES
Woman, from such a name refrain!

THE WITCH
Why so? What has it done to thee?

MEPHISTOPHELES
It's long been written in the Book of Fable;

Yet, therefore, no whit better men we see:
The Evil One has left, the evil ones are stable.
Sir Baron call me thou, then is the matter good;
A cavalier am I, like others in my bearing.
Thou hast no doubt about my noble blood:
See, here's the coat-of-arms that I am wearing!
(*He makes an indecent gesture.*)

THE WITCH (*laughs immoderately*)
Ha! ha! That's just your way, I know:
A rogue you are, and you were always so.

MEPHISTOPHELES (*to* FAUST)
My friend, take proper heed, I pray!
To manage witches, this is just the way.

THE WITCH
Wherein, Sirs, can I be of use?

MEPHISTOPHELES
Give us a goblet of the well-known juice!
But, I must beg you, of the oldest brewage;
The years a double strength produce.

But I can't see a cloven hoof,
And what happened to your pair of ravens?

I'll let you off this once,
As it's such a long time
Since we two met.
Civilisation, which smoothes all the edges off life,
Works on the Devil as well.
That old Devil from the North has had his day:
You'll note you can't see horns or a tail, nor claws.
As for the foot, to be honest I can't risk it,
It would only scare people off;
So like many kids who have matchstick legs,
I've disguised my calves for many years.

My mind's all in a whirl,
Now I see my Lord Satan here again!

Woman, don't call me that!

Why? What's the harm in it?

Men have thought I'm just a storybook character for
many years;
But of course men don't get any better:
They've banished the Devil but the evil stays behind.
Call me Sir Baron, that'll do;
I'm a gentleman just like many others.
You needn't question my noble blood:
Look, here's my coat-of-arms!

Ha ha! That's the way you always carry on:
You always were a rascal, and always will be.

Make a note of this, my friend!
This is how to manage witches.

How can I help you gentlemen?

Give us a glass of your famous potion!
But, I must ask, make it the oldest you have;
The passing years make it twice as strong.

THE WITH

With all my heart! Now, here's a bottle,
Wherefrom, sometimes, I wet my throttle,
Which, also, not the slightest, stinks;
And willingly a glass I'll fill him.
(*Whispering*)
Yet, if this man without due preparation drinks,
As well thou know'st, within an hour 'twill kill him.

Very glad to! Now, here's a bottle,
Which I sometimes have a swig from,
Which doesn't stink at all;
I'll be happy to give him a glassful
(Whispering)
But if a man drinks this without preparing himself,
You know as well as I do he'll be dead within the hour.

MEPHISTOPHELES

He is a friend of mine, with whom it will agree,
And he deserves thy kitchen's best potation:
Come, draw thy circle, speak thine adjuration,
And fill thy goblet full and free!

He's a pal of mine, it will do him good,
And he deserves the best your kitchen can offer:
Come on, draw the circle, speak the spell,
And fill the glass to the brim!

THE WITCH

(with fantastic gestures draws a circle and places mysterious articles therein; meanwhile the glasses begin to ring, the caldron to sound, and make a musical accompaniment. Finally she brings a great book, and stations in the circle the Apes, who are obliged to serve as reading-desk, and to hold the torches. She then beckons FAUST *to approach*.)

FAUST (*to* MEPHISTOPHELES)

Now, what shall come of this? the creatures antic,
The crazy stuff, the gestures frantic,--
All the repulsive cheats I view,--
Are known to me, and hated, too.

Now, what's going on here? The mad creatures,
The weird substances, the flailing gestures –
All these disgusting tricks I see here,
I know them, and I hate them.

MEPHISTOPHELES

O, nonsense! That's a thing for laughter;
Don't be so terribly severe!
She juggles you as doctor now, that, after,
The beverage may work the proper cheer.
(*He persuades FAUST to step into the circle*)

What rubbish! Why man, that's a joke;
Don't be so pompous!
She's working on you like a doctor so that afterwards
The drink will have its desired effect.

THE WITCH

(*begins to declaim, with much emphasis, from the book*)
See, thus it's done!
Make ten of one,
And two let be,
Make even three,
And rich thou 'It be.
Cast o'er the four!
From five and six
(The witch's tricks)
Make seven and eight,
'Tis finished straight!
And nine is one,
And ten is none.
This is the witch's once-one's-one!

Now see how it's done!
Make ten from one,
Carry the two,
Make three even,
And you'll be rich.
Carry the four!
From five and six
(The witch's tricks)
Make seven and eight,
Now it's finished!
Nine is one,
Ten is none,
This is the witch's times table!

FAUST

She talks like one who raves in fever.

She talks like someone gibbering with fever.

MEPHISTOPHELES

Thou'lt hear much more before we leave her.
'Tis all the same: the book I can repeat,
Such time I've squandered o'er the history:
A contradiction thus complete
Is always for the wise, no less than fools, a mystery.
The art is old and new, for verily
All ages have been taught the matter,--
By Three and One, and One and Three,
Error instead of Truth to scatter.
They prate and teach, and no one interferes;
All from the fellowship of fools are shrinking.
Man usually believes, if only words he hears,
That also with them goes material for thinking!

You'll hear much more of it before we go.
It's all the same thing: I can recite the lot,
I've spent so long studying it:
It's completely contradictory, which is
As difficult to understand for wise men as for fools.
The skill is old and new, for truly,
Every time has learned about it,
Three and One, One and Three,
They broadcast Falsehood instead of Truth.
They babble and teach, and nobody stops them;
Nobody wants to be thought a fool.
If Man hears the words, he usually believes
That there's thought behind them somewhere!

THE WITCH (*continues*)

The lofty skill
Of Science, still
From all men deeply hidden!
Who takes no thought,
To him 'tis brought,
'Tis given unsought, unbidden!

The high skills
Of Science are still
Hidden away from all men!
To the one who doesn't think,
He'll get them;
It comes unasked for to those who don't seek it.

FAUST

What nonsense she declaims before us!
My head is nigh to split, I fear:
It seems to me as if I hear
A hundred thousand fools in chorus.

What rot she's spouting!
I feel my head will explode:
It feels like listening to
A hundred thousand fools all talking together.

MEPHISTOPHELES

O Sibyl excellent, enough of adjuration!
But hither bring us thy potation,
And quickly fill the beaker to the brim!
This drink will bring my friend no injuries:
He is a man of manifold degrees,
And many draughts are known to him.

Most excellent witch, that's enough of the spells!
Just bring us the potion here,
And fill the glass to the brim!
The drink won't do my friend any harm:
He's a man of much learning,
And he knows all about potions.

(*The* WITCH, *with many ceremonies, pours the drink into a cup; as* FAUST *sets it to his lips, a light flame arises.*)

Down with it quickly! Drain it off!
'Twill warm thy heart with new desire:
Art with the Devil hand and glove,
And wilt thou be afraid of fire?
 (*The* WITCH *breaks the circle:* FAUST *steps forth*)

Get it down you! Finish the lot!
It'll warm your heart with fresh passion:
You've thrown your lot in with the Devil,
You can't be afraid of fire!

MEPHISTOPHELES

And now, away! Thou dar'st not rest.

Now, let's get moving! You mustn't stop.

THE WITCH

And much good may the liquor do thee!

And I hope the potion works for you!

MEPHISTOPHELES (*to the* WITCH)

Thy wish be on Walpurgis Night expressed;
What boon I have, shall then be given unto thee.

On Walpurgis Night, when you make a wish,
If it's within my power I'll grant it.

THE WITCH
Here is a song, which, if you sometimes sing,
You'll find it of peculiar operation.

Here's a song for you; sing it sometimes
And you'll find it has strange powers.

MEPHISTOPHELES (*to* FAUST)
Come, walk at once! A rapid occupation
Must start the needful perspiration,
And through thy frame the liquor's potence fling.
The noble indolence I'll teach thee then to treasure,
And soon thou'lt be aware, with keenest thrills of
pleasure, How Cupid stirs and leaps, on light and
restless wing.

Come on, get moving! You need to exercise
To start the sweat you need,
And spread the potion through your system.
I'll teach you how to enjoy leisure another time,
Soon you're going to learn, with great pleasure,
How Cupid flits about on his quick light wings.

FAUST
One rapid glance within the mirror give me,
How beautiful that woman-form!

Just let me have one more look in the mirror,
How gorgeous that woman is!

MEPHISTOPHELES
No, no! The paragon of all, believe me,
Thou soon shalt see, alive and warm.
(Aside)
Thou'lt find, this drink thy blood compelling,
Each woman beautiful as Helen!

No time for that! You'll soon see that perfection
In the living breathing flesh!
(Aside)
And with this potion inside you,
Every woman will look like Helen of Troy!

VII

STREET

FAUST MARGARET (passing by)

FAUST
Fair lady, let it not offend you,
That arm and escort I would lend you!

Beautiful lady, don't take it amiss,
If I ask you to take my arm and let me walk with you!

MARGARET
I'm neither lady, neither fair,
And home I can go without your care.
[*She releases herself, and exit*]

I'm not a lady, I'm not beautiful,
And I can get home without your help.

FAUST
By Heaven, the girl is wondrous fair!
Of all I've seen, beyond compare;
So sweetly virtuous and pure,
And yet a little pert, be sure!
The lip so red, the cheek's clear dawn,
I'll not forget while the world rolls on!
How she cast down her timid eyes,
Deep in my heart imprinted lies:
How short and sharp of speech was she,
Why, 'twas a real ecstasy!

Good Lord, that girl's so beautiful!
The loveliest I've ever seen;
So sweet and innocent,
But there's a glint in her eye, count on it!
That ruby lip, that unblemished cheek,
I won't forget until the end of time!
How she modestly looked away,
Is written on my heart:
And how handy with her speech she was,
Why, it's an absolute delight!

(MEPHISTOPHELES *enters*)

FAUST
Hear, of that girl I'd have possession!

Listen, I want that girl!

MEPHISTOPHELES
Which, then?

Which one?

FAUST
The one who just went by.

The one who just passed me.

MEPHISTOPHELES
She, there? She's coming from confession,
Of every sin absolved; for I,
Behind her chair, was listening nigh.
So innocent is she, indeed,
That to confess she had no need.
I have no power o'er souls so green.

That one? She's coming from confession,
With all her sins forgiven;
I was behind her chair listening in.
In fact she's so innocent that
There was no need for her to be there.
I haven't any power over such uncorrupted souls.

FAUST
And yet, she's older than fourteen.

But she's of the legal age, eh?

MEPHISTOPHELES
How now! You're talking like Jack Rake,
Who every flower for himself would take,
And fancies there are no favors more,

Steady on! You're talking like some gigolo,
Who wants every woman for himself,
And thinks that all favours and virginities

76

Nor honors, save for him in store;
Yet always doesn't the thing succeed.

FAUST
Most Worthy Pedagogue, take heed!
Let not a word of moral law be spoken!
I claim, I tell thee, all my right;
And if that image of delight
Rest not within mine arms to-night,
At midnight is our compact broken.

MEPHISTOPHELES
But think, the chances of the case!
I need, at least, a fortnight's space,
To find an opportune occasion.

FAUST
Had I but seven hours for all,
I should not on the Devil call,
But win her by my own persuasion.

MEPHISTOPHELES
You almost like a Frenchman prate;
Yet, pray, don't take it as annoyance!
Why, all at once, exhaust the joyance?
Your bliss is by no means so great
As if you'd use, to get control,
All sorts of tender rigmarole,
And knead and shape her to your thought,
As in Italian tales 'tis taught.

FAUST
Without that, I have appetite.

MEPHISTOPHELES
But now, leave jesting out of sight!
I tell you, once for all, that speed
With this fair girl will not succeed;
By storm she cannot captured be;
We must make use of strategy.

FAUST
Get me something the angel keeps!
Lead me thither where she sleeps!
Get me a kerchief from her breast,--
A garter that her knee has pressed!

MEPHISTOPHELES
That you may see how much I'd fain
Further and satisfy your pain,
We will no longer lose a minute;
I'll find her room to-day, and take you in it.

Are lined up just for him;
But it doesn't always work like that.

Now look here, you Preacher!
Don't give me a load of morals!
I'm telling you, I claim my rights;
If that vision of beauty
Isn't in my arms this evening,
At midnight our deal's off.

But think what a difficult thing you're asking!
I need at least a couple of weeks
To set this up for you.

If I had seven hours for the job,
I wouldn't have to call on the Devil,
I could get her on my own account.

You're boasting away almost like a Frenchman;
But don't go getting annoyed!
Why blow all your pleasure in one go?
You won't enjoy instant success as much
As if you won her over
With all sorts of loving strategies,
Sculpting her to your way of thinking,
Like in Italian stories.

I want her enough, I don't need that to spice it up!

Come on now, this is no time for jokes!
I'm telling you, once and for all, speed
Won't work with this lady;
She can't be had by rushing her;
We have to think of a plan of action.

Get me something of this angel's!
Take me to her bedroom,
Give me a handkerchief she's kept in her bosom,
Or a garter she's worn round her knee!

So you can see how much I want
To help you ease your pain
We won't waste a moment;
I'll find where she lives today, and take you there.

FAUST
And shall I see--possess her?

And shall I see her – shall I have her?

MEPHISTOPHELES
No!
Unto a neighbor she must go,
And meanwhile thou, alone, mayst glow
With every hope of future pleasure,
Breathing her atmosphere in fullest measure.

No! We must get her out to a neighbour's,

While you can go in alone and bask
In the atmosphere to your heart's content,
With hopes of getting more in the future.

FAUST
Can we go thither?

Can we go there now?

MEPHISTOPHELES
'Tis too early yet.

It's too early.

FAUST
A gift for her I bid thee get!
[*Exit*]

I order you to get her a gift!

MEPHISTOPHELES
Presents at once? That's good: he's certain to get at her!
Full many a pleasant place I know,
And treasures, buried long ago:
I must, perforce, look up the matter. [Exit]

Giving gifts eh? That's good, he's bound to have her!
I know many pleasant places
Where ancient treasures have been buried:
I'll have to go and visit them.

VIII

EVENING A SMALL, NEATLY KEPT CHAMBER

MARGARET

(*plaiting and binding up the braids of her hair*)
I'd something give, could I but say
Who was that gentleman, to-day.
Surely a gallant man was he,
And of a noble family;
And much could I in his face behold,--
And he wouldn't, else, have been so bold!

I'd give something to know,
Who that chap I saw today was.
Surely he was a gentleman,
And from a noble family;
I could see it in his face,
And anyway, if he wasn't he wouldn't have been so forward!

[*Exit*]

MEPHISTOPHELES FAUST
MEPHISTOPHELES
Come in, but gently: follow me!

Come in, quietly: follow me!

FAUST (*after a moment's silence*)
Leave me alone, I beg of thee!

Could you please leave me here alone!

MEPHISTOPHELES (*prying about*)
Not every girl keeps things so neat.

It's not every girl who keeps things so neat.

FAUST (*looking around*)
O welcome, twilight soft and sweet,
That breathes throughout this hallowed shrine!
Sweet pain of love, bind thou with fetters fleet
The heart that on the dew of hope must pine!
How all around a sense impresses
Of quiet, order, and content!
This poverty what bounty blesses!
What bliss within this narrow den is pent!
(*He throws himself into a leathern arm-chair near the bed.*)
Receive me, thou, that in thine open arms
Departed joy and pain wert wont to gather!
How oft the children, with their ruddy charms,
Hung here, around this throne, where sat the father!
Perchance my love, amid the childish band,
Grateful for gifts the Holy Christmas gave her,
Here meekly kissed the grandsire's withered hand.
I feel, O maid! thy very soul
Of order and content around me whisper,--
Which leads thee with its motherly control,
The cloth upon thy board bids smoothly thee unroll,
The sand beneath thy feet makes whiter, crisper.

O dearest hand, to thee 'tis given
To change this hut into a lower heaven!
And here!

Oh, what a lovely soft twilight,
Permeates this sacred place!
Love's sweet pain, your quick chains
Are on my heart, that is yearning with hope!
What a feeling one gets from this place,
Of peace, order, and happiness!
What fortune blesses this poor place!
What happiness is contained in this low room!
(He throw himself into a leathern armchair near the bed)
Receive me, chair, within whose arms,
Joy and pain have gathered in days gone by!
How often the rosy cheeked children,
Hung around this throne of their father's!
Perhaps my love, in that throng of children,
Grateful for the Christmas presents she'd been given,
Meekly kissed her grandpa's shrivelled hand.
I can feel you, my girl! The order and happiness
Which whisper around me speak of your very soul,
Which guides your path with a mother's care,
Telling you to lay out the tablecloth perfectly,
You could make the sand beneath your feet whiter and softer.
Oh what a dear hand, which has the power,
To make this hovel a heaven on earth!
And look here!

(*He lifts one of the bed-curtains.*)
What sweetest thrill is in my blood!
Here could I spend whole hours, delaying:
Here Nature shaped, as if in sportive playing,
The angel blossom from the bud.
Here lay the child, with Life's warm essence
The tender bosom filled and fair,
And here was wrought, through holier, purer presence,
The form diviner beings wear!
And I? What drew me here with power?
How deeply am I moved, this hour!
What seek I? Why so full my heart, and sore?

Miserable Faust! I know thee now no more.
Is there a magic vapor here?
I came, with lust of instant pleasure,
And lie dissolved in dreams of love's sweet leisure!
Are we the sport of every changeful atmosphere?
And if, this moment, came she in to me,
How would I for the fault atonement render!
How small the giant lout would be,
Prone at her feet, relaxed and tender!

MEPHISTOPHELES
Be quick! I see her there, returning.

FAUST
Go! go! I never will retreat.

MEPHISTOPHELES
Here is a casket, not unmeet,
Which elsewhere I have just been earning.
Here, set it in the press, with haste!
I swear, 'twill turn her head, to spy it:
Some baubles I therein had placed,
That you might win another by it.
True, child is child, and play is play.

FAUST
I know not, should I do it?

MEPHISTOPHELES
Ask you, pray?
Yourself, perhaps, would keep the bubble?
Then I suggest, 'twere fair and just
To spare the lovely day your lust,
And spare to me the further trouble.
You are not miserly, I trust?
I rub my hands, in expectation tender--
(*He places the casket in the press, and locks it again.*)

Now quick, away!
The sweet young maiden to betray,

(*He lifts one of the bed-curtains*)
How this sight makes my blood pound!
I could waste hours on end here:
Here Nature sculpted, as if for fun,
The heavenly flower from the bud.
Here the child lay, as the warm essence of life
Was breathed into the tender bosom,
And here, through the Holy presence, was made
A shape like those that are truly Holy.
And me? What power has drawn me here?
How deeply I'm moved, here!
What am I looking for? Why is my heart so full and yet so sore?
Miserable Faust! I no longer know you.
Is there a magic mist in this place?
I came, looking for instant pleasure:
That feeling's melted into the dreams of true love!
Are we at the mercy of every change in the atmosphere?
And if she came in here right now,
How I'd make up for my earlier feelings!
What a pussycat this great lout would be,
Lying at her feet, sleepy and loving!

Shift yourself! I can see her coming back.

You go! I'm never leaving.

Here's a jewellery box, quite suitable,
Which I was just fetching for you.
Here, put it in her dresser, quickly!
I promise, it'll appeal to her when she sees it:
I've put a few jewels in it,
To help you win the jewel you want.
This is the game, and you're the children.

I don't know if I should do it?

You're asking that?
Perhaps you'd like to keep the jewels for yourself?
Then I'd say the thing to do
Is to stop going on about your feelings,
And stop putting me to all this trouble.
You're not a miser, are you?
I was looking forward to seeing –
(*He places the casket in the dresser, and locks it away again*)
Now, let's be off!
The plan is to capture this sweet young girl,

So that by wish and will you bend her;
And you look as though
To the lecture-hall you were forced to go,--
As if stood before you, gray and loath,
Physics and Metaphysics both!
But away! [*Exeunt*]

MARGARET (*with a lamp*)
It is so close, so sultry, here!
(*She opens the window*)
And yet 'tis not so warm outside.
I feel, I know not why, such fear!--
Would mother came!--where can she bide?
My body's chill and shuddering,--
I'm but a silly, fearsome thing!
(*She begins to sing while undressing*)
There was a King in Thule,
Was faithful till the grave,--
To whom his mistress, dying,
A golden goblet gave.
Naught was to him more precious;
He drained it at every bout:
His eyes with tears ran over,
As oft as he drank thereout.
When came his time of dying,
The towns in his land he told,
Naught else to his heir denying
Except the goblet of gold.
He sat at the royal banquet
With his knights of high degree,
In the lofty hall of his fathers
In the Castle by the Sea.
There stood the old carouser,
And drank the last life-glow;
And hurled the hallowed goblet
Into the tide below.
He saw it plunging and filling,
And sinking deep in the sea:
Then fell his eyelids forever,
And never more drank he!
(She opens the press in order to arrange her clothes,
and perceives the casket of jewels)
How comes that lovely casket here to me?
I locked the press, most certainly.
'Tis truly wonderful! What can within it be?
Perhaps 'twas brought by some one as a pawn,
And mother gave a loan thereon?
And here there hangs a key to fit:
I have a mind to open it.
What is that? God in Heaven! Whence came
Such things? Never beheld I aught so fair!

Rich ornaments, such as a noble dame

So you may bend her to your will;
And you look as though
You were being forced into a lecture,
As if you were facing, not love,
But dull, horrid Physics and Metaphysics!
Now come on!

It's so oppressive in here!
(She opens the window)
But it's cooler outside.
I don't know why I feel so scared!
I wish Mother would come, where can she have got to?
I feel all cold and shivery –
But I'm a silly coward!
(She begins to sing while undressing)
There was a King in Thule,
Faithful to his dying day,
To whom his dying mistress gave
A golden cup.
It was his most treasured possession;
He drank from it at every session,
And he often cried
As he drank from it.
When it came to his dying days,
He left all that he owned
To his heir, with one exception,
Which was his golden cup.
He sat at the royal feast,
With all his lofty knights,
In his great ancestral hall
In the Castle by the Sea.
The old reveller stood there
And drank one last drop;
And threw his golden cup
Into the tide below.
He saw it tossing and filling up
And sinking deep under the waves:
Then his eyes were closed for ever
And he never drank again!
(She opens the dresser in order to arrange her clothes,
and perceives the casket of jewels)
How does this lovely box come to be here?
I know I locked the dresser, I'm sure of it.
It's really beautiful! What can it hold?
Perhaps someone came here to pawn it,
And mother gave a loan against its value?
Here's the key to the lock,
I think I'll open it.
What's all this! Good God! Where did
All these things come from? I've never seen such
beauty!
These are the sort of jewels a noble lady

On highest holidays might wear!
How would the pearl-chain suit my hair?
Ah, who may all this splendor own?
(She adorns herself with the jewelry, and steps before the mirror)
Were but the ear-rings mine, alone!
One has at once another air.
What helps one's beauty, youthful blood?
One may possess them, well and good;
But none the more do others care.
They praise us half in pity, sure:
To gold still tends,
On gold depends
All, all! Alas, we poor!

Would wear on the most sacred holidays!
How would this rope of pearls suit my hair?
Ah, who can all these fine things belong to?
(She adorns herself with jewellery, and steps before the mirror)
If I could just have the earrings, just them!
They change one into something different at once.
What use is youth and beauty?
If one has them, well that's fine,
But they won't make others care about you.
They praise you almost pityingly; what's true
Is that all want wealth,
And wealth is
Everything, everything! Oh, pity the poor!

IX

PROMENADE

(FAUST, *walking thoughtfully up and down. To him* MEPHISTOPHELES)

MEPHISTOPHELES
By all love ever rejected! By hell-fire hot and
unsparing!
I wish I knew something worse, that I might use it for
swearing!

*In the name of all failed love! In the name of pitiless
hellfire!
I wish I knew some worse curses than these, I'd use
them!*

FAUST
What ails thee? What is't gripes thee, elf?

*What's the matter with you? What's bothering you, you
imp?*

A face like thine beheld I never.

I've never seen such a face as yours.

MEPHISTOPHELES
I would myself unto the Devil deliver,
If I were not a Devil myself!

*I tell you, if I weren't a Devil already,
I'd turn myself over to the Devil!*

FAUST
Thy head is out of order, sadly:
It much becomes thee to be raving madly.

*It seems that you've gone mad, I'm afraid:
Though this mad raving suits who you are.*

MEPHISTOPHELES
Just think, the pocket of a priest should get
The trinkets left for Margaret!
The mother saw them, and, instanter,
A secret dread began to haunt her.
Keen scent has she for tainted air;
She snuffs within her book of prayer,
And smells each article, to see
If sacred or profane it be;
So here she guessed, from every gem,
That not much blessing came with them.
"My child," she said, "ill-gotten good
Ensnares the soul, consumes the blood.
Before the Mother of God we'll lay it;
With heavenly manna she'll repay it!"
But Margaret thought, with sour grimace,
"A gift-horse is not out of place,
And, truly! godless cannot be
The one who brought such things to me."
A parson came, by the mother bidden:
He saw, at once, where the game was hidden,
And viewed it with a favor stealthy.
He spake: "That is the proper view,--
Who overcometh, winneth too.
The Holy Church has a stomach healthy:
Hath eaten many a land as forfeit,
And never yet complained of surfeit:
The Church alone, beyond all question,

*Can you imagine, the jewels we left for Margaret,
Are now lining the pocket of a priest!
Her mother saw them, and straight away,
She began to feel uneasy.
She's got a good nose for unholy things;
She snuffles through her prayerbook,
Smelling each passage to see
If it's really holy;
So, sniffing at these jewels, she guessed
That there wasn't much holy about them.
"My daughter," she said, "ill-gotten gains
Are a trap for the soul, a disease for the body:
We'll lay these before the Virgin Mary,
And she'll repay us with heavenly blessings!"
But Margaret pulled a face and thought,
"This is looking a gift horse in the mouth,
And surely, the person who left me these things
Is not Godless."
The mother called the priest, who came,
And certainly liked what he saw:
He said, "You did right to call me,*

*By rejecting temptation you'll be blessed.
The Holy Church has a good appetite:
It's gobbled up many lands taken in fines,
But it's never complained that it's too full!
There's no question that the Church*

Has for ill-gotten goods the right digestion."

FAUST
A general practice is the same,
Which Jew and King may also claim.

MEPHISTOPHELES
Then bagged the spangles, chains, and rings,
As if but toadstools were the things,
And thanked no less, and thanked no more
Than if a sack of nuts he bore,--
Promised them fullest heavenly pay,
And deeply edified were they.

FAUST
And Margaret?

MEPHISTOPHELES
Sits unrestful still,
And knows not what she should, or will;
Thinks on the jewels, day and night,
But more on him who gave her such delight.

FAUST
The darling's sorrow gives me pain.
Get thou a set for her again!
The first was not a great display.

MEPHISTOPHELES
O yes, the gentleman finds it all child's-play!

FAUST
Fix and arrange it to my will;
And on her neighbor try thy skill!
Don't be a Devil stiff as paste,
But get fresh jewels to her taste!

MEPHISTOPHELES
Yes, gracious Sir, in all obedience!
[*Exit* FAUST]
Such an enamored fool in air would blow
Sun, moon, and all the starry legions,
To give his sweetheart a diverting show.
[*Exit*]

Is the right place for ill-gotten gains."

This is the same way
That Jews and Kings carry on.

He parcelled up the bangles, chains and rings,
As if they were as worthless as toadstools,
And gave no more or less thanks
Than if they'd given him a bag of nuts:
He promised they would get their reward from Heaven
And they were most delighted.

And Margaret?

She's not happy,
And doesn't know what she should do;
She thinks of the jewels day and night,
And even more of the man who gave them to her.

It hurts me that my sweetheart should be sad.
Go and get her another set!
That first lot wasn't so great anyway.

Oh yes, I suppose you think they were easy to get!

Arrange for it as I order you;
And go and work your magic on her neighbor!
Don't be a spoilsport, you Devil,
But get some more jewels, ones she'll like!

Yes, my dear master, just as you say!
[Exit Faust]
This lovesick idiot would blow up
The sun, the moon and all the stars,
Just to give his sweetheart a good show.
[Exit]

X

THE NEIGHBOR'S HOUSE

MARTHA (*solus*)
God forgive my husband, yet he
Hasn't done his duty by me!
Off in the world he went straightway,--
Left me lie in the straw where I lay.
And, truly, I did naught to fret him:
God knows I loved, and can't forget him!
(*She weeps.*)
Perhaps he's even dead! Ah, woe!--
Had I a certificate to show!

My God forgive my husband, but
He hasn't done right by me!
Off he sailed into the wide world
And left me lying in the straw.
I swear I did nothing to annoy him:
God knows I loved him and can't forget him!
(She weeps)
Perhaps he's even dead! What sorrow!
I wish I had a death certificate to prove it!

MARGARET (*comes*)
Dame Martha!

Lady Martha!

MARTHA
Margaret! what's happened thee?

Margaret! Whatever's happened?

MARGARET
I scarce can stand, my knees are trembling!
I find a box, the first resembling,
Within my press! Of ebony,--
And things, all splendid to behold,
And richer far than were the old.

I can hardly stand, my knees are knocking!
I found a box, like the first one,
In my dresser! It was ebony,
And all the wonderful things in it
Were even richer than the first lot.

MARTHA
You mustn't tell it to your mother!
'Twould go to the priest, as did the other.

Don't tell your mother about it!
The priest'll get it, like he did the other lot!

MARGARET
Ah, look and see--just look and see!

Ah, have a look – just have a look!

MARTHA (*adorning her*)
O, what a blessed luck for thee!

Oh, how lucky you are!

MARGARET
But, ah! in the streets I dare not bear them,
Nor in the church be seen to wear them.

But I dare not have them on in the street,
Nor can I be seen wearing them in church.

MARTHA
Yet thou canst often this way wander,
And secretly the jewels don,
Walk up and down an hour, before the mirror yonder,--
We'll have our private joy thereon.
And then a chance will come, a holiday,
When, piece by piece, can one the things abroad display,
A chain at first, then other ornament:
Thy mother will not see, and stories we'll invent.

You can come round here as often as you like,
And put the jewels on in secret,
Parade before that mirror for an hour –
We'll enjoy them between ourselves.
And then when a holiday comes
You can start showing them off bit by bit,

First a chain, then some other piece:
Your mother will never know, we'll make up a cover story.

MARGARET
Whoever could have brought me things so precious?
That something's wrong, I feel suspicious.
(*A knock*)
Good Heaven! My mother can that have been?

Who could have brought me such expensive things?
It can't be right, I'm thinking.
(A knock)
Good Lord! That's not my mother?

MARTHA (*peeping through the blind*)
'Tis some strange gentleman.--Come in!
(MEPHISTOPHELES *enters.*)

No, it's a man, a stranger.

MEPHISTOPHELES
That I so boldly introduce me,
I beg you, ladies, to excuse me.
(*Steps back reverently, on seeing* MARGARET)
For Martha Schwerdtlein I'd inquire!

I hope you ladies will excuse me
For intruding?
(Steps back reverently, on seeing MARGARET)
I'm looking for Martha Schwerdtlein!

MARTHA
I'm she: what does the gentleman desire?

I'm her, what can I do for you?

MEPHISTOPHELES (*aside to her*)
It is enough that you are she:
You've a visitor of high degree.
Pardon the freedom I have ta'en,--
Will after noon return again.

That's all I needed to know:
I see you have a distinguished visitor.
Excuse the liberty of my intrusion,
I'll come back after noon.

MARTHA (*aloud*)
Of all things in the world! Just hear--
He takes thee for a lady, dear!

Well, just imagine that! Listen –
He thought you were a noblewoman, my dear!

MARGARET
I am a creature young and poor:
The gentleman's too kind, I'm sure.
The jewels don't belong to me.

I'm just a poor young girl:
The gentleman is flattering me.
These jewels aren't mine.

MEPHISTOPHELES
Ah, not alone the jewelry!
The look, the manner, both betray--
Rejoiced am I that I may stay!

Oh, it's not just the jewels!
It's your looks, you manners, that made me think it –
I'm glad to know I don't have to leave.

MARTHA
What is your business? I would fain--

What do you want? I'd like –

MEPHISTOPHELES
I would I had a more cheerful strain!
Take not unkindly its repeating:
Your husband's dead, and sends a greeting.

I wish I had better news to bring you!
Don't blame the messenger for the message:
Your husband's dead, and sends his regards.

MARTHA
Is dead? Alas, that heart so true!
My husband dead! Let me die, too!

He's dead! Alas, for that faithful heart!
My husband's dead! Let me die too!

MARGARET
Ah, dearest dame, let not your courage fail!

Oh, sweet lady, don't let on so!

86

MEPHISTOPHELES
Hear me relate the mournful tale!

Listen to me tell you the sad story!

MARGARET
Therefore I'd never love, believe me!
A loss like this to death would grieve me.

This is why, believe me, I'll never fall in love!
If I had a loss like this I'd die of a broken heart.

MEPHISTOPHELES
Joy follows woe, woe after joy comes flying.

Joy follows sadness, and sadness follows joy.

MARTHA
Relate his life's sad close to me!

Tell me of his sad end!

MEPHISTOPHELES
In Padua buried, he is lying
Beside the good Saint Antony,
Within a grave well consecrated,
For cool, eternal rest created.

He's buried in Padua, lying
Next to good St. Antony's tomb,
In a hallowed grave,
Made for blessed eternal rest.

MARTHA
He gave you, further, no commission?

Did he tell you to do anything for him?

MEPHISTOPHELES
Yes, one of weight, with many sighs:

Three hundred masses buy, to save him from perdition!

My hands are empty, otherwise.

Yes, something important, sighing all the time he told me:
You must buy three hundred masses, to save him from hell!
That's all that I've brought you.

MARTHA
What! Not a pocket-piece? no jewelry?
What every journeyman within his wallet spares,
And as a token with him bears,
And rather starves or begs, than loses?

What! No watch? No jewellery?
That little something every traveller keeps in his purse,
And carries with him as a keepsake,
And would rather starve or beg than give it up?

MEPHISTOPHELES
Madam, it is a grief to me;
Yet, on my word, his cash was put to proper uses.
Besides, his penitence was very sore,
And he lamented his ill fortune all the more.

Madam, I'm sorry but it's the truth;
But I swear, his money was put to good use.
Besides, he was very sorry for it himself,
And was most upset by his bad luck.

MARGARET
Alack, that men are so unfortunate!
Surely for his soul's sake full many a prayer I'll proffer.

Alas, that men can have such bad luck!
I'll offer up many prayers for his soul.

MEPHISTOPHELES
You well deserve a speedy marriage-offer:
You are so kind, compassionate.

You deserve a proposal of marriage, madam,
You're so kind and compassionate.

MARGARET
O, no! As yet, it would not do.

Oh no! I'm not ready for that yet!

87

MEPHISTOPHELES
If not a husband, then a beau for you!
It is the greatest heavenly blessing,
To have a dear thing for one's caressing.

If not a husband, then a lover!
It's the greatest gift of heaven,
To give you a lover to embrace.

MARGARET
The country's custom is not so.

That's frowned on in this country.

MEPHISTOPHELES
Custom, or not! It happens, though.

Whether it is or not, it still happens.

MARTHA
Continue, pray!

Carry on, please!

MEPHISTOPHELES
I stood beside his bed of dying.
'Twas something better than manure,--
Half-rotten straw: and yet, he died a Christian, sure,
And found that heavier scores to his account were lying.
He cried: "I find my conduct wholly hateful!
To leave my wife, my trade, in manner so ungrateful!

Ah, the remembrance makes me die!
Would of my wrong to her I might be shriven!"

I stood at his dying bedside.
It was better than dying in a dungheap –
It was half-rotten straw: but he died a Christian,
And found he was well on the wrong side of the ledger.
He cried, "I'm disgusted with myself!
To leave my wife and my job, what a selfish way to behave!"
Oh, I'll die of the shame of it!
I wish I could be forgiven for the wrong I've done her!"

MARTHA (*weeping*)
The dear, good man! Long since was he forgiven.

Oh, the sweetheart! I forgave him long ago.

MEPHISTOPHELES
"Yet she, God knows! was more to blame than I."

"Yet God knows, it was more her fault than mine!"

MARTHA
He lied! What! On the brink of death he slandered?

What! He lied! He slandered me on his deathbed?

MEPHISTOPHELES
In the last throes his senses wandered,
If I such things but half can judge.
He said: "I had no time for play, for gaping freedom:
First children, and then work for bread to feed 'em,--

For bread, in the widest sense, to drudge,
And could not even eat my share in peace and quiet!"

I think at the end he'd lost his mind,
If I'm any judge of these things.
He said, "I had no time for enjoyment, to be free:
First there were the children, then I had to work to feed 'em,
I had to slave for bread (in every sense of the word),
And I wasn't even allowed to eat my bit in peace!"

MARTHA
Had he all love, all faith forgotten in his riot?
My work and worry, day and night?

Had he forgotten all faith and love in his madness?
The way I worked and worried, day and night?

MEPHISTOPHELES
Not so: the memory of it touched him quite.
Said he: "When I from Malta went away
My prayers for wife and little ones were zealous,
And such a luck from Heaven befell us,
We made a Turkish merchantman our prey,

Not at all, he remembered it distinctly.
He said, "When I left Malta,
I prayed for the family night and day,
And Heaven sent us a great piece of luck:
We captured a Turkish trading boat,

That to the Soldan bore a mighty treasure.
Then I received, as was most fit,
Since bravery was paid in fullest measure,
My well-apportioned share of it."

MARTHA
Say, how? Say, where? If buried, did he own it?

MEPHISTOPHELES
Who knows, now, whither the four winds have blown it?
A fair young damsel took him in her care,
As he in Naples wandered round, unfriended;
And she much love, much faith to him did bear,
So that he felt it till his days were ended.

MARTHA
The villain! From his children thieving!
Even all the misery on him cast
Could not prevent his shameful way of living!

MEPHISTOPHELES
But see! He's dead therefrom, at last.
Were I in *your* place, do not doubt me,
I'd mourn him decently a year,
And for another keep, meanwhile, my eyes about me.

MARTHA
Ah, God! another one so dear
As was my first, this world will hardly give me.
There never was a sweeter fool than mine,
Only he loved to roam and leave me,
And foreign wenches and foreign wine,
And the damned throw of dice, indeed.

MEPHISTOPHELES
Well, well! That might have done, however,
If he had only been as clever,
And treated *your* slips with as little heed.
I swear, with this condition, too,
I would, myself, change rings with you.

MARTHA
The gentleman is pleased to jest.

MEPHISTOPHELES
I'll cut away, betimes, from here:
She'd take the Devil at his word, I fear.
(*To* MARGARET)
How fares the heart within your breast?

That was taking a great fortune to Soldan,
And I got a well deserved
(for we were paid according to our courage)
Share of the booty."

What? Where? If he had it buried somewhere, did he tell?

Who knows where it's ended up?

A pretty young lady took him under her wing,
As he wandered friendless round Naples;
And she gave him such love, was so true to him,
That he was glad of her until his dying day.

The swine! Thieving from his children!
All the guilt he should have felt,
Didn't stop him enjoying his lifestyle!

But you see, it killed him in the end.
If I were in your shoes, honestly,
I'd mourn him properly for a year,
While keeping my eye out for another husband.

Oh God! I'll never find another as sweet
As the first, I couldn't be so lucky.
There never was a sweeter man than him,
Except he loved to travel and leave me,
For foreign girls and foreign booze,
And of course the gambling.

Well well! Everything might have been alright,
If he had been as smart as you,
And treated your indiscretions so lightly.
I swear, if I could have such a relationship,
I'd marry you myself.

Get away, you're having a joke.

I think I'd better get out of here,
Before she takes this Devil at his word!
(To MARGARET)
And how is your heart, my lady?

MRGARET
What means the gentleman?

What can you mean?

MEPHISTOPHELES (*aside*)
Sweet innocent, thou art!
(*Aloud.*)
Ladies, farewell!

Oh, you're innocent!
(Aloud)
Ladies, goodbye!

MARGARET
Farewell!

Goodbye!

MARTHA
A moment, ere we part!
I'd like to have a legal witness,
Where, how, and when he died, to certify his fitness.

Irregular ways I've always hated;
I want his death in the weekly paper stated.

Just a minute, before you go!
I'd like to have a legal witness,
As to how, where and when he died, to prove it actually happened.
I can't stand loose ends:
I want to put a death notice in the newspaper.

MEPHISTOPHELES
Yes, my good dame, a pair of witnesses
Always the truth establishes.
I have a friend of high condition,
Who'll also add his deposition.
I'll bring him here.

Certainly my lady, two witnesses
Always prove the truth.
I have a high born friend
Who'll swear to it as well.
I'll bring him along.

MARTHA
Good Sir, pray do!

Please do, kind sir!

MEPHISTOPHELES
And this young lady will be present, too?
A gallant youth! has travelled far:
Ladies with him delighted are.

And will this young lady still be here?
He's a dashing lad, well travelled,
And the ladies love him.

MARGARET
Before him I should blush, ashamed.

I think I'd be shy and blush, if I met him.

MEPHISTOPHELES
Before no king that could be named!

Ah, you should not be shy before any king on earth!

MARTHA
Behind the house, in my garden, then,
This eve we'll expect the gentlemen.

Then behind the house, in my garden,
We'll be expecting you gentlemen this evening.

XI

A STREET

FAUST MEPHISTOPHELES

FAUST
How is it? under way? and soon complete?

How's it going? Have you got the ball rolling? Will we reach the goal soon?

MEPHISTOPHELES
Ah, bravo! Do I find you burning?
Well, Margaret soon will still your yearning:
At Neighbor Martha's you'll this evening meet.
A fitter woman ne'er was made
To ply the pimp and gypsy trade!

Ah, excellent! Are you on fire with your desire?
Well, Margaret will soon put those flames out:
You'll meet at her neighbor Martha's place this evening.
I never saw a woman better suited
To running a bawdy house!

FAUST
Tis well.

This is good.

MEPHISTOPHELES
Yet something is required from us.

But there's something we must do.

FAUST
One service pays the other thus.

There's always a tradeoff.

MEPHISTOPHELES
We've but to make a deposition valid
That now her husband's limbs, outstretched and pallid,
At Padua rest, in consecrated soil.

We've just got to make a sworn statement
That her husband's laid out and bleached bones
Are resting in a hallowed grave at Padua.

FAUST
Most wise! And first, of course, we'll make the journey thither?

Good idea! So of course to do that we'll have to make a trip there?

MEPHISTOPHELES
Sancta simplicitas! no need of such a toil;
Depose, with knowledge or without it, either!

What holy innocence! No need to put ourselves out;
Swear, whether you know the truth or not!

FAUST
If you've naught better, then, I'll tear your pretty plan!

If you can't do better than this, I reject your scheme!

MEPHISTOPHELES
Now, there you are! O holy man!
Is it the first time in your life you're driven
To bear false witness in a case?
Of God, the world and all that in it has a place,
Of Man, and all that moves the being of his race,
Have you not terms and definitions given
With brazen forehead, daring breast?
And, if you'll probe the thing profoundly,
Knew you so much--and you'll confess it roundly!--

Ah, now we see your character! What a pious man!
Is this the first time in your life you've had
To bear false witness?
When talking about God, the world and all that's in it,
About Men and all the things that motivate humanity,
Have you not given explanations
With a mask on your face and falsehood in your heart?
If you're honest with yourself you'll see
You didn't know as much about these things – be honest now! –

As here of Schwerdtlein's death and place of rest?

As you do about Schwerdtlein's death and resting place.

FAUST
Thou art, and thou remain'st, a sophist, liar.

You are, and always will be, a peddler of false logic and a liar.

MEPHISTOPHELES
Yes, knew I not more deeply thy desire.

For wilt thou not, no lover fairer,
Poor Margaret flatter, and ensnare her,
And all thy soul's devotion swear her?

True, if I didn't know that your desires will overcome your scruples.
For won't you find yourself the fairest lover,
Flatter poor Margaret and then trap her,
Swearing your eternal devotion?

FAUST
And from my heart.

With all my heart.

MEPHISTOPHELES
'Tis very fine!
Thine endless love, thy faith assuring,
The one almighty force enduring,--
Will that, too, prompt this heart of thine?

That's all grand!
And so your great love
Will be the greatest force in the world,
Moving your heart?

FAUST
Hold! hold! It will!--If such my flame,
And for the sense and power intense
I seek, and cannot find, a name;
Then range with all my senses through creation,
Craving the speech of inspiration,
And call this ardor, so supernal,
Endless, eternal and eternal,--
Is that a devilish lying game?

Stop! Stop! It will! If this is my passion,
And for a way to describe it
I search for a name in vain;
Then I wander through the universe
To try and find inspiration for my speech,
And call this love, so unearthly,
Endless, going on forever and forever;
Should that be part of the Devil's lying tricks?

MEPHISTOPHELES
And yet I'm right!

But I'm right!

FAUST
Mark this, I beg of thee!
And spare my lungs henceforth: whoever
Intends to have the right, if but his
tongue be clever,
Will have it, certainly.
But come: the further talking brings disgust,
For thou art right, especially since I must.

Make a good note of this, I ask you!
Don't make me waste my breath in future:
The chaps who wants right on his side,
If he's good with words,
Will have it for sure.
Come on, I'm sick of talking about it,

And you're right, needs must when the devil drives!

XII

GARDEN

(MARGARET *on* FAUST'S *arm.* MARTHA *and* MEPHISTOPHELES
walking up and down)

MARGARET

I feel, the gentleman allows for me,	*I feel that you are making allowances for me,*
Demeans himself, and shames me by it;	*And that demeans the both of us;*
A traveller is so used to be	*I know that travellers*
Kindly content with any diet.	*Have to take what they can get.*
I know too well that my poor gossip can	*I'm well aware that my dull chatter*
Ne'er entertain such an experienced man.	*Can't entertain such a man of the world.*

FAUST

A look from thee, a word, more entertains	*A glance, or a word, from you, means more to me*
Than all the lore of wisest brains.	*Than all wise men's works put together.*
(*He kisses her hand.*)	

MARGARET

Don't incommode yourself! How could you ever kiss it!	*Don't put yourself out! How could you ever kiss my hand?*
It is so ugly, rough to see!	*See how rough and ugly it is!*
What work I do,--how hard and steady is it!	*I have to do such endless hard work!*
Mother is much too close with me.	*My mother's a hard taskmaster.*
[*They pass*]	

MARTHA

And you, Sir, travel always, do you not?	*And you sir, are you always on the road, or do you put down roots sometimes?*

MEPHISTOPHELES

Alas, that trade and duty us so harry!	*Alas, business and duty drive us about so much!*
With what a pang one leaves so many a spot,	*One often leaves so many places with sorrow,*
And dares not even now and then to tarry!	*And dare not hang about for a moment!*

MARTHA

In young, wild years it suits your ways,	*When you're young and reckless it suits you,*
This round and round the world in freedom sweeping;	*To go charging about the world without any ties;*
But then come on the evil days,	*But then the bad days come:*
And so, as bachelor, into his grave a-creeping,	*A man creeping into his grave as a bachelor,*
None ever found a thing to praise.	*Nobody ever had a good word to say about!*

MEPHISTOPHELES

I dread to see how such a fate advances.	*I'm dreading what's coming.*

MARTHA

Then, worthy Sir, improve betimes your chances!	*Then, dear man, you'd better do something to prevent it!*
[*They pass*]	

MARGARET

Yes, out of sight is out of mind!	*Out of sight and out of mind!*

Your courtesy an easy grace is;
But you have friends in other places,
And sensibler than I, you'll find.

FAUST
Trust me, dear heart! what men call sensible
Is oft mere vanity and narrowness.

MARGARET
How so?

FAUST
Ah, that simplicity and innocence ne'er know
Themselves, their holy value, and their spell!
That meekness, lowliness, the highest graces
Which Nature portions out so lovingly—

MARGARET
So you but think a moment's space on me,
All times I'll have to think on you, all places!

FAUST
No doubt you're much alone?

MARGARET
Yes, for our household small has grown,
Yet must be cared for, you will own.
We have no maid: I do the knitting, sewing, sweeping,
The cooking, early work and late, in fact;
And mother, in her notions of housekeeping,
Is so exact!
Not that she needs so much to keep expenses down:
We, more than others, might take comfort, rather:
A nice estate was left us by my father,
A house, a little garden near the town.
But now my days have less of noise and hurry;
My brother is a soldier,
My little sister's dead.
True, with the child a troubled life I led,
Yet I would take again, and willing, all the worry,
So very dear was she.

FAUST
An angel, if like thee!

MARGARET
I brought it up, and it was fond of me.
Father had died before it saw the light,
And mother's case seemed hopeless quite,
So weak and miserable she lay;
And she recovered, then, so slowly, day by day.
She could not think, herself, of giving

You've got lovely easy manners,
But I bet you've got other girls,
And cleverer than me, I'm sure.

Trust me, darling! What men call cleverness,
Is often vain and shallow.

How's that?

Ah, the simple and the innocent never know
What a holy value they have, how captivating they are!
Meekness and humility are the highest of the graces
Which Nature so lovingly hands out –

If you just think about me for one moment,
I'll have to think about you all the time, everywhere!

I suppose you're on your own a lot?

Yes, we're a small household,
But you must appreciate it still has to be looked after.
We don't have a maid: I knit, I sew, I sweep,
I cook, do all the housework, in fact;
And my mother has such demanding standards!
It's not that she needs to scrimp and save:

In fact, we're better off than many.
My father left us a nice estate:
A house and a little plot near the town.
Still, I'm less rushed now than I used to be.
My brother's in the army,
And my little sister's dead.
I must admit she gave me a lot of trouble,
But I wish she were alive to trouble me all over again,
I loved her so much.

If she was anything like you she must have been an angel!

I raised her, and she was fond of me.
My father died before she was born
And mother seemed in a bad way too,
She was so weak and sick;
Her recovery was so slow
That she herself couldn't give

The poor wee thing its natural living;
And so I nursed it all alone
With milk and water: 'twas my own.
Lulled in my lap with many a song,
It smiled, and tumbled, and grew strong.

The poor little mite the food she needed;
So I looked after her on my own,
Giving her milk and water: she was my baby.
I sang her to sleep with lullabies,
And she smiled, romped about, grew strong.

FAUST
The purest bliss was surely then thy dower.

So you must have had the purest happiness.

MARGARET
But surely, also, many a weary hour.
I kept the baby's cradle near
My bed at night: if 't even stirred, I'd guess it,
And waking, hear.
And I must nurse it, warm beside me press it,
And oft, to quiet it, my bed forsake,
And dandling back and forth the restless creature take,
Then at the wash-tub stand, at morning's break;
And then the marketing and kitchen-tending,
Day after day, the same thing, never-ending.
One's spirits, Sir, are thus not always good,

But then one learns to relish rest and food.
[*They pass*]

Yes, but also a great wearing responsibility.
I kept the baby's cradle next to my bed at night:
If she so much as moved I'd sense it
And wake up to hear her.
I had to cuddle her, hold her tight to me for warmth,
And often, to calm her down, I'd have to get up
And rock her back and forth.
Then at the washtub she'd be with me, at elevenses;
When I went to market and worked in the kitchen,
Day after day, the same thing without a break.
It's difficult to keep always cheerful in such
circumstances sir,
And one certainly learns to enjoy one's rest and food.

MARTHA
Yes, the poor women are bad off, 'tis true:
A stubborn bachelor there's no converting.

Yes, it's no life for we poor women, it's true:
There's no swaying you stubborn bachelors.

MEPHISTOPHELES
It but depends upon the like of you,
And I should turn to better ways than flirting.

Well, if all women were like you,
I'd soon find better things to do than just flirt.

MARTHA
Speak plainly, Sir, have you no one detected?
Has not your heart been anywhere subjected?

Tell the truth sir, have you never found someone?
Haven't you ever given your heart away?

MEPHISTOPHELES
The proverb says: One's own warm hearth
And a good wife, are gold and jewels worth.

The proverb says: a nice home fire
And a good wife are worth more than gold and jewels.

MARTHA
I mean, have you not felt desire, though ne'er so
slightly?

I mean, haven't you ever felt desire, just a little bit?

MEPHISTOPHELES
I've everywhere, in fact, been entertained politely.

Everyone's always been very nice to me.

MARTHA
I meant to say, were you not touched in earnest, ever?

I meant, weren't you ever really touched?

MEPHISTOPHELES
One should allow one's self to jest with ladies never.

One should never try and joke with the ladies.

MARTHA
Ah, you don't understand!

Oh, you don't understand me!

MEPHISTOPHELES
I'm sorry I'm so blind:
But I am sure--that you are very kind.
[*They pass*]

I don't mean to be so obtuse:
But I'm sure of this: you're very kind.

FAUST
And me, thou angel! didst thou recognize,
As through the garden-gate I came?

And me, my angel! Did you recognize me,
As I came through the garden gate?

MARGARET
Did you not see it? I cast down my eyes.

Didn't you see me lowering my gaze?

FAUST
And thou forgiv'st my freedom, and the blame
To my impertinence befitting,
As the Cathedral thou wert quitting?

And have you forgiven me the liberty I took
And the censure my impudence deserves,
That time you were leaving the cathedral?

MARGARET
I was confused, the like ne'er happened me;

No one could ever speak to my discredit.
Ah, thought I, in my conduct has he read it--
Something immodest or unseemly free?
He seemed to have the sudden feeling
That with this wench 'twere very easy dealing.
I will confess, I knew not what appeal
On your behalf, here, in my bosom grew;
But I was angry with myself, to feel
That I could not be angrier with you.

I was in a whirl: nothing like that ever happened to me
before;
No one could ever say anything against my behavior.
Ah, I thought, has he seen something in my demeanor,
Which is immodest or unseemly?
He seemed to have the feeling
That this was a lass one could take liberties with.
I must admit I don't know what it was about you
That made feelings for you start up in my heart;
I was cross with myself for the fact
That I wasn't more cross with you.

FAUST
Sweet darling!

You sweetheart!

MARGARET
Wait a while!
(She plucks a star-flower, and pulls off the leaves, one after the other)

Stop a moment!

FAUST
Shall that a nosegay be?

Are you making a bouquet?

MARGARET
No, it is just in play.

No, I'm just playing.

FAUST
How?

How?

MARGARET
Go! you'll laugh at me.
(*She pulls off the leaves and murmurs.*)

I shan't tell! You'd laugh.

FAUST
What murmurest thou?

What's that you're saying?

MARGARET (*half aloud*)
He loves me--loves me not.

He loves me – he loves me not.

FAUST
Thou sweet, angelic soul!

You sweet angel!

MARGARET (*continues*)
Loves me--not--loves me--not--
(*plucking the last leaf, she cries with frank delight*:)
He loves me!

Loves me--not--loves me--not--
(*plucking the last leaf, she cries with frank delight:*)
He loves me!

FAUST
Yes, child! and let this blossom-word
For thee be speech divine! He loves thee!
Ah, know'st thou what it means? He loves thee!
(*He grasps both her hands*)

Yes, my child! And let this message from the flower
Be to you like the word of God! He loves you!
Ah, do you know what that means? He loves you!

MARGARET
I'm all a-tremble!

I'm shaking!

FAUST
O tremble not! but let this look,
Let this warm clasp of hands declare thee
What is unspeakable!
To yield one wholly, and to feel a rapture
In yielding, that must be eternal!
Eternal!--for the end would be despair.
No, no,--no ending! no ending!

Oh, don't shake! But let this look,
And these warm hands holding yours, tell you
Those things which can't be said!
To give in completely and feel the ecstasy
Of doing so, that must be forever.
Forever! Because it would mean despair to end it.
No! No! Never end it!

MARTHA (*coming forward*)
The night is falling.

The night's coming on.

MEPHISTOPHELES
Ay! we must away.

Yes, we must get going.

MARTHA
I'd ask you, longer here to tarry,
But evil tongues in this town have full play.
It's as if nobody had nothing to fetch and carry,
Nor other labor,
But spying all the doings of one's neighbor:
And one becomes the talk, do whatsoe'er one may.

Where is our couple now?

I'd invite you to stop for longer,
But there are too many gossips in this town.
It's as if there was no fetching and carrying to be done,
No other work at all,
Than to spy on one's neighbor.
One becomes the centre of gossip, no matter what one's done.
Where have our lovers got to?

MEPHISTOPHELES
Flown up the alley yonder,
The wilful summer-birds!

They've popped up that alley there,
The flighty young things!

MARTHA
He seems of her still fonder.

MEPHISTOPHELES
And she of him. So runs the world away!

He seems be getting even fonder of her.

And she of him. And that's the way the world goes!

XIII

A GARDEN-ARBOR

(MARGARET comes in, conceals herself behind the door, puts her finger to her lips, and peeps through the crack)

MARGARET

He comes!

He's coming!

FAUST (*entering*)

Ah, rogue! a tease thou art:
I have thee!
(*He kisses her.*)

Ah, you rascal, you tease!
I've got you now!

MARGARET

(*clasping him, and returning the kiss*)
Dearest man! I love thee from my heart.

You darling man! I love you from the bottom of my heart!

(MEPHISTOPHELES *knocks*)

FAUST (*stamping his foot*)

Who's there?

Who's there!

MEPHISTOPHELES

A friend!

A friend!

FAUST

A beast!

A brute!

MEPHISTOPHELES

Tis time to separate.

It's time to say goodbye.

MARTHA (*coming*)

Yes, Sir, 'tis late.

Yes, sir, it's late.

FAUST

May I not, then, upon you wait?

Can't I stay with you?

MARGARET

My mother would--farewell!

My mother wouldn't have it – goodbye!

FAUST

Ah, can I not remain?
Farewell!

Oh, can't I stay?
Goodbye!

MARTHA

Adieu!

Goodbye!

MARGARET

And soon to meet again!

And we'll meet again soon!

[*Exeunt FAUST and MEPHISTOPHELES*]

MARGARET

Dear God! However is it, such
A man can think and know so much?
I stand ashamed and in amaze,
And answer "Yes" to all he says,
A poor, unknowing child! and he--
I can't think what he finds in me! [*Exit*]

Dear God! How on earth
Can a man like this think and know so much?
I stand there embarrassed and astonished.
And say "yes" to everything he says,
Like an ignorant child! And he —
I can't imagine what he sees in me!

XIV

FOREST AND CAVERN

FAUST (*solus*)

Spirit sublime, thou gav'st me, gav'st me all	*Wonderful spirit, you gave me everything*
For which I prayed. Not unto me in vain	*Which I asked for. You have lived up to the promise*
Hast thou thy countenance revealed in fire.	*Of your fiery face.*
Thou gav'st me Nature as a kingdom grand,	*You gave me the keys to Nature's kingdom,*
With power to feel and to enjoy it. Thou	*With the power to feel it and enjoy it.*
Not only cold, amazed acquaintance yield'st,	*You not only melted her reserve for me,*
But grantest, that in her profoundest breast	*But have made it so that I have access to her innermost thoughts*
I gaze, as in the bosom of a friend.	*As though I were her dearest friend.*
The ranks of living creatures thou dost lead	*You parade the creatures of the earth before me,*
Before me, teaching me to know my brothers	*Teaching me to know my fellow animals*
In air and water and the silent wood.	*Of the air, the water and the silent woods.*
And when the storm in forests roars and grinds,	*And when the storm tears through the forest,*
The giant firs, in falling, neighbor boughs	*And the giant firs fall, bring down with them*
And neighbor trunks with crushing weight bear down,	*Their neighboring trunks and branches with their weight*
And falling, fill the hills with hollow thunders,--	*And their crash echoes around the hills,*
Then to the cave secure thou leadest me,	*Then you took me to a safe cave*
Then show'st me mine own self, and in my breast	*And showed me my true nature, and in my heart,*
The deep, mysterious miracles unfold.	*Revealed the mysteries of life.*
And when the perfect moon before my gaze	*And when, as I looked, the perfect moon*
Comes up with soothing light, around me float	*Rose with its soothing light, all around me floated,*
From every precipice and thicket damp	*From the hilltops and damp thickets,*
The silvery phantoms of the ages past,	*The ghosts of times gone by,*
And temper the austere delight of thought.	*So that I wouldn't just have the dry pleasure of thought.*
That nothing can be perfect unto Man	*I now understand that nothing can be perfect*
I now am conscious. With this ecstasy,	*In this life of Man. These visions,*
Which brings me near and nearer to the Gods,	*Which bring me close to Heaven,*
Thou gav'st the comrade, whom I now no more	*Were a gift from you, my friend, whom I now*
Can do without, though, cold and scornful, he	*Can't manage without, although, cold and mocking,*
Demeans me to myself, and with a breath,	*He puts me down and in the blink of an eye,*
A word, transforms thy gifts to nothingness.	*With one word, he can change beauty into nothing.*
Within my breast he fans a lawless fire,	*Within my heart he's lit the forbidden flame,*
Unwearied, for that fair and lovely form:	*Which makes me want that lovely body day and night:*
Thus in desire I hasten to enjoyment,	*Thus in love I hurry towards lust,*
And in enjoyment pine to feel desire.	*And in lust I want to feel love.*
(MEPHISTOPHELES *enters*)	

MEPHISTOPHELES

Have you not led this life quite long enough?	*Haven't you had enough of this game?*
How can a further test delight you?	*How can more of the same please you?*
'Tis very well, that once one tries the stuff,	*It's all very well to try something once*
But something new must then requite you.	*But surely you then want something new?*

FAUST

Would there were other work for thee!	*I wish you had something else to do!*
To plague my day auspicious thou returnest.	*You've come back to darken my happy day.*

MEPHISTOPHELES

Well! I'll engage to let thee be:
Thou darest not tell me so in earnest.
The loss of thee were truly very slight,--
comrade crazy, rude, repelling:
One has one's hands full all the day and night;
If what one does, or leaves undone, is right,

From such a face as thine there is no telling.

Fine, I'll leave you alone then:
You haven't the guts to tell me to go outright.
Honestly, I wouldn't miss you anyway
You mad, rude, revolting companion:
Looking after you is a full time job;
And whether what one does, or doesn't do, is what you want,
You can't tell from the look on your face.

FAUST

There is, again, thy proper tone!--
That thou hast bored me, I must thankful be!

There you go again, that's what you're like!
You've bored me and I'm supposed to be grateful for it!

MEPHISTOPHELES

Poor Son of Earth, how couldst thou thus alone
Have led thy life, bereft of me?
I, for a time, at least, have worked thy cure;
Thy fancy's rickets plague thee not at all:
Had I not been, so hadst thou, sure,
Walked thyself off this earthly ball
Why here to caverns, rocky hollows slinking,
Sit'st thou, as 'twere an owl a-blinking?
Why suck'st, from sodden moss and dripping stone,
Toad-like, thy nourishment alone?
A fine way, this, thy time to fill!
The Doctor's in thy body still.

You pathetic man, how could you, alone,
Have lived your life without me?
I've cured you, temporarily at least,
Of the depression that was plaguing you:
Had I not done so it's certain
That you would have taken yourself off this planet.
Why do you creep up to these caves,
And sit here like a stupid blinking owl?
Why do you, like a toad, suck your food
From the dank stone and wet moss?
What a way to spend your time!
You've still got the mind of the Doctor.

FAUST

What fresh and vital forces, canst thou guess,
Spring from my commerce with the wilderness?
But, if thou hadst the power of guessing,
Thou wouldst be devil enough to grudge my soul the blessing.

Can't you guess what wonderful inspiration
I get from spending my time in the wilds?
But if you did know, devil that you are,
You would begrudge me my happiness.

MEPHISTOPHELES

A blessing drawn from supernatural fountains!
In night and dew to lie upon the mountains;
All Heaven and Earth in rapture penetrating;
Thyself to Godhood haughtily inflating;
To grub with yearning force through Earth's dark marrow,
Compress the six days' work within thy bosom narrow,--
To taste, I know not what, in haughty power,
Thine own ecstatic life on all things shower,
Thine earthly self behind thee cast,
And then the lofty instinct, thus--
(*With a gesture*:)
at last,--
daren't say how--to pluck the final flower!

A blessing you've taken from the holy fountains!
You lie in the mountains in the wet night,
Feeling the pulse of Heaven and Earth in your joy,
Arrogantly thinking you're like a God yourself.
You want to tunnel through the soul of the Earth,

To squash all of Creation into your heart,

To taste goodness knows what, in your arrogant power,
To get everything you can for yourself,
To throw off the bonds of your body,
And then what you'll want to do, like this –
(*Makes a gesture*)
At last,
I can't say how – you'll pick that final flower!

FAUST
Shame on thee!

You should be ashamed!

MEPHISTOPHELES
Yes, thou findest that unpleasant!
Thou hast the moral right to cry me "shame!" at present.
One dares not that before chaste ears declare,
Which chaste hearts, notwithstanding, cannot spare;
And, once for all, I grudge thee not the pleasure
Of lying to thyself in moderate measure.
But such a course thou wilt not long endure;
Already art thou o'er-excited,
And, if it last, wilt soon be plighted
To madness and to horror, sure.
Enough of that! Thy love sits lonely yonder,
By all things saddened and oppressed;
Her thoughts and yearnings seek thee, tenderer, fonder,--
mighty love is in her breast.
First came thy passion's flood and poured around her
As when from melted snow a streamlet overflows;
Thou hast therewith so filled and drowned her,

That now *thy* stream all shallow shows.
Methinks, instead of in the forests lording,
The noble Sir should find it good,
The love of this young silly blood
At once to set about rewarding.
Her time is miserably long;
She haunts her window, watching clouds that stray
O'er the old city-wall, and far away.
"Were I a little bird!" so runs her song,
Day long, and half night long.
Now she is lively, mostly sad,
Now, wept beyond her tears;
Then again quiet she appears,--Always
love-mad.

Ah, you don't like that!
Just for now you can say I should be ashamed.
One can't talk of things before the pure,
That nevertheless their hearts can't manage without;
I'm telling you, I don't mind the pleasure you're getting,
From lying to yourself a bit.
But you won't be able to hold out for long,
You're on the boil already,
And if you stay in this state for long
You can be sure you'll go mad.
Give it up! You love sits there lonely,
Saddened and depressed by everything;
Her thoughts and desires are all of you, fond and sweet,

There's a great love in her heart.
First the tide of your passion crashed over her,
Like a stream flooding from the melted snow waters;
You've filled her up and drowned her so deep with passion,
That your reservoir seems to be empty.
I think, instead of swanning around in the forest,
This great man would be better off,
To set about the task
Of reciprocating the love of this silly young thing.
Time drags by for her;
She sits at her window, watching the clouds drifting
Over the city wall and off into the distance.
"I wish I were a bird!" That's what she sings
All day and half the night.
Now she's lively, now she's sad,
Now she cries herself out,
The she seems calm again, and all the time,
She's mad with love.

FAUST
Serpent! Serpent!

You snake!

MEPHISTOPHELES (aside)
Ha! do I trap thee!

Ha, that's got you!

FAUST
Get thee away with thine offences,
Reprobate! Name not that fairest thing,
Nor the desire for her sweet body bring
Again before my half-distracted senses!

Clear off and take your dirty mind with you,
You scoundrel! Don't name that beautiful thing,
And don't conjure up the desire for her sweet body
In front of my half mad senses again!

MEPHISTOPHELES
What wouldst thou, then? She thinks that thou art flown;

What are you going to do then? She thinks you've given up on her,

And half and half thou art, I own.

FAUST
Yet am I near, and love keeps watch and ward;
Though I were ne'er so far, it cannot falter:
I envy even the Body of the Lord
The touching of her lips, before the altar.

MEPHISTOPHELES
'Tis very well! *My* envy oft reposes
On your twin-pair, that feed among the roses.

FAUST
Away, thou pimp!

MEPHISTOPHELES
You rail, and it is fun to me.
The God, who fashioned youth and maid,
Perceived the noblest purpose of His trade,
And also made their opportunity.
Go on! It is a woe profound!
'Tis for your sweetheart's room you're bound,
And not for death, indeed.

FAUST
What are, within her arms, the heavenly blisses?
Though I be glowing with her kisses,
Do I not always share her need?
I am the fugitive, all houseless roaming,
The monster without air or rest,
That like a cataract, down rocks and gorges foaming,
Leaps, maddened, into the abyss's breast!
And side-wards she, with young unwakened senses,

Within her cabin on the Alpine field
Her simple, homely life commences,
Her little world therein concealed.
And I, God's hate flung o'er me,
Had not enough, to thrust
The stubborn rocks before me
And strike them into dust!
She and her peace I yet must undermine:
Thou, Hell, hast claimed this sacrifice as thine!
Help, Devil! through the coming pangs to push me;
What must be, let it quickly be!
Let fall on me her fate, and also crush me,--
One ruin whelm both her and me!

MEPHISTOPHELES
Again it seethes, again it glows!
Thou fool, go in and comfort her!
When such a head as thine no outlet knows,
It thinks the end must soon occur.

And it looks to me as though you almost have.

But I've stayed close, and love is still on duty;
However far away I was it would not die:
I'm jealous even of the communion wafer
That gets to touch her lips when she's in church.

That's all well and good! I'm often thinking
Of another pair of lips, you know the ones I mean!

Get lost, you filthy beast!

You tell me off if you like, it's all a laugh to me.
When God made men and women,
He knew what he was up to,
And he meant them to use what he gave them.
Go on! It'd be a crime not to!
You're headed for your sweetheart's room, I reckon,
And not for death.

What are the heavenly delights to be found in her arms?
Though she covers me with burning kisses,
Don't I always have the same desire as her?
I'm like the homeless stray,
A monster choking and restless,
Like that crashing waterfall
Which hurls itself down into the abyss!
And by the side of that torrent she sits with her innocence,
In her simple little mountain shack,
Living a quiet, demure life,
The four walls encompassing her whole existence.
And I, drowning in the hatred of God,
Am not strong enough
To push temptation aside
And smash it into pieces!
I must destroy the quiet love we have:
You've claimed this as your tribute, Hell!
Help me, Devil, through what's coming:
If it's going to happen, let it be quick!
Whatever's going to fall on her let me suffer the same,
Let us share the same ruinous fate!

Aha, you're hot again eh?
You idiot, go and give her what she wants!
When your sort of mind can't let off steam
It convinces itself the end's coming.

Hail him, who keeps a steadfast mind!
Thou, else, dost well the devil-nature wear:
Naught so insipid in the world I find
As is a devil in despair.

My hat's off to the man who doesn't give in to despair!
You make quite a good devil most of the time:
There's nothing worse, I reckon,
Than a devil with depression.

XV

MARGARET'S ROOM

MARGARET
(*at the spinning-wheel, alone*)

My peace is gone,	*I have no peace,*
My heart is sore:	*My heart's broken,*
I never shall find it,	*I'll never get it back,*
Ah, nevermore!	*Never again!*
Save I have him near.	*Unless he's with me.*
The grave is here;	*I can see the grave;*
The world is gall	*The world is all*
And bitterness all.	*Pain and bitterness.*
My poor weak head	*My poor weak mind*
Is racked and crazed;	*Is spinning round;*
My thought is lost,	*I can't think,*
My senses mazed.	*My senses are all mixed up.*
My peace is gone,	*I have no peace,*
My heart is sore:	*My heart's broken,*
I never shall find it,	*I'll never get it back,*
Ah, nevermore!	*Never again!*
To see him, him only,	*To see him, just him,*
At the pane I sit;	*I sit at the window;*
To meet him, him only,	*To meet him, just him,*
The house I quit.	*I leave the house.*
His lofty gait,	*His sweet movements,*
His noble size,	*His manly bulk,*
The smile of his mouth,	*His smiling mouth,*
The power of his eyes,	*His compelling eyes,*
And the magic flow	*And the magical stream*
Of his talk, the bliss	*Of his talk, the joy*
In the clasp of his hand,	*In holding his hand,*
And, ah! his kiss!	*Ah oh! His kiss!*
My peace is gone,	*I have no peace,*
My heart is sore:	*My heart's broken,*
I never shall find it,	*I'll never get it back,*
Ah, nevermore!	*Never again!*
My bosom yearns	*My heart pines*
For him alone;	*Just for him;*
Ah, dared I clasp him,	*Oh, if only I dared,*
And hold, and own!	*To hold him and make him mine!*
And kiss his mouth,	*To kiss his mouth,*
To heart's desire,	*As the heart desires,*
And on his kisses	*And at last,*
At last expire!	*To die of kissing!*

XVI

MARTHA'S GARDEN

MARGARET FAUST

MARGARET
Promise me, Henry!—

Promise me, Henry –

FAUST
What I can!

Anything!

MARGARET
How is't with thy religion, pray?
Thou art a dear, good-hearted man,
And yet, I think, dost not incline that way.

What's the position with you and religion?
You're a sweet and good man,
But I don't think you're that way inclined.

FAUST
Leave that, my child! Thou know'st my love is tender;

For love, my blood and life would I surrender,
And as for Faith and Church, I grant to each his own.

Don't fuss about that, sweetheart! You know that I love
you truly;
I would gladly give up my life for love,
And as for faith and religion, I say live and let live.

MARGARET
That's not enough: we must believe thereon.

That's not good enough, we must have faith.

FAUST
Must we?

Must we?

MARGARET
Would that I had some influence!
Then, too, thou honorest not the Holy Sacraments.

I wish I had some hold over you!
So you don't venerate the Holy Sacrements?

FAUST
I honor them.

I do.

MARGARET
Desiring no possession
'Tis long since thou hast been to mass or to confession.

Believest thou in God?

But you don't want any part of it.
It's a long time since you've been to mass or to
confession.
Do you believe in God?

FAUST
My darling, who shall dare
"I believe in God!" to say?
Ask priest or sage the answer to declare,
And it will seem a mocking play,
A sarcasm on the asker.

Darling, who dares say,
"I believe in God"?
If you ask a priest or a wise man that question,
The answer would seem like a joke
Played on the one who asked.

MARGARET
Then thou believest not!

Then you don't believe!

FAUST

Hear me not falsely, sweetest countenance!
Who dare express Him?
And who profess Him,
Saying: I believe in Him!
Who, feeling, seeing,

Deny His being,
Saying: I believe Him not!
The All-enfolding,
The All-upholding,
Folds and upholds he not
Thee, me, Himself?
Arches not there the sky above us?
Lies not beneath us, firm, the earth?
And rise not, on us shining,
Friendly, the everlasting stars?
Look I not, eye to eye, on thee,
And feel'st not, thronging
To head and heart, the force,
Still weaving its eternal secret,
Invisible, visible, round thy life?
Vast as it is, fill with that force thy heart,
And when thou in the feeling wholly blessed art,
Call it, then, what thou wilt,--
Call it Bliss! Heart! Love! God!
I have no name to give it!
Feeling is all in all:
The Name is sound and smoke,
Obscuring Heaven's clear glow.

MARGARET

All that is fine and good, to hear it so:
Much the same way the preacher spoke,
Only with slightly different phrases.

FAUST

The same thing, in all places,
All hearts that beat beneath the heavenly day--
Each in its language--say;
Then why not I, in mine, as well?

MARGARET

To hear it thus, it may seem passable;
And yet, some hitch in't there must be
For thou hast no Christianity.

FAUST

Dear love!

MARGARET

I've long been grieved to see
That thou art in such company.

Don't misunderstand me, you beautiful girl!
Who can name Him?
Who can confess,
"I believe in Him!"
But who,
If they're alive,
Can deny Him,
And say, "He doesn't exist!"
He is wrapped in everything,
He supports the world,
Doesn't he support
You, me, Himself?
Isn't that the sky overhead?
Isn't this the firm earth below us?
And don't the shining, friendly, eternal stars,
Rise above us?
Don't I look you in the face,
And don't you feel, swarming
Over the heart and the head,
That force which wraps the everlasting mystery,
Visible and invisible, round your life?
Fill your heart with that mystery,
And when you're quite full of it,
You can call it what you want –
Happiness! Heart! Love! God!
I can't say what it is!
Feelings are feelings:
Giving them names just obscures
Their Holy beauty.

It's good to hear it put like that:
The preacher said much the same thing,
Though he expressed it rather differently.

It's the same thing for everyone, wherever they are,
For all the hearts that beat beneath the rule of Heaven.
Each one has its own language,
So why can't I have my own, too?

Hearing the way you put it, it sounds reasonable;
But there's a catch in it somewhere,
For you're not a Christian.

Sweetheart!

I've been bothered for a long time,
By the company you keep.

FAUST
How so?

What do you mean?

MARGARET
The man who with thee goes, thy mate,
Within my deepest, inmost soul I hate.
In all my life there's nothing
Has given my heart so keen a pang of loathing,
As his repulsive face has done.

That chap who hangs around with you, your friend,
I despise him from the bottom of my heart.
I've never seen anything in my life,
That disgusts me as much
As his revolting face.

FAUST
Nay, fear him not, my sweetest one!

Darling, don't let him bother you!

MARGARET
I feel his presence like something ill.
I've else, for all, a kindly will,
But, much as my heart to see thee yearneth,
The secret horror of him returneth;
And I think the man a knave, as I live!
If I do him wrong, may God forgive!

He gives me the creeps.
I've got a good word for everyone,
But though my heart ached to see you,
Knowing he would come too gave me the horrors;
I swear the man's a scoundrel!
If I'm wrong about him then may God forgive me!

FAUST
There must be such queer birds, however.

But we're all different, aren't we?

MARGARET
Live with the like of him, may I never!
When once inside the door comes he,
He looks around so sneeringly,
And half in wrath:
One sees that in nothing no interest he hath:
'Tis written on his very forehead
That love, to him, is a thing abhorréd.
I am so happy on thine arm,
So free, so yielding, and so warm,
And in his presence stifled seems my heart.

I couldn't live with his sort!
When he comes in the door,
He looks around with contempt,
And angrily too:
You can see her cares for nothing:
It's written plainly in his face
That he hates love.
I am so happy with you,
So free, so relaxed, so warm,
But when he comes I feel suffocated.

FAUST
Foreboding angel that thou art!

What a suspicious darling you are!

MARGARET
It overcomes me in such degree,
That wheresoe'er he meets us, even,
I feel as though I'd lost my love for thee.
When he is by, I could not pray to Heaven.
That burns within me like a flame,
And surely, Henry, 'tis with thee the same.

The feeling's so powerful,
That whenever we meet him,
I even feel as if I don't love you.
I can't pray while he's around,
And that burns me up.
Surely, Henry, you must feel the same?

FAUST
There, now, is thine antipathy!

It's just a feeling, don't worry!

MARGARET
But I must go.

But I must leave.

FAUST
Ah, shall there never be
A quiet hour, to see us fondly plighted,
With breast to breast, and soul to soul united?

Are we never going to get
A quiet hour when we can join together,
Body to body and soul to soul?

MARGARET
Ah, if I only slept alone!
I'd draw the bolts to-night, for thy desire;

Ah, if only I had my own place!
I'd leave the door unlocked tonight, for you to come and
get what you want.

But mother's sleep so light has grown,
And if we were discovered by her,
'Twould be my death upon the spot!

But Mother sleeps so lightly now,
And if she caught us,
It would be the death of me!

FAUST
Thou angel, fear it not!
Here is a phial: in her drink
But three drops of it measure,
And deepest sleep will on her senses sink.

You sweetheart, don't let that bother you!
Take this bottle, and just slip
Three drops of the liquid in her drink
And she'll be off into the deepest sleep.

MARGARET
What would I not, to give thee pleasure?
It will not harm her, when one tries it?

I'd do anything to make you happy.
It won't do her harm though, will it?

FAUST
If 'twould, my love, would I advise it?

If it would, would I suggest it?

MARGARET
Ah, dearest man, if but thy face I see,
I know not what compels me to thy will:
So much have I already done for thee,
That scarcely more is left me to fulfil.
(*Enter* MEPHISTOPHELES) [*Exit*]

Ah, you dear man, when I look on your face,
I hardly know what rules over me:
I've given you so much already,
I've hardly anything left to give.

MEPHISTOPHELES
The monkey! Is she gone?

The cheeky monkey! Gone, is she?

FAUST
Hast played the spy again?

Eavesdropping again?

MEPHISTOPHELES
I've heard, most fully, how she drew thee.
The Doctor has been catechised, 'tis plain;
Great good, I hope, the thing will do thee.
The girls have much desire to ascertain
If one is prim and good, as ancient rules compel:

I heard all about how she tested you on religion.
The Doctor's been put through his paces, I can see.
I think it's going to do you a lot of good.
These girls want to know
If a chap's good and holy, as the old rules say he should
be.

If there he's led, they think, he'll follow them as well.

They think if a man can follow those rules, he'll follow
them too.

FAUST
Thou, monster, wilt nor see nor own
How this pure soul, of faith so lowly,
So loving and ineffable,--

You monster, you can't see or won't admit
How her pure soul, with such humble faith,
So loving and close to God –

110

The faith alone
That her salvation is,--with scruples holy
Pines, lest she hold as lost the man she loves so well!

Her faith, which is her only salvation,
Is sorely tested: she doesn't want to lose it
Nor to lose the man she loves.

MEPHISTOPHELES
Thou, full of sensual, super-sensual desire,
A girl by the nose is leading thee.

You're mad with desire,
And letting a girl lead you up the garden path.

FAUST
Abortion, thou, of filth and fire!

You foul creature, made of muck and flame!

MEPHISTOPHELES
And then, how masterly she reads physiognomy!
When I am present she's impressed, she knows not how;

She in my mask a hidden sense would read:
She feels that surely I'm a genius now,--
Perhaps the very Devil, indeed!
Well, well,--to-night--?

And how well she can read a face!
When I'm around she feels something, though she
doesn't know what:
She reads something underneath my disguise:
She can feel that I've got the power,
Maybe she even knows I'm the Devil!
Come on then, is it going to happen tonight?

FAUST
What's that to thee?

What business is it of yours?

MEPHISTOPHELES
Yet my delight 'twill also be!

It'll give me as much pleasure as it'll give you!

XVII

AT THE FOUNTAIN

MARGARET *and* LISBETH *with pitchers.*

LISBETH
Hast nothing heard of Barbara?

Did you hear about Barbara?

MARGARET
No, not a word. I go so little out.

No, nothing. I hardly get out.

LISBETH
It's true, Sibylla said, to-day.
She's played the fool at last, there's not a doubt.
Such taking-on of airs!

Well it's true, Sybilla told me today.
She's done the deed at last, that's for sure.
She thinks she's all that now!

MARGARET
How so?

What do you mean?

LISBETH
It stinks!
She's feeding two, whene'er she eats and drinks.

You can smell it!
You can see she's eating for two.

MARGARET
Ah!

Aha!

LISBETH
And so, at last, it serves her rightly.
She clung to the fellow so long and tightly!
That was a promenading!
At village and dance parading!
As the first they must everywhere shine,
And he treated her always to pies and wine,
And she made a to-do with her face so fine;
So mean and shameless was her behavior,
She took all the presents the fellow gave her.
'Twas kissing and coddling, on and on!
So now, at the end, the flower is gone.

And it serves her right.
She was chasing after that chap so desperately!
That was a sight to see!
Showing him off in the village and at the dance!
They had to be the best couple everywhere,
And he was always treating her to pies and wine,
And she showed off, all made up;
She was so greedy, so shameless in her behaviour,
She took everything the chap could give.
First kissing, the cuddling, then more and more!
Until, in the end, now she's lost everything!

MARGARET
The poor, poor thing!

Oh, the poor thing!

LISBETH
Dost pity her, at that?
When one of us at spinning sat,
And mother, nights, ne'er let us out the door
She sported with her paramour.
On the door-bench, in the passage dark,
The length of the time they'd never mark.
So now her head no more she'll lift,
But do church-penance in her sinner's shift!

Why feel sorry for her?
When the likes of us were home spinning,
With our mothers keeping us in at night,
She was off enjoying herself with her fellow.
On the tavern bench, in the dark alleys,
Never thinking about the time.
Now she can't hold her head up in public,
And she'll have to ask forgiveness at church in sinners'
clothes!

MARGARET
He'll surely take her for his wife.

LISBETH
He'd be a fool! A brisk young blade
Has room, elsewhere, to ply his trade.
Besides, he's gone.

MARGARET
That is not fair!

LISBETH
If him she gets, why let her beware!
The boys shall dash her wreath on the floor,
And we'll scatter chaff before her door!
[*Exit*]

MARGARET (*returning home*)
How scornfully I once reviled,
When some poor maiden was beguiled!
More speech than any tongue suffices
I craved, to censure others' vices.
Black as it seemed, I blackened still,
And blacker yet was in my will;
And blessed myself, and boasted high,--
And now--a living sin am I!
Yet--all that drove my heart thereto,
God! was so good, so dear, so true!

Well, surely he'll marry her?

He'd be mad to! A dashing young chap like him,
Will doubtless get other invitations.
Anyway, he's gone.

That's not right!

Anyone who ends up with him had better watch out!
The lads will bust up all she has,
And we'll throw rubbish round her doorway!

How I used to sit in judgement,
When some poor girl got into trouble!
I liked nothing better
Than to criticize the behavior of others.
However bad it was, I made it worse,
And wanted to believe it was even worse than that:
I praised myself and was so proud of my virtue,
And now – I'm the very image of sin!
Yet everything that led me to it -
Believe me, God! - was good and pure and true!

XVIII

DONJON *(Tower)*

(In a niche of the wall a shrine, with an image of the Mater Dolorosa. Pots of flowers before it)

MARGARET
(putting fresh flowers in the pots)

Incline, O Maiden,	*Please bend, oh Holy Virgin,*
Thou sorrow-laden,	*Your sorrowing and gracious*
Thy gracious countenance upon my pain!	*Face to look upon my pain!*
The sword Thy heart in,	*The sword pierced your heart,*
With anguish smarting,	*With such sharp anguish,*
Thou lookest up to where Thy Son is slain!	*When you looked up to see your son killed!*
Thou seest the Father;	*You see God,*
Thy sad sighs gather,	*And gather up your sadness and His pain*
And bear aloft Thy sorrow and His pain!	*And send them up to heaven!*
Ah, past guessing,	*Ah, you can't guess,*
Beyond expressing,	*And I can't say,*
The pangs that wring my flesh and bone!	*What agonies I am suffering!*
Why this anxious heart so burneth,	*Why my heart is burning,*
Why it trembleth, why it yearneth,	*Trembling with desire,*
Knowest Thou, and Thou alone!	*Only you know!*
Where'er I go, what sorrow,	*Everywhere I go, what sorrow,*
What woe, what woe and sorrow	*What sorrow and sadness,*
Within my bosom aches!	*Weigh down my heart!*
Alone, and ah! unsleeping,	*All alone and unable to sleep,*
I'm weeping, weeping, weeping,	*I cry, and cry, and cry,*
The heart within me breaks.	*And my heart is breaking.*
The pots before my window,	*My window box*
Alas! my tears did wet,	*Was soaked with my tears*
As in the early morning	*As I picked these flowers*
For thee these flowers I set.	*For you this morning.*
Within my lonely chamber	*In my lonely room,*
The morning sun shone red:	*The sunrise shone in red,*
I sat, in utter sorrow,	*And I sat in utter sorrow*
Already on my bed.	*On my bed.*
Help! rescue me from death and stain!	*Help! Save me from death and dishonor!*
O Maiden!	*Oh Holy Maid!*
Thou sorrow-laden,	*You who know what it is to have sorrow,*
Incline Thy countenance upon my pain!	*Turn the light of your face upon my agony!*

XIX

NIGHT

STREET BEFORE MARGARET'S DOOR

VALENTINE (*a soldier,* MARGARET'S *brother*)

When I have sat at some carouse.	When I've been on some spree,
Where each to each his brag allows,	Where everyone's allowed to boast as he pleases,
And many a comrade praised to me	And many of my comrades would tell me
His pink of girls right lustily,	How great his girl was,
With brimming glass that spilled the toast,	With his full glass slopping over as he raised it to her,
And elbows planted as in boast:	And his elbows on the table, showing off:
I sat in unconcerned repose,	I'd just sit there, undisturbed,
And heard the swagger as it rose.	As the boasts got bigger and bigger.
And stroking then my beard, I'd say,	Then, stroking my beard, I'd say,
Smiling, the bumper in my hand:	With a smile and with my glass in hand:
"Each well enough in her own way.	"They're all nice enough in their way,
But is there one in all the land	But is there a lass in the land,
Like sister Margaret, good as gold,--	Who can hold an candle to
One that to her can a candle hold?"	My good sister Margaret?"
Cling! clang! "Here's to her!" went around	Cling! Clang! "Here's to her!" they'd all toast
The board: "He speaks the truth!" cried some;	Round the table: "He's right there!" some would shout;
"In her the flower o' the sex is found!"	"She is the fairest of women!"
And all the swaggerers were dumb.	And all the boasters would have to shut up.
And now!--I could tear my hair with vexation.	And now! I could tear my hair out,
And dash out my brains in desperation!	Smash my brains out with frustration!
With turned-up nose each scamp may face me,	Each rascal can turn his nose up at me,
With sneers and stinging taunts disgrace me,	Disgrace me with sneering and taunting,
And, like a bankrupt debtor sitting,	And like someone who owes money,
A chance-dropped word may set me sweating!	A chance overheard word can send me into a sweat!
Yet, though I thresh them all together,	Yet, though I beat them for what they say,
I cannot call them liars, either.	I know that it's the truth.
But what comes sneaking, there, to view?	But what's this, sneaking along?
If I mistake not, there are two.	If I'm not mistaken there are two of them.
If *he's* one, let me at him drive!	If one of them's the fellow, let me have at him!
He shall not leave the spot alive.	He won't get out of here alive.

FAUST MEPHISTOPHELES

FAUST

How from the window of the sacristy	How the Holy light is shining
Upward th'eternal lamp sends forth a glimmer,	Up from the windows of the church,
That, lessening side-wards, fainter grows and dimmer,	That as it spreads gets fainter,
Till darkness closes from the sky!	Until darkness wins over the sky.
The shadows thus within my bosom gather.	This is how the darkness has gathered in my heart.

MEPHISTOPHELES

I'm like a sentimental tom-cat, rather,	I'm feeling like a tomcat,
That round the tall fire-ladders sweeps,	That goes creeping round the fire escapes,
And stealthy, then, along the coping creeps:	And stealthily along the roofs;
Quite virtuous, withal, I come,	I'm quite virtuous really,
A little thievish and a little frolicsome.	Just fond of a bit of thieving, a bit of fun.
I feel in every limb the presage	I can feel in my bones the coming

Forerunning the grand Walpurgis-Night:
Day after to-morrow brings its message,
And one keeps watch then with delight.

FAUST

Meanwhile, may not the treasure risen be,

Which there, behind, I glimmering see?

MEPHISTOPHELES

Shalt soon experience the pleasure,
To lift the kettle with its treasure.
I lately gave therein a squint--
Saw splendid lion-dollars in 't.

FAUST

Not even a jewel, not a ring,
To deck therewith my darling girl?

MEPHISTOPHELES

I saw, among the rest, a thing
That seemed to be a chain of pearl.

FAUST

That's well, indeed! For painful is it
To bring no gift when her I visit.

MEPHISTOPHELES

Thou shouldst not find it so annoying,
Without return to be enjoying.
Now, while the sky leads forth its starry throng,
Thou'lt hear a masterpiece, no work completer:
I'll sing her, first, a moral song,
The surer, afterwards, to cheat her.
(*Sings to the cither.*)
What dost thou here
In daybreak clear,
Kathrina dear,
Before thy lover's door?
Beware! the blade
Lets in a maid.
That out a maid
Departeth nevermore!
The coaxing shun
Of such an one!
When once 'tis done
Good-night to thee, poor thing!
Love's time is brief:
Unto no thief
Be warm and lief,
But with the wedding-ring!

Of the great time of Walpurgis-Night:
The day after tomorrow it'll be here,
And that's when I'll be having fun.

In the meantime, haven't you dug up some more treasure,
Which I can see shining behind your back?

You'll soon be having the pleasure
Of getting your hands on the lot.
I took a peek inside just now –
I saw there's good hard cash in there.

Don't you have some jewel or ring
That I can put on my lovely girl?

Amongst the rest I saw something
That looked like a pearl necklace.

Ah, that's good! For I'm ashamed
Not to bring her a present when I visit.

You shouldn't get so bothered about it,
Enjoy getting something for nothing!
Now, as the stars are coming out,
You'll hear a masterpiece, the best thing imaginable:
First I'll sing her a moral song,
Which will make her give in later.
(Sings to cither)
What are you doing,
In the light of day,
Dear Katherine,
At your lover's door?
Look out! The dashing chap,
Lets a virgin in,
But a virgin,
Won't come out!
Don't let his type
Talk you round!
Give him his way
And that's the end of you, poor thing!
Love doesn't last:
Don't give yourself
To any thief,
Unless he offers you a wedding ring!

VALENTINE (*comes forward*)
Whom wilt thou lure? God's-element!
Rat-catching piper, thou!--perdition!
To the Devil, first, the instrument!
To the Devil, then, the curst musician!

Who are you trying to catch? By heavens!
Damn you, you piping rat catcher!
I'll send your instrument to hell,
And then I'll send you the same way!

MEPHISTOPHELES
The cither's smashed! For nothing more 'tis fitting.

The cither's broken! It's useless now.

VALENTINE
There's yet a skull I must be splitting!

And now there's a head needs breaking too!

MEPHISTOPHELES (*to* FAUST)
Sir Doctor, don't retreat, I pray!
Stand by: I'll lead, if you'll but tarry:
Out with your spit, without delay!
You've but to lunge, and I will parry.

Good Doctor, please don't run away!
Stand by, if you'll wait here I'll take the lead:
Out with your sword, hurry!
You attack and I'll block.

VALENTINE
Then parry that!

Block that then!

MEPHISTOPHELES
Why not? 'tis light.

Why not, it wasn't much of a blow.

VALENTINE
That, too!

And that!

MEPHISTOPHELES
Of course.

Certainly.

VALENTINE
I think the Devil must fight!
How is it, then? my hand's already lame:

I think I must be fighting the devil!
What's happening? Already my hands are tired.

MEPHISTOPHELES (*to* FAUST)
Thrust home!

Now stab him!

VALENTINE (*falls*)
O God!

Oh God!

MEPHISTOPHELES
Now is the lubber tame!
But come, away! 'Tis time for us to fly;
For there arises now a murderous cry.
With the police 'twere easy to compound it,
But here the penal court will sift and sound it.
[*Exit with* FAUST]

That's settled that lout!
But come on, we must run for it,
The shout of "murder" has gone up.
If it were just the police we could easily fool them
But round here we'll end up investigated by the judges.

MARTHA (*at the window*)

Come out! Come out!

Come out! Come out!

MARGARET (*at the window*)
Quick, bring a light!

Quick, bring a light!

MARTHA (*as above*)
They swear and storm, they yell and fight!

They're swearing and rowing, it's a proper punchup!

PEOPLE
Here lies one dead already--see!

Look, here's one lying dead!

MARTHA (*coming from the house*)
The murderers, whither have they run?

Which way did the murderers run?

MARGARET (*coming out*)
Who lies here?

Who's this lying here?

PEOPLE
'Tis thy mother's son!

It's your brother!

MARGARET
Almighty God! what misery!

Oh God! What sorrow!

VALENTINE
I'm dying! That is quickly said,
And quicker yet 'tis done.
Why howl, you women there? Instead,
Come here and listen, every one!
(*All gather around him*)
My Margaret, see! still young thou art,
But not the least bit shrewd or smart,
Thy business thus to slight:
So this advice I bid thee heed--
Now that thou art a whore indeed,
Why, be one then, outright!

I'm dying! It doesn't take long to say,
And it can be over and done with even quicker.
Stop wailing, all you women.
Gather round and listen to me.
(*All gather round him*)
There's my Margaret! You're still young,

And you haven't got the brains to promote your trade:
So listen to what I tell you:
Now you've become a whore,
You might as well be one in public!

MARGARET
My brother! God! such words to me?

My brother! God! How can you talk to me like this?

VALENTINE
In this game let our Lord God be!
What's done's already done, alas!
What follows it, must come to pass.
With one begin'st thou secretly,
Then soon will others come to thee,
And when a dozen thee have known,
Thou'rt also free to all the town.
When Shame is born and first appears,
She is in secret brought to light,
And then they draw the veil of night
Over her head and ears;
Her life, in fact, they're loath to spare her.
But let her growth and strength display,
She walks abroad unveiled by day,
Yet is not grown a whit the fairer.

Leave the good Lord out of this!
Alas, what's done is done,
And what follows on must happen.
You begin secretly with one,
Then soon you'll get some others,
And when you've had a dozen,
You'll be available to all.
When Shame first arrives,
She grows in secret,
And hides herself in the cloak of night,
And people want to cut her down,
But as she grows stronger,
She'll flaunt herself in broad daylight.

She won't get any more pleasant looking,

The uglier she is to sight,
The more she seeks the day's broad light.
The time I verily can discern
When all the honest folk will turn
From thee, thou jade! and seek protection
As from a corpse that breeds infection.
Thy guilty heart shall then dismay thee.
When they but look thee in the face:--
Shalt not in a golden chain array thee,
Nor at the altar take thy place!
Shalt not, in lace and ribbons flowing,
Make merry when the dance is going!
But in some corner, woe betide thee!
Among the beggars and cripples hide thee;
And so, though even God forgive,
On earth a damned existence live!

MARTHA
Commend your soul to God for pardon,
That you your heart with slander harden!

VALENTINE
Thou pimp most infamous, be still!
Could I thy withered body kill,
'Twould bring, for all my sinful pleasure,
Forgiveness in the richest measure.

MARGARET
My brother! This is Hell's own pain!

VALENTINE
I tell thee, from thy tears refrain!
When thou from honor didst depart
It stabbed me to the very heart.
Now through the slumber of the grave
I go to God as a soldier brave.
(*Dies*)

But the uglier she is,
The more she likes to show off.
I can see a time
When all honest folk will reject you,
You tart! And they'll back away from you,
As if you were an infectious corpse.
Then you'll be stabbed by your guilty conscience,
Any time they look you in the eye:
You won't have a golden chain,
And you won't be allowed at the altar!
You shan't dress in lace and ribbons,
And be allowed to enjoy the dance!

Hide yourself amongst the beggars and cripples,
And even though God may forgive you,
Lead a hellish life here on earth!

May God forgive you,
For letting these lies into your heart!

Shut up, you old bawd!
If I could kill you
I would get full forgiveness
For all the pleasure it gave me.

My brother! You're giving me devilish pain!

Don't you bother with crying!
When you chose the the way of dishonor,
It stabbed me to the heart.
Now I go to my rest, and to God,
As a brave soldier.

XX

CATHEDRAL

SERVICE, ORGAN *and* ANTHEM.

(MARGARET *among much people: the EVIL SPIRIT behind*
MARGARET)

EVIL SPIRIT
HOW otherwise was it, Margaret,	*How different it was, Margaret,*
When thou, still innocent,	*When you, still innocent,*
Here to the altar cam'st,	*Came up to the altar,*
And from the worn and fingered book	*And from your well-thumbed book,*
Thy prayers didst prattle,	*Would say your prayers,*
Half sport of childhood,	*Half a child playing a game,*
Half God within thee!	*And half filled with the spirit of God!*
Margaret!	*Margaret!*
Where tends thy thought?	*What are you thinking?*
Within thy bosom	*There in your heart*
What hidden crime?	*What crimes are you hiding?*
Pray'st thou for mercy on thy mother's soul,	*Are you asking mercy for your mother's soul,*
That fell asleep to long, long torment, and through thee?	*Your mother who died of the long torture you put her through?*
Upon thy threshold whose the blood?	*Whose blood is on your hands?*
And stirreth not and quickens	*Doesn't your heart tremble*
Something beneath thy heart,	*At the thought of some evil presence,*
Thy life disquieting	*Which terrifies your life?*
With most foreboding presence?	

MARGARET
Woe! woe!	*Alas! Alas!*
Would I were free from the thoughts	*I wish I could escape these thoughts,*
That cross me, drawing hither and thither	*That run through my mind, dragging me here and there,*
Despite me!	*However I try and shut them out!*

CHORUS
Dies ira, dies illa,	*This is the day of anger and of wrath,*
Solvet soeclum in favilla!	*When the earth shall be dissolved into ashes.*
(Sound of the organ)	

EVIL SPIRIT
Wrath takes thee!	*Anger takes you!*
The trumpet peals!	*The trumpet rings out!*
The graves tremble!	*The graves shake!*
And thy heart	*And the embers*
From ashy rest	*Of your heart*
To fiery torments	*Flare up again*
Now again requickened,	*Into a torturing flame!*
Throbs to life!	

MARGARET
Would I were forth!	*I wish I was out of here!*

I feel as if the organ here
My breath takes from me,
My very heart
Dissolved by the anthem!

This organ seems
To take my breath away,
And my heart
Is shattered by the song!

CHORUS
Judex ergo cum sedebit,
Quidquid latet, ad parebit,
Nil inultum remanebit.

When the judge takes His place,
All shall be revealed,
Nothing shall be left hidden.

MARGARET
I cannot breathe!
The massy pillars
Imprison me!
The vaulted arches
Crush me!--Air!

I can't breathe!
These great pillars
Are like a prison!
The arches
Are crushing me! Let me breathe!

EVIL SPIRIT
Hide thyself! Sin and shame
Stay never hidden.
Air? Light?
Woe to thee!

Hide yourself away! But sin and shame
Can never hide.
You want air and light?
They'll expose you!

CHORUS
Quid sum miser tunc dicturus,
Quem patronem rogaturus,
Cum vix Justus sit securus?

For what should I, weak man, be pleading?
Who will intercede for me
When the just are begging for mercy?

EVIL SPIRIT
They turn their faces,
The glorified, from thee:
The pure, their hands to offer,
Shuddering, refuse thee!
Woe!

All these who are blessed,
Turn their faces away from you:
They refuse
To offer you their hands.
Alas!

CHORUS
Quid sum miser tune dicturus?

For what should I, weak man, be pleading?

MARGARET
Neighbor! your cordial! (*She falls in a swoon.*)

Neighbor! Give me medicine!

XXI

WALPURGIS-NIGHT

THE HARTZ MOUNTAINS.   *District of Schierke and Elend.*

FAUST MEPHISTOPHELES
MEPHISTOPHELES
DOST thou not wish a broomstick-steed's assistance?   *Don't you wish we had a broomstick to ride on?*
The sturdiest he-goat I would gladly see: *I'd be glad of a sturdy billy goat for transport:*
The way we take, our goal is yet some distance.   *The way we're going, our destination is still a fair way off.*

FAUST
So long as in my legs I feel the fresh existence.   *As long as my legs don't give out,*
This knotted staff suffices me.   *This walking stick's enough for me.*
What need to shorten so the way?   *Why do you want to go any quicker?*
Along this labyrinth of vales to wander,   *Wandering through this maze of valleys,*
Then climb the rocky ramparts yonder,   *Then climbing up those rocky cliffs ahead,*
Wherefrom the fountain flings eternal spray,   *With the waterfalls tumbling down them,*
Is such delight, my steps would fain delay.   *Is such a pleasure, I'd sooner walk more slowly.*
The spring-time stirs within the fragrant birches,   *The birch trees are budding with the Spring,*
And even the fir-tree feels it now: *And even the fir tree is coming to life:*
Should then our limbs escape its gentle searches?   *Shouldn't we let ourselves feel it too?*

MEPHISTOPHELES
I notice no such thing, I vow!   *I promise you, I can't feel a thing!*
'Tis winter still within my body: *It's still winter inside me:*
Upon my path I wish for frost and snow.   *I want to see frost and snow on my journey.*
How sadly rises, incomplete and ruddy,   *How sad, dark and red,*
The moon's lone disk, with its belated glow,   *The moon rises alone with its poor light,*
And lights so dimly, that, as one advances,   *So dim that one trips over a rock or root at every step!*
At every step one strikes a rock or tree!
Let us, then, use a Jack-o'-lantern's glances: *Let's use the light of a will-o'-the-wisp:*
I see one yonder, burning merrily.   *I can see one burning away over there.*
Ho, there! my friend! I'll levy thine attendance: *Ahoy, my friend! I'll press you into service:*
Why waste so vainly thy resplendence?   *Why do you burn for nothing?*
Be kind enough to light us up the steep!   *Be kind enough to light our way up the slope!*

WILL-O'-THE-WISP
My reverence, I hope, will me enable   *I hope my respect for you*
To curb my temperament unstable;   *Can calm my flighty instincts;*
For zigzag courses we are wont to keep.   *I'm used to following crooked paths.*

MEPHISTOPHELES
Indeed? he'd like mankind to imitate!   *Is that so? That sounds like humanity!*
Now, in the Devil's name, go straight,   *Now, in the name of Satan, you go straight,*
Or I'll blow out his being's flickering spark!   *Or I'll blow your light out!*

WILL-O'-THE-WISP
You are the master of the house, I mark,   *I see you're the boss here,*
And I shall try to serve you nicely.   *And I'll do my best for you.*
But then, reflect: the mountain's magic-mad to-day,   *But be aware, the magic of the mountain is crazy today,*

And if a will-o'-the-wisp must guide you on the way,
You mustn't take things too precisely.

FAUST, MEPHISTOPHELES, WILL-O'-THE-WISP
(*in alternating song*)
We, it seems, have entered newly
In the sphere of dreams enchanted.
Do thy bidding, guide us truly,
That our feet be forwards planted
In the vast, the desert spaces!
See them swiftly changing places,
Trees on trees beside us trooping,
And the crags above us stooping,
And the rocky snouts, outgrowing,--
Hear them snoring, hear them blowing!
O'er the stones, the grasses, flowing
Stream and streamlet seek the hollow.
Hear I noises? songs that follow?
Hear I tender love-petitions?
Voices of those heavenly visions?
Sounds of hope, of love undying!
And the echoes, like traditions
Of old days, come faint and hollow.
Hoo-hoo! Shoo-hoo! Nearer hover
Jay and screech-owl, and the plover,--
Are they all awake and crying?
Is't the salamander pushes,
Bloated-bellied, through the bushes?
And the roots, like serpents twisted,
Through the sand and boulders toiling,
Fright us, weirdest links uncoiling
To entrap us, unresisted:
Living knots and gnarls uncanny
Feel with polypus-antennae
For the wanderer. Mice are flying,
Thousand-colored, herd-wise hieing
Through the moss and through the heather!
And the fire-flies wink and darkle,
Crowded swarms that soar and sparkle,
And in wildering escort gather!
Tell me, if we still are standing,
Or if further we're ascending?
All is turning, whirling, blending,
Trees and rocks with grinning faces,
Wandering lights that spin in mazes,
Still increasing and expanding!

MEPHISTOPHELES
Grasp my skirt with heart undaunted!
Here a middle-peak is planted,
Whence one seeth, with amaze,
Mammon in the mountain blaze.

And if you want follow the will-o'-the-wisp,
You mustn't hope for a dead-straight path.

It seems we have come in
To a world of magic dreams.
Do your bidding, so we are truly guided
As our feet walk on
Into the vast desert places!
Look how quickly they replace each other,
The trees marching along beside us,
The cliffs bending over us,
With their rocking peaks above them,
Hear them snoring and puffing!
Over the stones and the grass
The trickles and streams are seeking the low places.
Can I hear noises? Are there songs following us?
Are they the words of love?
Are they the voices of angels?
The sounds of hope, of undying love!
And the echoes, like the customs
Of days gone by, come soft and hollow.
Twit-twoo! Nearer hover
The jay, the screech owl and the plover.
Are they all awake and singing?
Is that a salamander pushing
His bloated belly through the bushes?
And the roots, like twisted snakes,
Pushing through the sand and rocks,
Frighten us, their strange shapes uncoiling
To catch us unawares:
The twisted, unearthly shapes,
Grope out with their feelers
To snare the traveller. The mice are flying,
Multicolored, like a great herd,
Through the moss and heather!

And the fireflies blink and sparkle
As they gather together!
Tell me, are we standing still,
Or are we still climbing?
Everything's spinning, whirling, mixing together,
The trees and rocks with their grinning faces,
Wandering lights spinning round,
Increasing and expanding.

Hang on to my jacket, don't be afraid!
Here's a summit right in the middle,
On which, incredibly,
You can see Mammon blazing.

FAUST

How strangely glimmers through the hollows
A dreary light, like that of dawn!
Its exhalation tracks and follows
The deepest gorges, faint and wan.
Here steam, there rolling vapor sweepeth;
Here burns the glow through film and haze:
Now like a tender thread it creepeth,
Now like a fountain leaps and plays.
Here winds away, and in a hundred
Divided veins the valley braids:
There, in a corner pressed and sundered,
Itself detaches, spreads and fades.
Here gush the sparkles incandescent
Like scattered showers of golden sand;--
But, see! in all their height, at present,
The rocky ramparts blazing stand.

How oddly through the hollows
There's a dull grey light like dawn!
Its seems to follow
The deepest gorges, faint and pale.
Here steam, there a boiling fog erupts:
Here you see the fire through the mist and smoke:
Now it creeps like a delicate shoot,
Now it leaps up and sprays like a fountain.
Here the valley splits
Into a hundred branches:
There, pressed up in a corner, divided,
It dissipates, spreads and fades.
Here the glittering sparks fly out,
Like showers of golden sand;
But look! Right up there, at the highest point,
The rocky cliffs are aflame.

MEPHISTOPHELES

Has not Sir Mammon grandly lighted
His palace for this festal night?
'Tis lucky thou hast seen the sight;
The boisterous guests approach that were invited.

Hasn't great Mammon lit up
His palace well for this special night?
You're lucky, seeing this;
The jolly guests are on their way.

FAUST

How raves the tempest through the air!
With what fierce blows upon my neck 'tis beating!

How the storm blows through the air!
How fiercely it's beating on my neck!

MEPHISTOPHELES

Under the old ribs of the rock retreating,
Hold fast, lest thou be hurled down the abysses there!
The night with the mist is black;
Hark! how the forests grind and crack!
Frightened, the owlets are scattered:
Hearken! the pillars are shattered.
The evergreen palaces shaking!
Boughs are groaning and breaking,
The tree-trunks terribly thunder,
The roots are twisting asunder!
In frightfully intricate crashing
Each on the other is dashing,
And over the wreck-strewn gorges
The tempest whistles and surges!
Hear'st thou voices higher ringing?
Far away, or nearer singing?
Yes, the mountain's side along,
Sweeps an infuriate glamouring song!

Keep in the shelter of the cliffs,
Or you'll be blown down into the gorge!
The night is thick with fog;
Hear how the forests groan and creak!
The owls are scared and scattered,

Their leafy homes are shaking!
The branches are moaning and snapping,
The tree trunks roar frightfully,
And the roots are tearing from the ground!
In the terrible, intricate disaster,
Each smashes into the other,
And over the gorges, littered with debris,
The storm whistles and whines!
Can you hear voices singing above it?
Sometime near, sometimes far?
Yes, all along the mountainside,
There's a maddening, enticing song!

WITCHES (*in chorus*)

The witches ride to the Brocken's top,
The stubble is yellow, and green the crop.
There gathers the crowd for carnival:
Sir Urian sits over all.

The witches are riding to the top of the Brocken,
The stubble is yellow and the crops are green.
The crowd is gathering for the party:
Sir Urian is the master of all.

And so they go over stone and stock;
The witch she-----s, and-----s the buck.

Here we go over wood and stone,
The stinking buck and puking witch.

A VOICE
Alone, old Baubo's coming now;
She rides upon a farrow-sow.

Here comes old Baubo now,
Riding on a pregnant pig.

CHORUS
Then honor to whom the honor is due!
Dame Baubo first, to lead the crew!
A tough old sow and the mother thereon,
Then follow the witches, every one.

Then give honor to those who've earned it!
Dame Baubo, the leader of them all!
A tough old sow carries the mother,
And then come all the witches.

A VOICE
Which way com'st thou hither?

How did you come here?

VOICE
O'er the Ilsen-stone.
I peeped at the owl in her nest alone:
How she stared and glared!

Over the Ilsen Stone.
I peeped in at the owl who sat alone,
How she glared at me!

VOICE
Betake thee to Hell!
Why so fast and so fell?

Of you go to Hell!
Why are you making such haste?

VOICE
She has scored and has flayed me:
See the wounds she has made me!

She's scratched and scarred me,
Look at the wounds she's given me!

WITCHES (*chorus*)
The way is wide, the way is long:
See, what a wild and crazy throng!
The broom it scratches, the fork it thrusts,
The child is stifled, the mother bursts.

It's a long wide trail we're taking:
Look at this crazy rioting crowd!
The broom scratches, the fork stabs,
The child will be smothered and the mother will burst.

WIZARDS (*semichorus*)
As doth the snail in shell, we crawl:
Before us go the women all.
When towards the Devil's House we tread,
Woman's a thousand steps ahead.

We crawl along like snails in their shells:
The women rush on before us.
When you're journeying to Hell,
Woman are always way ahead of you.

OTHER SEMICHORUS
We do not measure with such care:
Woman in thousand steps is theft.
But howsoe'er she hasten may,
Man in one leap has cleared the way.

We don't measure it all so carefully:
A woman can be a thousand steps ahead,
But however quickly she makes her way,
Man can get there in one bound.

VOICE (*from above*)
Come on, come on, from Rocky Lake!

Come on, come on, from the Rocky Lake!

VOICE (*from below*)
Aloft we'd fain ourselves betake.
We've washed, and are bright as ever you will,

We'd like to get ourselves to the heights.
We've washed and are as bright as you could wish,

Yet we're eternally sterile still.

BOTH CHORUSES
The wind is hushed, the star shoots by.
The dreary moon forsakes the sky;
The magic notes, like spark on spark,
Drizzle, whistling through the dark.

VOICE (*from below*)
Halt, there! Ho, there!

VOICE (*from above*)
Who calls from the rocky cleft below there?

VOICE (*below*)
Take me, too! take me, too!
I'm climbing now three hundred years,
And yet the summit cannot see:
Among my equals I would be.

BOTH CHORUSES
Bears the broom and bears the stock,
Bears the fork and bears the buck:
Who cannot raise himself to-night
Is evermore a ruined wight.

HALF-WITCH (*below*)
So long I stumble, ill bestead,
And the others are now so far ahead!
At home I've neither rest nor cheer,
And yet I cannot gain them here.

CHORUS OF WITCHES
To cheer the witch will salve avail;
A rag will answer for a sail;
Each trough a goodly ship supplies;
He ne'er will fly, who now not flies.

BOTH CHORUSES
When round the summit whirls our flight,
Then lower, and on the ground alight;
And far and wide the heather press
With witchhood's swarms of wantonness!
(*They settle down.*)

MEPHISTOPHELES
They crowd and push, they roar and clatter!
They whirl and whistle, pull and chatter!
They shine, and spirt, and stink, and burn!
The true witch-element we learn.
Keep close! or we are parted, in our turn,
Where art thou?

But we can never breed at all.

The wind has calmed, the stars have gone,
The waning moon has set;
The magic notes, like a fire's sparks,
Go on streaming through the dark.

You there! Stop now!

Who's calling from that rocky gap down there?

Take me, too! Take me, too!
I've been climbing for three hundred years,
But I still can't see the peak:
I want to join my equals.

Here's the broom, here's the stick,
Here's the fork and here's the goat:
The one who can't get up for tonight
Will be ruined for ever more.

How long I've stumbled round and round,
And how far ahead the others have got.
There's no rest or happiness for me at home,
And I can't get them here either.

Ointment will do to cheer a witch,
A rag will make do for a sail;
A tub is good enough for a boat;
If you don't fly tonight then you never will.

We fly around the summit's top,
Then fly down lower and settle on the ground;
And all around the heather's flattened,
By the hordes of depraved witches.

They crowd and push, they roar and clatter!
They whirl and whistle, pull and chatter!
They shine, and spurt, and stink, and burn!
We see what witches are really like.
Stay close to me or we'll get split up!
Where are you?

FAUST (*in the distance*)
Here!

Here!

MEPHISTOPHELES
What! whirled so far astray?
Then house-right I must use, and clear the way.
Make room! Squire Voland comes! Room, gentle rabble, room!
Here, Doctor, hold to me: in one jump we'll resume
An easier space, and from the crowd be free:
It's too much, even for the like of me.
Yonder, with special light, there's something shining clearer Within those bushes; I've a mind to see.
Come on! well slip a little nearer.

What? Blown so far away?
Then I must claim my privileges and make a path.
Make room! The squire's here, make way you scum!

Here, Doctor, hold on to me: with one bound we'll find
A clearer space and escape this crowd:
They're too much even for my taste.
Over that way, there's a special light,
Shining within the bushes; I'd like to investigate.
Come on, we'll creep a bit closer.

FAUST
Spirit of Contradiction! On! I'll follow straight.
'Tis planned most wisely, if I judge aright:
We climb the Brocken's top in the Walpurgis-Night,
That arbitrarily, here, ourselves we isolate.

You old Devil! Go on, I'll follow straight after.
It's a cunning plan, if I'm reading it right:
We're walking on the Brocken on Walpurgis-Night,
Yet still we can keep ourselves apart.

MEPHISTOPHELES
But see, what motley flames among the heather!
There is a lively club together:
In smaller circles one is not alone.

But look at these colourful flames in the heather!
This looks like a lively gathering:
One is not alone in smaller groups.

FAUST
Better the summit, I must own:
There fire and whirling smoke I see.
They seek the Evil One in wild confusion:
Many enigmas there might find solution.

I'd like to be up at the summit:
I can see fire and smoke there.
In the riot they seek the Evil One:
The answers to many mysteries might be revealed up there.

MEPHISTOPHELES
But there enigmas also knotted be.
Leave to the multitude their riot!
Here will we house ourselves in quiet.
It is an old, transmitted trade,
That in the greater world the little worlds are made.
I see stark-nude young witches congregate,
And old ones, veiled and hidden shrewdly:
On my account be kind, nor treat them rudely!
The trouble's small, the fun is great.

I hear the noise of instruments attuning,--
Vile din! yet one must learn to bear the crooning.
Come, come along! It *must* be, I declare!

I'll go ahead and introduce thee there,
Thine obligation newly earning.
That is no little space: what say'st thou, friend?
Look yonder! thou canst scarcely see the end:
A hundred fires along the ranks are burning.

But mysteries are also created up there.
Leave the mob to their riot!
We'll keep ourselves here in peace.
It's a well established rule
That small worlds can be made within bigger ones.
Here I see stark naked young witches,
And old ones veiled and cleverly disguised:
For my sake be polite, don't be rude!
It won't be a hardship, and there's plenty of fun to be had.
I can hear the band tuning up;
It's a terrible racket, but you just have to get used to it.
Come along, come along! This is what we must do, I say!
I'll go first and introduce you,
Earning your fresh thanks.
There's plenty of room: what do you say?
Look over there! You can hardly see the finish:
The line is a hundred fires long.

They dance, they chat, they cook, they drink, they court:
Now where, just tell me, is there better sport?

FAUST
Wilt thou, to introduce us to the revel,
Assume the part of wizard or of devil?

MEPHISTOPHELES
I'm mostly used, 'tis true, to go incognito,
But on a gala-day one may his orders show.
The Garter does not deck my suit,
But honored and at home is here the cloven foot.
Perceiv'st thou yonder snail? It cometh, slow and steady;
So delicately its feelers pry,
That it hath scented me already:
I cannot here disguise me, if I try.
But come! we'll go from this fire to a newer:
I am the go-between, and thou the wooer.
(*To some, who are sitting around dying embers*:)
Old gentlemen, why at the outskirts? Enter!

I'd praise you if I found you snugly in the centre,
With youth and revel round you like a zone:
You each, at home, are quite enough alone.

GENERAL
Say, who would put his trust in nations,
Howe'er for them one may have worked and planned?
For with the people, as with women,
Youth always has the upper hand.

MINISTER
They're now too far from what is just and sage.
I praise the old ones, not unduly:
When we were all-in-all, then, truly,
Then was the real golden age.

PARVENU
We also were not stupid, either,
And what we should not, often did;
But now all things have from their bases slid,
Just as we meant to hold them fast together.

AUTHOR
Who, now, a work of moderate sense will read?
Such works are held as antiquate and mossy;
And as regards the younger folk, indeed,
They never yet have been so pert and saucy.

MEPHISTOPHELES
(*who all at once appears very old*)
I feel that men are ripe for Judgment-Day,

They're dancing and chatting, cooking, drinking and courting:
Now you tell me where we could find better fun?

To get us into their party
Are you going to play a wizard or be a devil?

It's true that I usually go disguised,
But on this special day one can show one's true status:
I don't have a Garter medal to smarten up my chest,
But the cloven hoof is honored here.
You see that snail? It's coming here, slow and sure;
It's got its feelers out,
And it's spotted me already:
I couldn't disguise myself even if I wanted to.
But come on, we'll go from this fire to a better one:
I'm the pimp and you're the client.
(To some, who are sitting around dying embers)
Old gentlemen, why are you on the fringes? Come on in!
I'd like to see you in the middle of things,
With youth and fun surrounding you:
You surely get enough of loneliness at home.

Who would put his faith in the country,
However hard one's worked for it?
The people are just like women:
They'll always prefer youth over age.

They don't understand what's right and wise.
I don't praise the old ones for no reason:
When we were at the heart of matters,
That was the real Golden Age.

We weren't exactly stupid either,
And got up to plenty we shouldn't have;
But now everything has fallen apart
Just as we tried to keep it whole.

Who'd read a book which spoke some sense?
They're looked upon as out of date:
And as for the young folk, why,
They're cheekier than they've ever been.

I think it's time for Judgement Day;

128

Now for the last time I've the witches'-hill
ascended:
Since to the lees *my* cask is drained away,
The world's, as well, must soon be ended.

HUCKSTER-WITCH
Ye gentlemen, don't pass me thus!
Let not the chance neglected be!
Behold my wares attentively:
The stock is rare and various.
And yet, there's nothing I've collected--
No shop, on earth, like this you'll find!--

Which has not, once, sore hurt inflicted
Upon the world, and on mankind.
No dagger's here, that set not blood to flowing;
No cup, that hath not once, within a healthy frame
Poured speedy death, in poison glowing:
No gems, that have not brought a maid to shame;
No sword, but severed ties for the unwary,
Or from behind struck down the adversary.

MEPHISTOPHELES
Gossip! the times thou badly comprehendest:
What's done has happed--what haps, is done!
'Twere better if for novelties thou sendest:
By such alone can we be won.

FAUST
Let me not lose myself in all this pother!
This is a fair, as never was another!

MEPHISTOPHELES
The whirlpool swirls to get above:
Thou'rt shoved thyself, imagining to shove.

FAUST
But who is that?

MEPHISTOPHELES
Note her especially,
Tis Lilith.

FAUST
Who?

MEPHISTOPHELES
Adam's first wife is she.
Beware the lure within her lovely tresses,
The splendid sole adornment of her hair!
When she succeeds therewith a youth to snare,
Not soon again she frees him from her jesses.

This is the last time I'll climb the witches' hill.

I've almost finished my journey,
And so the earth's must finish soon.

You gentlemen, don't pass me by!
Don't miss your opportunity!
Have a look at what I've got,
Rare things for every taste.
There's nothing I have here –
I promise you, you won't find a shop like this anywhere
else –
That hasn't done humanity
Serious damage at some time.
There's no dagger here that hasn't drawn blood;
No cup that hasn't poured deadly poison
Into a healthy body;
No jewels that haven't tempted a girl to dishonor,
No swords which haven't cut loose the careless,
Or struck a foe down from behind.

You old fool! You don't undertand the times:
What's done has happened, what's happened is done!
You'd be better of selling novelties:
They're the things that sell these days.

Don't let me get lost in the confusion!
This is a fair, the like of which I've never seen!

They're all trying to get up there:
You're being pushed along, even when you think you're
doing the pushing.

But who's that?

Ah, pay special attention to her.
That's Lilith.

Who?

She is Adam's first wife.
Look out for the lure of those lovely curls,
That splendid hair which adorns her!
Once she catches a young man with those snares,
She won't be letting him go in a hurry.

FAUST
Those two, the old one with the young one sitting,
They've danced already more than fitting.

Those two, the old and the young sitting together,
They've already danced more than they should.

MEPHISTOPHELES
No rest to-night for young or old!
They start another dance: come now, let us take hold!

Nobody gets any rest tonight!
Another dance is starting, let's grab out partners!

FAUST (*dancing with the young witch*)
A lovely dream once came to me;
I then beheld an apple-tree,
And there two fairest apples shone:
They lured me so, I climbed thereon.

I once had a lovely dream;
In it I saw an apple tree,
And two of the most beautiful apples hung on it:
They called to me, and I climbed up.

THE FAIR ONE
Apples have been desired by you,
Since first in Paradise they grew;
And I am moved with joy, to know
That such within my garden grow.

Your sort have always wanted apples,
Since you saw them in Eden;
And it makes me happy to know,
They grow within my garden.

MEPHISTOPHELES (*dancing with the old one*)
A dissolute dream once came to me:
Therein I saw a cloven tree,
Which had a----------------;
Yet,-----as 'twas, I fancied it.

I once had a depraved dream,
That I saw a split tree,
Which had a great crack in it,
But gross as it was, I liked it.

THE OLD ONE
I offer here my best salute
Unto the knight with cloven foot!
Let him a-----------prepare,
If him-----------------does not scare.

I offer up my best salute,
To the knight with the cloven hoof!
If he really likes that crack,
He'd better have something to put in it!

PROKTOPHANTASMIST
Accurséd folk! How dare you venture thus?
Had you not, long since, demonstration
That ghosts can't stand on ordinary foundation?
And now you even dance, like one of us!

You cursed people! How can you carry on like this?
I think you'll find that it's been proved,
That ghosts cannot exist,
And yet you're dancing around, large as life!

THE FAIR ONE (*dancing*)
Why does he come, then, to our ball?

Why does he come to our dance, then?

FAUST (*dancing*)
O, everywhere on him you fall!
When others dance, he weighs the matter:
If he can't every step bechatter,
Then 'tis the same as were the step not made;
But if you forwards go, his ire is most displayed.
If you would whirl in regular gyration
As he does in his dull old mill,
He'd show, at any rate, good-will,--
Especially if you heard and heeded his hortation.

Oh, you find the likes of him everywhere!
When others dance he studies it,
And if he cannot measure a step,
Then to him it's like it never happened;
He doesn't like progress, that makes him angry.
If you go round in circles,
Like his dull old mind does,
He'll be happy with you,
Especially if you pay him some attention.

PROKTOPHANTASMIST

You still are here? Nay, 'tis a thing unheard!
Vanish, at once! We've said the enlightening word.
The pack of devils by no rules is daunted:
We are so wise, and yet is Tegel haunted.
To clear the folly out, how have I swept and stirred!
Twill ne'er be clean: why, 'tis a thing unheard!

THE FAIR ONE

Then cease to bore us at our ball!

PROKTOPHANTASMIST

I tell you, spirits, to your face,
I give to spirit-despotism no place;
My spirit cannot practise it at all.
(*The dance continues*)
Naught will succeed, I see, amid such revels;
Yet something from a tour I always save,
And hope, before my last step to the grave,
To overcome the poets and the devils.

MEPHISTOPHELES

He now will seat him in the nearest puddle;
The solace this, whereof he's most assured:
And when upon his rump the leeches hang and fuddle,
He'll be of spirits and of Spirit cured.
(*To* FAUST, *who has left the dance*:)
Wherefore forsakest thou the lovely maiden,
That in the dance so sweetly sang?

FAUST

Ah! in the midst of it there sprang
A red mouse from her mouth--sufficient reason.

MEPHISTOPHELES

That's nothing! One must not so squeamish be;
So the mouse was not gray, enough for thee.
Who'd think of that in love's selected season?

FAUST

Then saw I--.

MEPHISTOPHELES

What?

FAUST

Mephisto, seest thou there,
Alone and far, a girl most pale and fair?
She falters on, her way scarce knowing,
As if with fettered feet that stay her going.
I must confess, it seems to me
As if my kindly Margaret were she.

You're still here? This is unheard of!
Be off, the lot of you! We're all enlightened now.
The Devil's mob doesn't play by the rules:
We've proved it can't be, but Tegel is still haunted.
To get rid of this idiocy, what efforts I've made!
But it's never-ending: why, it's unheard of!

Then stop boring us at our dance!

I'm telling you straight, you spirits,
I'm not going to acknowledge your power;
I'm just not having it at all.
(The dance continues)
I see nothing's going to stop your party.
But every time I come here I learn a bit more,
And before I die I hope
To have beaten the devils and *the poets!*

Now he'll go and sit in a puddle,
And take comfort from the thought,
That if he sticks leeches all over his backside,
He'll be cheered up and exorcised of Ghosts.
(To FAUST, who has left the dance)
Why have you left that lovely girl,
Who sang so prettily in the dance?

Ah! Right in the middle of it all a red mouse
Jumped out of her mouth – that was enough for me.

That's nothing! You shouldn't be so fussy;
At least it wasn't a grey mouse.
Who makes a fuss about that sort of thing at harvest
time?

Then I saw –

What?

Mephisto, do you see there,
Alone and far off, that pale beautiful girl?
She looks lost, she staggers about,
As if her feet were in chains.
I must say, it looks to me,
As if she were my sweet Margaret.

MEPHISTOPHELES

Let the thing be! All thence have evil drawn:
It is a magic shape, a lifeless eidolon.
Such to encounter is not good:
Their blank, set stare benumbs the human blood,
And one is almost turned to stone.
Medusa's tale to thee is known.

FAUST

Forsooth, the eyes they are of one whom, dying,
No hand with loving pressure closed;
That is the breast whereon I once was lying,--
The body sweet, beside which I reposed!

MEPHISTOPHELES

Tis magic all, thou fool, seduced so easily!
Unto each man his love she seems to be.

FAUST

The woe, the rapture, so ensnare me,
That from her gaze I cannot tear me!
And, strange! around her fairest throat
A single scarlet band is gleaming,
No broader than a knife-blade seeming!

MEPHISTOPHELES

Quite right! The mark I also note.
Her head beneath her arm she'll sometimes carry;
Twas Perseus lopped it, her old adversary.
Thou crav'st the same illusion still!
Come, let us mount this little hill;
The Prater shows no livelier stir,
And, if they've not bewitched my sense,
I verily see a theatre.
What's going on?

SERVIBILIS

'Twill shortly recommence:
A new performance--'tis the last of seven.
To give that number is the custom here:
'Twas by a Dilettante written,
And Dilettanti in the parts appear.
That now I vanish, pardon, I entreat you!
As Dilettante I the curtain raise.

MEPHISTOPHELES

When I upon the Blocksberg meet you,
I find it good: for that's your proper place.

Just let it be! Evil has drawn everything to it:
It's just a magic shape, a lifeless apparition.
It wouldn't do you any good to meet it:
Their blank look freezes the blood,
And one is almost turned to stone.
You know the story of Medusa.

The eyes are like those of one who has died,
And hasn't had a loved one to close the lids:
That's the breast I once laid my head on,
The sweet body I lay beside!

It's just magic, you easily tricked fool!
Every man who sees her thinks she's his love.

The sadness, the enchantment, have me so caught,
That I can't tear my eyes away from her!
And that's odd! Around her lovely throat
There's a single scarlet line,
No wider than the blade of a knife.

Yes, you're right, I can see it too.
Sometimes she carries her head under her arm;
It was Perseus, her old enemy, who took it off.
You're still chasing after the old mirage!
Come on, let's get up on this hillock;
It's as lively as the amusement park in Vienna,
And if it's not a trick,
I see they've set up a theatre.
What's happening?

It's coming on again shortly,
For a new performance – it's the last of seven.
That's our traditional number:
It was written by an amateur,
And amateurs play all the parts.
Now you must forgive me, I have to go!
I'm the amateur curtain raiser.

I'm glad I've met you here on the Block –
It's the right place for you.

XXII

WALPURGIS-NIGHT'S DREAM

OBERON AND TITANIA's GOLDEN WEDDING
INTERMEZZO

MANAGER
Sons of Mieding, rest to-day!
Needless your machinery:
Misty vale and mountain gray,
That is all the scenery.

HERALD
That the wedding golden be.
Must fifty years be rounded:
But *the Golden* give to me,
When the strife's compounded.

OBERON
Spirits, if you're here, be seen--
Show yourselves, delighted!
Fairy king and fairy queen,
They are newly plighted.

PUCK
Cometh Puck, and, light of limb,
Whisks and whirls in measure:
Come a hundred after him,
To share with him the pleasure.

ARIEL
Ariel's song is heavenly-pure,
His tones are sweet and rare ones:
Though ugly faces he allure,
Yet he allures the fair ones.

OBERON
Spouses, who would fain agree,
Learn how we were mated!
If your pairs would loving be,
First be separated!

TITANIA
If her whims the wife control,
And the man berate her,
Take him to the Northern Pole,
And her to the Equator!

ORCHESTRA. TUTTI.
Fortissimo.
Snout of fly, mosquito-bill,
And kin of all conditions,

You stagehands, take a rest today!
We don't need your gear:
Just the misty valleys and grey mountains,
That's all the scenery we need.

For it to be a golden wedding,
Fifty years must pass:
But when all's been said and done
Let me have the gold.

Spirits, if you're here, appear,
Show yourselves and be merry!
Here are the fairy king and queen,
Newly engaged.

Here comes Puck, with dancing feet,
Who whirls around in time:
Another hundred are following
To join him in the dance.

Ariel has a lovely song,
His tone is sweet and rare:
Though ugly faces like his song
It attracts fair ones as well.

Partners, who would like to stay together,
Learn how we were joined!
If you want a loving marriage,
First you must split up!

If a wife is headstrong,
And her husband criticises her,
Put him at the North Pole,
Dump her on the equator!

The nose of a fly, mosquito's beak,
And all things that are like them,

Frog in grass, and cricket-trill,--
These are the musicians!

SOLO
See the bagpipe on our track!
'Tis the soap-blown bubble:
Hear the *schnecke-schnicke-schnack*
Through his nostrils double!

SPIRIT, JUST GROWING INTO FORM
Spider's foot and paunch of toad,
And little wings--we know 'em!
A little creature 'twill not be,
But yet, a little poem.

A LITTLE COUPLE
Little step and lofty leap
Through honey-dew and fragrance:
You'll never mount the airy steep
With all your tripping vagrance.

INQUISITIVE TRAVELLER
Is't but masquerading play?
See I with precision?
Oberon, the beauteous fay,
Meets, to-night, my vision!

ORTHODOX
Not a claw, no tail I see!
And yet, beyond a cavil,
Like "the Gods of Greece," must he
Also be a devil.

NORTHERN ARTIST
I only seize, with sketchy air,
Some outlines of the tourney;
Yet I betimes myself prepare
For my Italian journey.

PURIST
My bad luck brings me here, alas!
How roars the orgy louder!
And of the witches in the mass,
But only two wear powder.

YOUNG WITCH
Powder becomes, like petticoat,
A gray and wrinkled noddy;
So I sit naked on my goat,
And show a strapping body.

MATRON
We've too much tact and policy

The frog in the grass, the song of a cricket,
These are our musicians!

Along here comes the bagpipe,
Made from a soap bubble,
And here's a great hullaballoo,
Blowing through his nose!

A spider's foot and a toad's belly,
And little wings, we know what they are!
They won't make a little creature,
But they make a little poem.

With a little step and a big jump,
Through the honeydew and sweetness:
For all your jumping travelling,
You'll never reach the top.

Is this just a masquerade?
Do I see things correctly?
I can see, if I'm not mistaken,
Oberon, that fair king.

I can't see a claw, nor a tail,
And yet without doubt,
Like the Grecian gods,
He must be a devil as well.

I can only grasp, with a faint sketch,
The outlines of what's happening;
But I preparing myself in readiness
For the Italian journey I'll one day make.

Alas, it's bad luck brings me here!
How loud this orgy's getting!
Of all the witches in the crowd,
Only two are wearing makeup.

Makeup is like a petticoat,
To cover up the grey and the wrinkled;
So I sit naked on my goat
To show off my fine young body.

We're too polite and sensible,

To rate with gibes a scolder;
Yet, young and tender though you be,
I hope to see you moulder.

To trade insults with a braggart:
But young and tender as you are,
We hope to see you rot.

LEADER OF THE BAND

Fly-snout and mosquito-bill,
Don't swarm so round the Naked!
Frog in grass and cricket-trill,
Observe the time, and make it!

Nose of fly, mosquito's beak,
Don't swarm around the naked!
Frog in grass and cricket's song,
Look at the beat, and keep it up!

WEATHERCOCK (*towards one side*)

Society to one's desire!
Brides only, and the sweetest!
And bachelors of youth and fire.
And prospects the completest!

This is the society that one likes!
Only the sweetest brides,
And young bachelors full of passion,
This is a fine prospect!

WEATHERCOCK (*towards the other side*)

And if the Earth don't open now
To swallow up each ranter,
Why, then will I myself, I vow,
Jump into hell instanter!

And if the earth doesn't open now,
And swallow up the lot,
Then I promise that I myself,
Will take a leap into hell!

XENIES

Us as little insects see!
With sharpest nippers flitting,
That our Papa Satan we
May honor as is fitting.

See us little insects!
We run around with the sharpest claws,
So that we can do proper honor
To our father, Satan.

HENNINGS

How, in crowds together massed,
They are jesting, shameless!
They will even say, at last,
That their hearts are blameless.

How in crowds as they gather together,
They are laughing without shame!
They'll even try to claim, in the end,
That they have pure hearts.

MUSAGETES

Among this witches' revelry
His way one gladly loses;
And, truly, it would easier be
Than to command the Muses.

Amongst all this witches' party
One's happy to get lost;
And it's definitely easier,
Than trying to control the Muses.

CI-DEVANT GENIUS OF THE AGE

The proper folks one's talents laud:
Come on, and none shall pass us!
The Blocksberg has a summit broad,
Like Germany's Parnassus.

The best people praised my work,
No-one will surpass me!
The Blocksberg has a wide summit,
It can be the Parnassus of Germany.

INQUISITIVE TRAVELLER

Say, who's the stiff and pompous man?
He walks with haughty paces:
He snuffles all he snuffle can:
"He scents the Jesuits' traces."

Hey, who's that stiff and pompous chap?
He walks around with his nose in the air:
He's sniffing around all he can,
"He's sniffing out Jesuits."

CRANE

Both clear and muddy streams, for me
Are good to fish and sport in:
And thus the pious man you see
With even devils consorting.

I like both clear and muddy streams,
For fishing and for bathing:
And so you can see a pious man,
Mixing with the devils.

WORLDLING

Yes, for the pious, I suspect,
All instruments are fitting;
And on the Blocksberg they erect
Full many a place of meeting.

For pious men, I think it's true,
Everywhere is valid;
And on the Blocksberg they put up
Plenty of meeting houses.

DANCER

A newer chorus now succeeds!
I hear the distant drumming.
"Don't be disturbed! 'tis, in the reeds,
The bittern's changeless booming."

Now a new chorus takes over!
I can hear the sound of distant drums.
"Don't worry! It's just, within the reeds,
A booming bittern."

DANCING-MASTER

How each his legs in nimble trip
Lifts up, and makes a clearance!
The crooked jump, the heavy skip,
Nor care for the appearance.

How each one throws his legs about,
Lifts up and turns around!
Their jumps are skewed, their skips are plods,
They don't care how they look.

GOOD FELLOW

The rabble by such hate are held,
To maim and slay delights them:
As Orpheus' lyre the brutes compelled,
The bagpipe here unites them.

The mob are held together with hate,
They love to hurt and kill.
Just like Orpheus' harp calmed the animals,
The bagpipe holds this lot.

DOGMATIST

I'll not be led by any lure
Of doubts or critic-cavils:
The Devil must be something, sure,--
Or how should there be devils?

I'll not be tricked by any talk,
Of doubts or arguments:
The Devil must exist,
Or how would there be any devils?

IDEALIST

This once, the fancy wrought in me
Is really too despotic:
Forsooth, if I am all I see,
I must be idiotic!

I think that the idea that I have now,
Is really too controlling:
Really, if I'm to see everything,
I must be an idiot!

REALIST

This racking fuss on every hand,
It gives me great vexation;
And, for the first time, here I stand
On insecure foundation.

The great commotion all around,
Is making me disturbed;
For the first time I'm not sure
That what I think is right.

SUPERNATURALIST

With much delight I see the play,
And grant to these their merits,
Since from the devils I also may
Infer the better spirits.

I love to see what's going on,
And acknowledge these base spirits,
Since if devils exist then we can say
That angels must as well.

SCEPTIC
The flame they follow, on and on,
And think they're near the treasure:
But *Devil rhymes with Doubt* alone,
So I am here with pleasure.

They keep on chasing this illusion,
And think they'll find an answer,
But Devil and Doubt are the same thing,
So I'm happy to be here.

LEADER OF THE BAND
Frog in green, and cricket-trill.
Such dilettants!--perdition!
Fly-snout and mosquito-bill,--
Each one's a fine musician!

Frog in the grass, cricket's song.
Damnation to all amateurs!
Snout of fly, mosquito's beak,
They're all fine musicians!

THE ADROIT
Sans souci, we call the clan
Of merry creatures so, then;
Go a-foot no more we can,
And on our heads we go, then.

Without a care, we call this band
All of merry creatures;
See when we cannot go on foot,
We'll walk along on our heads.

THE AWKWARD
Once many a bit we sponged, but now,
God help us! that is done with:
Our shoes are all danced out, we trow,
We've but naked soles to run with.

We once picked up things here and there,
But those days are gone, God help us:
We've danced our way right through our shoes,
And have just our bare feet left.

WILL-O'-THE WISPS
From the marshes we appear,
Where we originated;
Yet in the ranks, at once, we're here
As glittering gallants rated.

We come from out of the marshes,
That's where we were born,
Yet in this company we are seen
As the best of shining knights.

SHOOTING-STAR
Darting hither from the sky,
In star and fire light shooting,
Cross-wise now in grass I lie:
Who'll help me to my footing?

I shot here from out the sky,
Trailing light and fire,
Now I'm stuck here in the grass,
Who'll help me to my feet?

THE HEAVY FELLOWS
Room! and round about us, room!
Trodden are the grasses:
Spirits also, spirits come,
And they are bulky masses.

Give us room, give us room!
The grass is all flattened down.
The spirits are coming,
And they need plenty of room.

PUCK
Enter not so stall-fed quite,
Like elephant-calves about one!
And the heaviest weight to-night
Be Puck, himself, the stout one!

Don't thump around the place so much,
Like a bunch of baby elephants!
Let the heaviest person tonight,
Be Puck, I'll be the stout one!

ARIEL
If loving Nature at your back,
Or Mind, the wings uncloses,
Follow up my airy track
To the mount of roses!

If loving nature gives you wings,
Either on your back or in your mind,
You can follow my path in the sky
Up to the hill of roses.

ORCHESTRA
pianissimo
Cloud and trailing mist o'erhead
Are now illuminated:
Air in leaves, and wind in reed,
And all is dissipated.

The cloud and trailing mist overhead
Are now lit up by sunrise:
The air stirs the leaves, the wind the reeds,
And all has blown away.

XXIII

DREARY DAY

A FIELD

FAUST MEPHISTOPHELES

FAUST

In misery! In despair! Long wretchedly astray on the face of the earth, and now imprisoned! That gracious, ill-starred creature shut in a dungeon as a criminal, and given up to fearful torments! To this has it come! to this!--Treacherous, contemptible spirit, and thou hast concealed it from me!--Stand, then,--stand! Roll the devilish eyes wrathfully in thy head! Stand and defy me with thine intolerable presence! Imprisoned! In irretrievable misery! Delivered up to evil spirits, and to condemning, unfeeling Man! And thou hast lulled me, meanwhile, with the most insipid dissipations, hast concealed from me her increasing wretchedness, and suffered her to go helplessly to ruin!

In misery! In despair! Left to roam the earth for ages, and now imprisoned! That beautiful, unlucky creature shut up in a dungeon as a criminal and tortured! That it's come down to this! You treacherous, pathetic Spirit, you kept this from me! Come on, stand up to me! Roll your devil's eyes in your head! Defy me with your appalling existence! Imprisoned!. Shut away in misery! And you distracted me, meanwhile, with the dullest sins, hiding from me what was happening to her and letting her go to her ruin unaided!

MEPHISTOPHELES

She is not the first.

She's not the first.

FAUST

Dog! Abominable monster! Transform him, thou Infinite Spirit! transform the reptile again into his dog-shape? in which it pleased him often at night to scamper on before me, to roll himself at the feet of the unsuspecting wanderer, and hang upon his shoulders when he fell! Transform him again into his favorite likeness, that he may crawl upon his belly in the dust before me,--that I may trample him, the outlawed, under foot! Not the first! O woe! woe which no human soul can grasp, that more than one being should sink into the depths of this misery,--that the first, in its writhing death-agony under the eyes of the Eternal Forgiver, did not expiate the guilt of all others! The misery of this single one pierces to the very marrow of my life; and thou art calmly grinning at the fate of thousands!

You dog! You foul monster! You Infinite Spirit, change him again! Change this reptile back into dog form! The shape in which he used to scamper on in front of me, to roll himself at the feet of unsuspecting walkers, to pull him up when he fell! Turn him into his favourite shape, so he can crawl on his belly in the dust before me and I can trample him, the outcast! Not the first! Oh sorrow! Sorrow which no human soul can grasp, knowing that more than one should have to suffer this misery – that the first, dying in agony beneath the gaze of the Eternal Forgiver, didn't pay for the guilt of all the others! That just this one should have suffered in this way cuts me to the heart, and you're calmly grinning, knowing it has happened to thousands more!

MEPHISTOPHELES

Now we are already again at the end of our wits, where the understanding of you men runs wild. Why didst thou enter into fellowship with us, if thou canst not carry it out? Wilt fly, and art not

Now we're really in a mad place, where men go completely off the rails. Why did you go into partnership with me, if you didn't want to follow through? You want to fly, but you don't want to leave the

secure against dizziness? Did we thrust ourselves upon thee, or thou thyself upon us?

ground? Did I force myself on you, or was it the other way about?

FAUST
Gnash not thus thy devouring teeth at me? It fills me with horrible disgust. Mighty, glorious Spirit, who hast vouchsafed to me Thine apparition, who knowest my heart and my soul, why fetter me to the felon-comrade, who feeds on mischief and gluts himself with ruin?

Don't gnash your killer's teeth at me! You fill me with disgust. You mighty, glorious Spirit, who has appeared to me in person, why chain me to this criminal, who feeds on trouble and stuffs himself on ruin?

MEPHISTOPHELES
Hast thou done?

Are you finished?

FAUST
Rescue her, or woe to thee! The fearfullest curse be upon thee for thousands of ages!

Rescue her, or it'll be the worse for you! The greatest curse be on you for aeons!

MEPHISTOPHELES
I cannot loosen the bonds of the Avenger, nor undo his bolts. Rescue her? Who was it that plunged her into ruin? I, or thou?
(FAUST *looks around wildly*.)
Wilt thou grasp the thunder? Well that it has not been given to you, miserable mortals! To crush to pieces the innocent respondent--that is the tyrant-fashion of relieving one's self in embarrassments.

I can't loosen the ropes of the Avenger, or undo his bolts. Rescue her? Who pushed her into this fate, you or me?
(FAUST *looks around wildly*.)
Do you think you can catch the thunder? Well you can't, you miserable mortal! To shoot the messenger – that's what tyrants do when they want to avoid the blame for their actions.

FAUST
Take me thither! She shall be free!

Take me to her! I shall free her!

MEPHISTOPHELES
And the danger to which thou wilt expose thyself? Know that the guilt of blood, from thy hand, still lies upon the town! Avenging spirits hover over the spot where the victim fell, and lie in wait for the returning murderer.

What about the risk you'll be taking? You know that in the town there is still the guilt of blood which you spilt. Avenging spirits are at the spot where the victim fell, waiting for the murderer to come back.

FAUST
That, too, from thee? Murder and death of a world upon thee, monster! Take me thither, I say, and liberate her!

Now you're using that as an excuse? May murder and the death of the world fall on you, monster! Take me there, I say, and free her!

MEPHISTOPHELES
I will convey thee there; and hear, what I can do! Have I all the power in Heaven and on Earth? I will becloud the jailer's senses: get possession of the key, and lead her forth with human hand! I will keep watch: the magic steeds are ready, I will carry you off. So much is in my power.

I'll take you there; and listen, this is what I can do! Have I power over Heaven and Earth? I'll confuse the jailer, get the key, and let you bring her out of there! I'll keep watch: the magic horses are ready, I'll help your escape. This much I can do.

FAUST
Up and away!   *Then let's go!*

XXIV

NIGHT

OPEN FIELD

(FAUST *and* MEPHISTOPHELES *speeding onward on black horses.*)

FAUST
What weave they there round the raven-stone?   *What are they wrapping around the ravenstone?*

MEPHISTOPHELES
I know not what they are brewing and doing.   *I don't know what they're up to.*

FAUST
Soaring up, sweeping down, bowing and bending!   *Soaring, sweeping, swooping and bowing!*

MEPHISTOPHELES
A witches'-guild.   *It's a witches' coven.*

FAUST
They scatter, devote and doom!   *They've scattered, they've made their devotions!*

MEPHISTOPHELES
On! on!   *On! On!*

XXV

DUNGEON

FAUST
(*with a bunch of keys and a lamp, before an iron door*)
A shudder, long unfelt, comes o'er me;
Mankind's collected woe o'erwhelms me, here.
She dwells within the dark, damp walls before me,
And all her crime was a delusion dear!
What! I delay to free her?
I dread, once again to see her?
On! my shrinking but lingers Death more near.

A fear I've not felt for an age comes over me;
All of mankind's sadness crushes me, here.
She lives within these dark, damp walls,
And her only crime was to be tricked!
What! Am I going to delay her freedom?
Do I dread seeing her again?
Get on with it! Wasting time just lets Death come closer.

(*He grasps the lock: the sound of singing is heard inside.*)

(*He grasps the lock: the sound of singing is heard inside.*)

My mother, the harlot,
Who put me to death;
My father, the varlet,
Who eaten me hath!
Little sister, so good,
Laid my bones in the wood,
In the damp moss and clay:
Then was I a beautiful bird o' the wood;
Fly away! Fly away!

My mother, the tart,
She had me killed;
My father, the scoundrel,
He ate me up!
My little sister, so good,
Laid out my bones
In the damp moss and clay in the wood:
Then I was a beautiful bird in the wood.
Fly away! Fly away!

FAUST (*unlocking*)
She does not dream her lover listens near;
That he the rattling chain, the rustling straw, can hear.
(*He enters*)

She has no idea that her lover is listening nearby;
That he can hear her rattling chain, the rustling straw.

MARGARET (*hiding herself on the pallet*)
Woe! woe! They come. O death of bitterness!

Oh no! No! They're coming! Oh bitter death!

FAUST (*whispering*)
Hush! hush! The hour is come that frees thee.

Hush, hush! The time of your freedom is here!

MARGARET (*throwing herself before him*)
Art thou a man, then pity my distress!

If you're a man, pity my plight!

FAUST
Thy cries will wake the guards, and they will seize thee!
(*He takes hold of the fetters to unlock them.*)

Your cries will wake the guards, they'll take you!

MARGARET (*on her knees*)
Who, headsman! unto thee such power
Over me could give?
Thou'rt come for me at midnight-hour:
Have mercy on me, let me live!
Is't not soon enough when morning chime has run?
(*She rises.*)
And I am yet so young, so young!

Who gave you, executioner,
Such power over me?
You've come for me at midnight:
Have mercy on me, let me live!
Isn't the morning early enough?
(she rises)
I'm still so young!

142

And now Death comes, and ruin!
I, too, was fair, and that was my undoing.
My love was near, but now he's far;
Torn lies the wreath, scattered the blossoms are.
Seize me not thus so violently!
Spare me! What have I done to thee?
Let me not vainly entreat thee!
I never chanced, in all my days, to meet thee!

FAUST
Shall I outlive this misery?

MARGARET
Now am I wholly in thy might.
But let me suckle, first, my baby!
I blissed it all this livelong night;
They took 't away, to vex me, maybe,
And now they say I killed the child outright.
And never shall I be glad again.
They sing songs about me! 'tis bad of the folk to do it!

There's an old story has the same refrain;
Who bade them so construe it?

FAUST (*falling upon his knees*)
Here lieth one who loves thee ever,
The thraldom of thy woe to sever.

MARGARET (*flinging herself beside him*)
O let us kneel, and call the Saints to hide us!
Under the steps beside us,
The threshold under,
Hell heaves in thunder!
The Evil One
With terrible wrath
Seeketh a path
His prey to discover!

FAUST (*aloud*)
Margaret! Margaret!

MARGARET (*attentively listening*)
That was the voice of my lover!
(*She springs to her feet: the fetters fall off.*)
Where is he? I heard him call me.
I am free! No one shall enthrall me.
To his neck will I fly,
On his bosom lie!
On the threshold he stood, and *Margaret*! calling,
Midst of Hell's howling and noises appalling,
Midst of the wrathful, infernal derision,
I knew the sweet sound of the voice of the vision!

And now Death and disgrace come to me!
I was beautiful, and that was my downfall.
My love was here, but now he's far away;
The garland is torn, the flowers are thrown away.
Don't grab me so roughly!
Spare me! What have I done to you?
Don't make me beg in vain!
I've never even met you!

Can I survive such misery?

Now I'm completely in your power.
But let me feed my baby first!
I caressed it all night;
They took it away, maybe to annoy me,
And now they say I killed it.
I shall never know happiness again.
They sing songs about me! It's not right that people should do it!
There's an old song on the same theme;
Who told them to adapt it?

Here's one who still loves you,
And has come to take you from your sadness.

Let's kneel, and pray for the saints to hide us!
Under these steps here,
Just under the threshold,
Hell is heaving with thunder!
The Evil One
With great anger,
Is trying to find
A way to his victims!

Margaret! Margaret!

That was my lover's voice!
(*She springs to her feet: the fetters fall off*)
Where is he? I heard him call me!
I'm free, nobody can hold me now.
I'll fly to his arms,
And lie on his chest.
He stood in the doorway and called Margaret!,
Over Hell's appalling shrieks and howls,
Over all the hellish mockery,
I knew I heard the sweet sound of that vision's voice!

FAUST
'Tis I!

It's me!

MARGARET
'Tis thou! O, say it once again!
(*Clasping him.*)
'Tis he! 'tis he! Where now is all my pain?
The anguish of the dungeon, and the chain?
'Tis thou! Thou comest to save me,
And I am saved!--
Again the street I see
Where first I looked on thee;
And the garden, brightly blooming,
Where I and Martha wait thy coming.

It's you! Oh, say it again!
(Clasping him)
It's him, it's him! Now where has all my pain gone?
Where is the suffering,
Of the prison and my chains?
It's you! You've come to get me,
And I'm saved!
I can see the street again
Where I first saw you,
And the brightly blooming garden,
Where Martha and I waited for your arrival.

FAUST (*struggling to leave*)
Come! Come with me!

Come on! Come with me!

MARGARET
Delay, now!
So fain I stay, when thou delayest!
(*Caressing him.*)

Oh, wait!
I'll be happy to stay here if you're with me.

FAUST
Away, now!
If longer here thou stayest,
We shall be made to dearly rue it.

Come away!
If you stay here any longer,
We shall pay for it dearly.

MARGARET
Kiss me!--canst no longer do it?
My friend, so short a time thou'rt missing,
And hast unlearned thy kissing?
Why is my heart so anxious, on thy breast?
Where once a heaven thy glances did create me,
A heaven thy loving words expressed,
And thou didst kiss, as thou wouldst suffocate me--
Kiss me!
Or I'll kiss thee!
(*She embraces him.*)
Ah, woe! thy lips are chill,
And still.
How changed in fashion
Thy passion!
Who has done me this ill?
(*She turns away from him.*)

Kiss me! Can't you kiss me any more?
My friend, you've been gone such a short time,
And you've forgotten how to kiss?
Why do I feel so anxious, here in your arms?
Once to be looked at by you was heaven,
Your words made a heaven,
And you kissed me as if you wanted to steal my breath –
Kiss me!
Or I'll kiss you!
(She embraces him)
Oh! Your lips are cold
And unyielding.
How your passion has changed!

Who's done this wrong to me?
(She turns away from him)

FAUST
Come, follow me! My darling, be more bold:
I'll clasp thee, soon, with warmth a thousand-fold;
But follow now! 'Tis all I beg of thee.

Come, follow me! My darling, take heart!
I'll hug you soon, with warmth a thousand times this,
But all I ask you to do now is to come with me!

MARGARET (*turning to him*)
And is it thou? Thou, surely, certainly?

FAUST
'Tis I! Come on!

MARGARET
Thou wilt unloose my chain,
And in thy lap wilt take me once again.
How comes it that thou dost not shrink from me?--
Say, dost thou know, my friend, whom thou mak'st
free?

FAUST
Come! come! The night already vanisheth.

MARGARET
My mother have I put to death;
I've drowned the baby born to thee.
Was it not given to thee and me?
Thee, too!--'Tis thou! It scarcely true doth seem--
Give me thy hand! 'Tis not a dream!
Thy dear, dear hand!--But, ah, 'tis wet!
Why, wipe it off! Methinks that yet
There's blood thereon.
Ah, God! what hast thou done?
Nay, sheathe thy sword at last!
Do not affray me!

FAUST
O, let the past be past!
Thy words will slay me!

MARGARET
No, no! Thou must outlive us.
Now I'll tell thee the graves to give us:
Thou must begin to-morrow
The work of sorrow!
The best place give to my mother,
Then close at her side my brother,
And me a little away,
But not too very far, I pray!
And here, on my right breast, my baby lay!
Nobody else will lie beside me!--
Ah, within thine arms to hide me,
That was a sweet and a gracious bliss,
But no more, no more can I attain it!
I would force myself on thee and constrain it,
And it seems thou repellest my kiss:
And yet 'tis thou, so good, so kind to see!

FAUST
If thou feel'st it is I, then come with me!

And it is you? Definitely, certainly you?

It's me! Now come on!

You'll undo my chains,
And sit me in your lap again?
Why don't you recoil from me?
Hang on, my friend, do you know whom you're
releasing?

Come on! The night is slipping away.

I've killed my mother;
I've drowned your baby.
Wasn't it given to you and me?
You as well! It's you! It hardly seems –
Give me your hand! It's not a dream!
Your dear, dear hand! But ah, it's wet!
Come, dry it! I think that
There's blood on it.
Oh God! What have you done?
No, put away your sword!
Don't frighten me!

Oh, let the past disappear!
Your words will kill me!

No, no, you must live on.
Now, I'll tell you how to organise the graves:
You must begin
The sad work tomorrow!
Give my mother the best spot,
With my brother close by her side,
And me a little way away –
But not too far, I beg you!
And here, on my right breast, put my baby!
Nobody else can lie beside me!
Ah, to hide in your arms once
Was a sweet and lovely feeling,
But I can't have that pleasure any more!
It's as if I'd be forcing you to do it,
And it seems you turn away my kiss:
But it is you, and it's so good to see you!

If you know it's me then come with me!

145

MARGARET
Out yonder?

FAUST
To freedom.

MARGARET
If the grave is there,
Death lying in wait, then come!
From here to eternal rest:
No further step--no, no!
Thou goest away! O Henry, if I could go!

FAUST
Thou canst! Just will it! Open stands the door.

MARGARET
I dare not go: there's no hope any more.
Why should I fly? They'll still my steps waylay!
It is so wretched, forced to beg my living,
And a bad conscience sharper misery giving!
It is so wretched, to be strange, forsaken,
And I'd still be followed and taken!

FAUST
I'll stay with thee.

MARGARET
Be quick! Be quick!
Save thy perishing child!
Away! Follow the ridge
Up by the brook,
Over the bridge,
Into the wood,
To the left, where the plank is placed
In the pool!
Seize it in haste!
'Tis trying to rise,
'Tis struggling still!
Save it! Save it!

FAUST
Recall thy wandering will!
One step, and thou art free at last!

MARGARET
If the mountain we had only passed!
There sits my mother upon a stone,--
I feel an icy shiver!
There sits my mother upon a stone,
And her head is wagging ever.
She beckons, she nods not, her heavy head falls o'er;

Out there?

To freedom.

If the grave is out there,
With Death waiting for me, then let's go!
I won't take another step from here,
Except to go to my death, no, no!
You go! Oh Henry, if I could go too!

You can! You just have to want it! The door is open.

I dare not go: there's no hope to be had.
Why should I run?
They'll only hunt me down!
It's so awful, having to beg for my life,
And my guilt gives me even worse pain!
It is so awful to be outcast, abandoned,
And still they would track me down!

I'll stay here with you.

Hurry! Hurry!
Save your dying child!
Go now! Follow the ridge,
Up by the stream,
Cross over the bridge,
Into the wood,
Go to the left,
Where there's a plank over the pool!
Grab it quickly!
It's trying to get out,
It's still struggling! Save it! Save it!

Get a grip on your mind!
One step and you'll be free!

If only we'd gone past the mountain!
There my mother sits on a stone,
I feel an icy shiver!
There my mother sits on a stone,
And she's shaking her head at me.
She doesn't call or nod to me, her head falls;

She slept so long that she wakes no more.
She slept, while we were caressing:
Ah, those were the days of blessing!

FAUST
Here words and prayers are nothing worth;
I'll venture, then, to bear thee forth.

MARGARET
No--let me go! I'll suffer no force!
Grasp me not so murderously!
I've done, else, all things for the love of thee.

FAUST
The day dawns: Dearest! Dearest!

MARGARET
Day? Yes, the day comes,--the last day breaks for me!
My wedding-day it was to be!
Tell no one thou has been with Margaret!
Woe for my garland! The chances
Are over--'tis all in vain!
We shall meet once again,
But not at the dances!
The crowd is thronging, no word is spoken:
The square below
And the streets overflow:
The death-bell tolls, the wand is broken.
I am seized, and bound, and delivered--
Shoved to the block--they give the sign!
Now over each neck has quivered
The blade that is quivering over mine.

Dumb lies the world like the grave!

FAUST
O had I ne'er been born!

MEPHISTOPHELES (*appears outside*)
Off! or you're lost ere morn.
Useless talking, delaying and praying!
My horses are neighing:
The morning twilight is near.

MARGARET
What rises up from the threshold here?
He! he! suffer him not!
What does he want in this holy spot?
He seeks me!

FAUST
Thou shalt live.

She sleep so long and never wakes.
She slept while we were together:
Oh what happy days they were!

Here words and prayers won't work;
Then I'll try to carry you out.

No, let me go! I shan't be forced!
Don't grab me so roughly!
I've done everything else for the love of you.

It's daybreak! Sweetheart, sweetheart!

Day? Yes, the day has come, this is my last day!
It was going to be my wedding day!
Don't tell anyone you were with Margaret!
Alas for my bouquet! Everything is lost,
It was all in vain!
We shall meet again,
But not at a dance!
The crowd has gathered, nothing is said;
The square and the streets
Are packed:
The death bell rings, the stick is snapped.
I am seized, tied, delivered,
Shoved onto the block, the sign is made!
The blade which quivers above my neck,
Has done the same over all the necks which came before.
The world's as quiet as the grave!

I wish I'd never been born!

Go! Or you'll be done for before morning.
There's no point talking, delaying and praying!
My horses are restless:
Dawn's first light is almost here.

What's that on the doorstep there?
Him! Him! Don't let him in!
What does he want in this holy place?
He's after me!

You shall live.

MARGARET
Judgment of God! myself to thee I give.

God, I give myself up to your mercy!

MEPHISTOPHELES (*to* FAUST)
Come! or I'll leave her in the lurch, and thee!

Come on! Or I'll leave her in the lurch, and you too!

MARGARET
Thine am I, Father! rescue me!
Ye angels, holy cohorts, guard me,
Camp around, and from evil ward me!
Henry! I shudder to think of thee.

Father, I'm yours! Rescue me!
You angels of heaven, guard me,
Gather round and save me from evil!
Henry! I shiver when I think of you!

MEPHISTOPHELES
She is judged!

She is judged!

VOICE (*from above*)
She is saved!

She is saved!

MEPHISTOPHELES (*to* FAUST)
Hither to me!

Come with me!

(*He disappears with* FAUST)
VOICE (*from within, dying away*)
Henry! Henry!

Henry! Henry!

27288419R00083

Made in the USA
Columbia, SC
21 September 2018